THE OLIVE PICKERS

Pete Burnell

I am indebted to those of my friends who have read earlier drafts of this book, and given useful feedback.

And especially indebted to the real Matina and Scott!

Special thanks go out to my wife, Julia, for putting up with me for the last 46 years.

And finally, I must mention Peggy Choucair, who provided the image that I have used for the book's cover.

CONTENTS

PROLOGUE.

Joe had left university two years earlier with a mediocre degree and absolutely no idea of what to do with the rest of his life. Throughout his university years he had embraced a hippy lifestyle (long hair, cannabis, free love, naïve left-wing ideals) and now he decided to drop out and travel to India - the fashionable adventure of his generation.

He made his farewells to his family and friends, persuaded his mother to sew a Union Jack onto his backpack, and then hitch-hiked to Athens. He drifted around the Greek Islands for a few months: Paros, Naxos, Santorini, Crete, Rhodes. Sleeping rough on beaches, smoking dope, drinking beer, ouzo, and cheap wine, and sleeping with the occasional girl. Generally having a good time. Eventually he found himself on a plane to Tel Aviv, in the company of an American couple that he had befriended. They intended to work as volunteers on a kibbutz, having heard tales of kibbutz life from other travellers. Although he liked Bruce and Jane, the Americans, Joe had different reasons for travelling to Israel: the Americans were fired with enthusiasm towards Zionist ideals, Joe wasn't. If anything, he leaned towards sympathy towards the Palestinians (who, in his view, had been there first). Naturally he kept this to himself. His main reason for travelling with the Americans was that he did actually enjoy their company, and he was starting to get a bit fed up of always travelling on his own. Also, he rather fancied Jane, although he was careful to keep that to himself as well.

When they arrived in Tel Aviv, the three of them checked in at the Youth Hostel, where they stayed for a few days, enjoying evenings in the numerous bars nearby, and with their days split between sight-seeing and the beach. Eventually they made their way to the kibbutz office. After being interviewed by a very attractive Israeli lady (originally from Liverpool it transpired), they were all assigned to kibbutz Ashdot Yaakov Meuhad, just south of the Sea of Galilee.

***

Most of the next day was spent travelling on buses to the Kibbutz. Finally they arrived at the entrance gates to the kibbutz and they were – in no particular order - hungry, thirsty, and tired. It was quite a long walk of a couple of kilometres from the entrance gate to the centre of the kibbutz, and by the time they arrived, they were even more fed up. However, things very quickly improved from then on. After they were given an orientation talk by an old lady called Malka, who was responsible for organising the volunteers, about pocket money, cigarette rations, and so on, they were allocated rooms. Bruce and Jane shared a room, Joe finished up in a room which he shared with two other guys. They were also allocated to work details – Joe was picking olives, Bruce picking bananas, and Jane working in the kitchen. It was then time for the evening meal, which was served in a large communal dining hall. The three of them mingled with the other kibbutz volunteers, and soon started feeling at home.

From then on, Joe picked olives. He picked olives six days a week. On alternate weeks, he worked either on a shift from four in the morning until noon, or on a shift from noon until eight in the evening. Had it been at all practical to operate a shift from eight in the evening until four in the morning, then he felt sure that he would have been working on that shift as well, one week in three.

At times there was a very 'them and us' mentality between the Israelis and the volunteers: the Israelis were often seen as bossy towards the volunteers; the volunteers were seen as lazy. After every refreshment break, the Israelis would be urging them back to work: "Hurry, hurry, pick more olives." The volunteers would slowly dawdle their way back. They found the work hot and boring. "Right lads, tea-break over, back on your heads!" Joe would say. The Brits in the group would laugh, the Israelis looked puzzled.

Nevertheless, relations between the two, were generally friendly. On each shift of olive-pickers, there were eight people – two or three Israelis, and the rest volunteers. One of the Israelis who Joe *got quite friendly with was an older man in his early thirties called Chaim, who was a Major with the Israeli Defence Force reservists. Chaim spoke good English, and had a dry sense of humour, and a witty turn of phrase, which Joe enjoyed. Chaim tried to teach Joe a few phrases of Hebrew, with rather mixed success. Another Israeli, who Joe got friendly with, was a woman called Leah. This friendship took a lot longer to develop. Leah was about five years older than Joe. She rarely smiled and sometimes seemed quite sad. She was a widow; her husband had been a friend of Chaim's, and had been killed in the Yom Kippur war scarcely a year earlier, whilst on active service with the Israeli Defence Force.*

Leah had lovely red hair and freckles, and was very pretty. Joe found himself strongly attracted to her. However, Joe was on occasions a little bit shy with women, and this time his shyness was made worse by Leah being older than him, but more significantly by the fact that she was a widow. He did not know how he could possibly approach her, without risking being seen as insensitive. Over the next few weeks, he grew increasingly desperate – torn between his growing attraction to Leah, and his worries about what to do about it. He constantly manoeuvred to be working on the same shift as Leah. He found himself secretly watching her and trying to sit near her when they had refreshment breaks in the olive groves. Occasionally catching her eye, and smiling at her. And acutely aware that his behaviour seemed a little bit pathetic and puerile, like that of a love-struck fourteen-year old.

Other people noticed. Bruce and Jane, the Americans, observed all this with some amusement, waiting for Joe to pluck up courage to make a move, indeed willing him to do so. Gradually, Joe became aware that Leah was also surreptitiously watching him. At first, he thought that she had simply noticed his interest and was being wary of him. That thought scared him even more. Maybe she was at first, but before too much longer it became obvious that there was more to it than that. The glances became more frequent, along with smiles, and eventually turned into friendly, and increasingly intimate, chats.

***

One day, while they were both emptying their individual baskets of olives that they had picked into the main container, Leah suddenly said, "Joe, please can I ask you a question?"

"Sure, Leah, ask away."

"What do you mean when you say 'Right lads, tea-break over, back on your heads'?"

Joe smiled at her. "It's the punch-line of an old English joke." She raised her eyebrows and looked at him with an interested expression on her face. So he grinned and told her the whole joke:

"This guy dies and goes off down to hell. He wasn't a good person, see, so hell was where he ended up. But he wasn't really _very_ bad, so when he gets down there he's met by the Devil who says to him: 'I'm afraid you've been bad and so you're here to be punished for the rest of eternity. But, because you haven't really been _very_ bad, I'm going to do you a favour and allow you to choose what sort of punishment you'd prefer.' He starts to show him around.

"The first room they come to has fires, molten brimstone, that sort of stuff, and the people there have blackened and burnt skin continually peeling from their bodies. Horrible. 'I don't fancy this one' he says.

"The Devil shows him a second room where people were tied up with barbed wire, being flogged with whips. He shudders. 'Don't fancy this one either.'

"The third room was simply a large deep pool of piss, shit, vomit, puss, rotting flesh, everything disgusting that you could possibly think of. And there were a bunch of naked people sitting round in this revolting stuff, in it up to their chests. They were happily drinking tea from fancy china teacups. "This is pretty horrible, but it doesn't look _too_ bad, I think that I'll take this one.' he says. So he strips off and jumps into the disgusting pool to join the others. And starts drinking tea from a fancy china teacup. But just then a demon comes in cracking his whip. 'Right lads, tea-break over, back on your heads' he says."

Leah looked at him blankly for a couple of seconds, then burst out laughing. Joe joined in, and they started laughing together. Eventually they calmed down, smiled at each other and went back to work.

***

This continued for several more weeks, with Bruce and Jane, and Chaim, increasingly despairing of Joe's slow progress. But eventually Leah took matters into her own hands. One day, whilst they were busy picking olives, Leah wandered over to the tree where Joe was working. She silently beckoned to him, and, as he approached, she grabbed hold of the front of his T-shirt, pulled him towards her, and gave him a long and tender kiss. Then, without saying anything, she smiled at him, and went back to her own tree to continue picking. The ball was now in Joe's court. That night he went around to the house where Leah lived on her own, with a feeling that was somewhere between excitement and terror. But, as Leah opened the door to him, they fell in each other's arms and started kissing passionately. They virtually tore each other's clothes off and frantically made love then and there in the middle of the floor. The evening was warm and humid, and their passion was sweaty and frenzied. Later, they retreated to Leah's bedroom, where they made love again, in a much more leisurely and gentle way, taking time to explore each other's bodies. A few days later, Joe moved in with Leah, and they became inseparable. Most people, volunteers and Israelis alike, approved. Both Joe and Leah were well liked, and everyone could see that they were very happy, and seemed to be in love.

One day they were sat together in the restaurant, on a table by themselves. Malka suddenly wandered over and plonked herself down at the same table. "Shalom, Joe."

"Shalom, Malka."

"You are a very naughty boy, Joe."

"Oh. Why's that, Malka?" he asked cautiously.

"Because when you came here, you did not tell me that you were a magician." He looked at her blankly. "Yes," she continued, "you come into the kibbutz, and you wave your magic wand, and then you turn our Leah from a sad girl to a happy girl who is always smiling. You must be a magician."

"Would you like me to wave my magic wand at you, Malka?" he asked with a wicked grin on his face. Malka roared with laughter, *and slapped him across his back as she wandered off.*

***

Leah took Joe on visits to other parts of Israel. They had a few days in Haifa, staying at a small hotel overlooking the Mediterranean sea, and rarely leaving their bedroom, except to eat. They visited the Golan Heights, which impressed Joe with its dramatic beauty. Then later they travelled to Jerusalem. They stayed in another small hotel, but this time divided their time between their bed, and visiting the sights around the city. Joe was not religious in the slightest, and neither was Leah, but despite that, they found themselves inspired by the sights around the city, such as the Wailing Wall, and the Church of the Holy Sepulchre.

And, in Jerusalem, Joe introduced Leah to the delights of cannabis. Whilst wandering through the old city market, he was offered, and eagerly bought, a 'finger' of 'Red Leb' – hashish that had been 'imported' from Lebanon. Leah happily smoked it with him, and thoroughly enjoyed getting stoned.

***

By now, Joe's views on the dispute between the Palestinians and the Israelis had started to mellow. He had grown to fully understand the desire of the Jewish people to have their own state in their historic homeland, and had grown to love the country of Israel, and (some of) its people. And one Israeli in particular! While he was not unsympathetic towards the Palestinian Arabs, and had met and befriended several, he had become seriously troubled by the activities of the extremists who were engaged in terrorist activities. The Munich Olympic games massacre of 1972, an earlier school bus massacre at a place called Avivim, and only a few months before his arrival in Israel, the Ma'alot massacre in which some twenty five Israelis had been murdered....

***

After Jerusalem, they headed back to the kibbutz. On their arrival, they were met by a rather tense and worried looking Chaim. Clearly something was wrong. With him was a tough-looking man wearing a military uniform. Joe and Leah greeted Chaim warily, wondering what was going on.

Chaim led them to his own quarters in the kibbutz, and offered them drinks. They both declined. "Joe and Leah, I would like to introduce General Shavit," said Chaim, indicating the other man. He was clearly uncomfortable. "General Shavit wishes to have a word with you both."

"Good evening Joe. Very good to meet you," smiled the general. "I am from an organisation called Mossad. Maybe you've heard of us. We believe that you may be able to assist us...."

CHAPTER 1.

London, June 2004.

Joe sat in the lobby of the Dorchester hotel, in Park Lane. Definitely not the sort of hotel that he would normally stay in, but on this occasion the cost was being paid for by George, the man whom he was here to meet. He nursed a glass of beer, occasionally glancing at the newspaper he was holding. The last thirty years had been kind to Joe. Although in his fifties, he looked more like a man in his mid thirties - lean and tanned, with longish brown hair, and an easy smile. His jeans and leather jacket easily fitted in with this youthful appearance. On one occasion he had been highly amused when he had been mistaken for the lead guitarist of a famous rock band and had been asked for his autograph, which he had happily given in an illegible scribble.

However, in the thirty years since his initial involvement with Mossad, Joe had actually been working as a freelance agent (some might call him a mercenary) for a variety of organisations: both MI5 and MI6, the CIA, and DGSE, France's intelligence agency. (Amongst other languages, Joe spoke excellent French.) He had also kept in close contact with his ex-colleagues in Mossad, and over the years had done more than one freelance job for them. His activities had generally been relatively innocuous – gathering information and so on – although he had on more than one occasion been responsible for 'terminating with extreme prejudice' some really nasty people. Events from thirty years ago had hardened him considerably, and the free-spirited hippy was long gone.

Joe had first encountered George from MI5, the guy he was here to meet, some twelve years earlier, in Kuwait City. This was immediately after the Gulf War which followed the Iraqi invasion of Kuwait. At that time, Joe had participated in an MI5-initiated operation to rescue some hostages held by terrorists. The operation was successful, and subsequently Joe had carried out several assignments for George, and MI5.

He had been sitting there for about half an hour, half-hidden behind a pillar, furtively watching the hotel entrance. There were several other people sitting around in the lobby: a trio of businessmen having an informal discussion about something or other, a couple of groups of American tourists, complete with children, and one or two individuals sitting on their own. These, Joe paid careful attention to, though he saw nothing to arouse his suspicions.

The newspaper contained the usual stuff: a story about suicide bombers in Israel, the continuing saga about non-existent weapons of mass destruction in Iraq, and a somewhat bizarre piece about an exploding whale in Taiwan. He read more carefully the story about suicide bombers in Israel. Apparently, two suicide bombers, had killed a number of people on two buses in Beersheba in southern Israel. He remembered Beersheba from his time in Israel many years ago. His thoughts turned to the people in Israel who he stilled called friends, and, inevitably, to Leah. The familiar pangs of grief stabbed him, followed, inevitably by a fierce blaze of anger, and the renewal of his need for revenge. They say that 'Revenge is a dish best served cold', but for Joe the desire for revenge never cooled down, and was an ever-present emotion. He tried to bury the black thoughts that often troubled him, and turned his attention back to the newspaper story. Responsibility had been claimed by a group called 'Hamas', which Joe had heard of, although he knew few details, and he made a mental note to find out more about them from his contacts in Mossad.

He glanced at his watch, and turned his attention to the hotel's entrance from the street. He was starting to feel secure, and confident that he was not under surveillance. As he watched, a black cab pulled up in the street outside. A man got out – an oldish man in his early sixties, balding but fairly trim, wearing a smart suit, and carrying a briefcase. He watched the man approach the reception desk and speak to the receptionist. The receptionist picked up a phone and dialled. He listened to the phone for a while, and then shook his head at the older man. At this point, Joe got up and crossed over to reception. He gave the older man a tap on the shoulder.

"George!" he said. "Good to see you."

"Ah, Joe. You're looking well. Thank you for meeting with me. "

"From the telephone conversation that we had, I was led to believe that I didn't have much choice in the matter."

"Yes. That is correct." George gave Joe a thin smile. "Now, shall we retire to your suite, to have our conversation?"

"Certainly. And a very nice suite it is too. Please convey my thanks to the Home Secretary for it. I assume that it is he, who will be be picking up the tab."

George regarded Joe coolly. "I will give you all the information that you need to know, when we are in the seclusion of your room. But – according to section twenty-six, paragraph five - who is paying for your suite is not information that you need to know. OK?"

"Oh absolutely, George. Absolutely." They crossed the lobby, and entered the lift.

***

The two men entered Joe's room on the twelfth floor. George immediately turned on the television, with the volume turned up. He switched on the lights and crossed the room to draw the curtains. "Please sit down Joe." He indicated an armchair, and sat in another himself. He carefully placed his briefcase on a low table positioned between the two chairs.

Joe didn't immediately sit down. Instead, he he gave himself time to think by crossing the room to the drinks cabinet and taking out a bottle of whisky. It was clear to Joe that George was being very thorough in the precautions he was taking to avoid eavesdropping. George worked for MI5, and occasionally employed Joe on a freelance basis, but it was clear, from the clandestine nature of this meeting, that George had something unusual on his mind. Joe was intrigued.

He raised the bottle of whisky and showed it to George. "Shall we?"

"Why not?"

Joe poured generous measures of whisky into two tumblers. He crossed back across the room and sat down, handing one glass to George.

"Cheers, George."

"Cheers."

They each took a drink. Joe put his glass down on the table, and gave George a long steady look. "So, George, why, exactly, are you bringing me out of retirement yet again? The last time I worked for you was, what, five years ago? I swore then that I would never work for you again, and you swore that you would never use me again. You need to give me a very good reason why I should come back, now."

George put his own glass on the table, and studied it carefully. Then he looked directly at Joe. "Because I am willing to pay you a very large sum of money. A sum of money that is larger than any that I have ever paid you in the past. Is that a good enough reason?"

"OK, I'm listening. Go on."

"Do you remember someone called Michael Corrigan?"

"Wasn't he involved with the IRA, about ten years or so ago?"

"Yes, he was involved with them. But he never had any real idealogical commitment to their cause. He simply ran a commercial operation, supplying them with arms. He made a great deal of money, bringing guns from the States, paid for by IRA sympathisers over there. He also brought guns, and explosives, from Eastern Europe. In the process he built up a great many business relationships with the Russian Mafia, in addition to other relationships he forged with equally unsavoury elements in the States."

"Is he still active?"

"Yes. Although he no longer works with the IRA. But he is still heavily involved with gun-running, nowadays on behalf of organisations that are even more unsavoury than the IRA, if that were at all possible. In addition, he has diversified into many other areas – drugs, gambling clubs, protection rackets, and prostitution. His Russian contacts keep him supplied with trafficked women from all over Eastern Europe, who, once in this country, have a particularly short and brutal life working in one of his brothels. He also has a range of business interests in Amsterdam, which, I believe, is where he is currently to be found."

Joe grimaced. "Sounds rather a nasty bugger. But I've never heard of these more recent activities."

"He keeps a very low profile. But he is also involved in a number of legitimate, or perhaps more accurately, quasi-legitimate, businesses. Which are used to launder his illegal earnings. And most importantly, he is believed to have a number of people who are in his pocket, receiving payments to turn a blind eye to his activities, and in some cases to actively assist him. Senior policemen in the Met., judges, newspaper editors, and a couple of MPs. There is believed to be one member of the Shadow cabinet. And there may even be someone within MI5."

Joe looked hard at him. "So where do I come into all this?"

"He seems to be involved in some major new project. It involves large amounts of drugs coming from the Middle East – quite possibly heroin from Afghanistan – being sold to buy arms, which are then shipped back to the Middle East. Mostly ending up in the hands of Islamic militants, and Palestinian terrorist organisations, such as Hamas. Where do you come into this? I want you to find out everything you can about who is involved, where are the drugs coming from, and most especially I want to find out which MPs and policemen are corrupt, and being paid off by Corrigan. And, indeed, anyone else on Corrigan's payroll. And I want to know if there actually is a traitor within MI5. I want every detail. You have many contacts within the Middle East, that I hope you will be able to use. And once you have obtained all this information…"

"Yes?"

"…Michael Corrigan will never be arrested and brought to trial. He has too many powerful friends in the establishment, and in any case, he has considerable sums of money available to him, enabling him to buy the absolute best in terms of legal representation. So once you have obtained whatever information you can about these activities, I want Michael Corrigan dead. This is why I have brought you back in, and the reason for all this subterfuge. Killing people is one of your very special skills."

"I see. And I guess that this operation is not exactly official."

"Quite. Nobody knows about it apart from you, me, and a couple of other people."

"Like the Home Secretary?"

George grimly shook his head. "Need to know, Joe, need to know. OK, now for one or two details. On successful completion of the project, you will be paid a fee of two hundred thousand pounds."

Joe whistled softly.

"And while the project is in progress, you will have an unlimited expense budget. This hotel room is paid for for the next two weeks. In the briefcase there are twenty thousand pounds to cover your expenses, together with a return air ticket to Amsterdam, travelling out tomorrow afternoon, and a reservation for Hotel Krasnapolsky. Which is the same hotel as Corrigan is staying at, together with a couple of his bodyguards.

"There is also a folder in the briefcase, containing all the information that is available to us about Corrigan and his activities, both past and present. I will leave this with you, but I would appreciate it if you would destroy it once you have read it. You might also find it useful to research him on the internet. There are probably rather a lot of references to his various activities. But, from now on you will be largely on your own, on this project. However, you may contact me on this number, should you have need to do so."

He handed Joe a plain business card, which was completely empty, except for a telephone number.

"Is everything clear?"

"Completely. But two hundred thousand is not enough. Not for a job like this. A very special, high profile, execution. I want four hundred. Two hundred thousand up front, and the balance when I finish the job. When Michael Corrigan is dead."

They stared hard at each other. Finally George sighed, and said, "OK. Agreed. Wait here and I'll have the initial payment sent to you. But if you double cross me... If you even think of double crossing me..." He stared grimly at Joe as he got up to leave. "Now, if there are no further questions, I'll let you get started. Good luck." He shook Joe's hand, and then abruptly turned and left the room.

***

After George had left, Joe crossed over to the window, and stood there for a while, looking across into Hyde Park. He thought carefully about the discussion that had just taken place. Elements of it made him very uneasy. And especially George's ready capitulation over the fee that he was being paid, raised his suspicions. He knew that George frequently used people for his own ends - in the past, agents had been ruthlessly sacrificed to achieve the requisite objective. In George's mind, the end always justified the means. Indeed, the most recent job that Joe had carried out for him, some five years earlier in Kosovo, had gone disastrously wrong, and had very nearly cost Joe his life. This had led to the acrimonious split between the two of them that Joe had hinted at earlier in his conversation with George. However, four hundred thousand pounds went an awful long way to helping him overcome his misgivings and his antipathy towards George, and so he brushed all these negative thoughts aside and decided to give George the benefit of the doubt. Well, at least for the time being...

Joe sighed and looked down into Hyde Park, just across the road from the hotel, watching people go about their normal daily lives, oblivious of the darker side of human nature. There were two young women chatting, each pushing a push-chair with a small child. A young couple, walking hand-in-hand down the path known as 'Lover's Walk'. A young blonde girl, jogging peacefully along the same path, unaware that she was being observed. He watched her for a few minutes, envious of her innocence.

He sighed again and crossing back to the table in the centre of the room, opened the briefcase, picked up his glass of whisky and took another sip. He started rummaging through the briefcase; as George had said, there were several large bundles of ten and twenty pound notes. Joe didn't bother counting the money – he didn't think that George would try to double-cross him on such a basic point as expenses. There was a business class open return from Heathrow to Amsterdam, with a reservation out for the next day, and details of the hotel that George had told him about. He took out Michael Corrigan's file, had another drink of his whisky, and then sat back to read. After he had finished reading the information that George had provided, he connected his own laptop to the hotel's network, and using the newfangled 'Google' thing, had a look to see if there was any additional information that could be found on the internet.

Interestingly, there was quite a number of seemingly legitimate businesses that Michael Corrigan was involved with. In London a rather upmarket nightclub called 'Tarantula', together with a somewhat more run-of-the-mill club called 'Crazy Horse'. He owned a betting shop in Hounslow, and had a half share in a pub called the 'Bay Horse' in East London. A pub that Joe thought that he had actually had a drink in on at least one occasion. Good atmosphere, decent beer. And in Amsterdam he had a couple of nightclubs (*"or were they brothels?"*). One was called 'Pink Lady' (*"definitely sounded like a brothel!"*), and one was called 'Bang Bang' (*"Hmmm'*). He also had a half share in a coffee-shop in an area called Leidseplein. In Amsterdam, the so-called coffee-shops were quite legal suppliers of cannabis. Joe found himself reminiscing about his earlier, hippy, lifestyle, and once again, his thoughts turned to Leah. He sighed.

During his researching he discovered that Michael Corrigan had once been married, but his wife had died a few years earlier in a car crash. He read the details with interest. It seemed that there were suspicious circumstances about this crash.

"*Hmmm.*" He filed this titbit of information away.

While he was researching Michael Corrigan, he was interrupted by a knock on the door. He looked up, then crossed the room, opened the door and looked out into the corridor. There was no-one there, but a briefcase had been left. He picked it up and carried it back into his room. He opened it, and smiled happily at the sight of bundles of fifty pound and twenty pound notes, which he then transferred into the hotel's room safe. His down payment for the job.

OK. Time to get started. Let's go out and kill someone...

CHAPTER 2.

London, June 2004.

Two days earlier, Vicki had flown in from New York. After the usual dreadful flight – God, how she hated overnight flights, especially in economy, which was all she ever aspired to – she was then faced with a long, slow-moving, queue to get through immigration. Luckily for all concerned she had not been able to bring a handgun with her as she would have liked; luckily, because if she had brought her gun, she would have been able to use it to shorten the queue in front of her. Then she would have definitely killed the arrogant, officious, prick of an immigration officer who treated her as though she were a fully paid up member of al-Qaida. She smiled sweetly at him, as she presented her passport and immigration card. Although secretly she wanted to blind him by pushing her thumbs into both his eyes, and then having popped his eyeballs out, grinding them into the floor under her boots. She successfully suppressed this urge, and continued smiling as he stamped her passport and handed it to her. She then stuck her tongue out at him and marched off to the baggage carousel. As always, her bag was one of the last to be delivered, and her internal fury achieved new heights.

Eventually having reclaimed her baggage, she passed successfully through customs, and caught the underground railway into the centre of London. She managed to find her hotel – a small private hotel just off Bayswater Road, north of Hyde Park – which she had found on the internet. It was surprisingly nice, and her mood started to improve somewhat. She took her boots off and lay on the bed, but she couldn't work out whether she was tired or not – her watch said twelve o'clock, which, after a moment's thought, she interpreted as noon.

A moment later she looked at her watch again, this time it

said six o'clock. *"Shit, shit, shit,"* she thought. Then, after deliberating for a while, she couldn't decide whether she was hungry, or whether she wasn't hungry, but she decided that she ought to eat anyway. She showered and changed her knickers, but put the rest of her clothes – jeans, T-shirt, and denim jacket – back on, having given them the sniff test first. Nearby, she found a restaurant which had a vaguely American menu, and ordered a burger with fries, or chips as the Brits liked to call them, and a beer. Then she decided that she actually was hungry after all, and ravenously wolfed the meal down. Afterwards she leaned back in her seat, and thought about why she had come to England.

***

Some six years earlier, Vicki had graduated from Penn State University with a degree in law. She then worked for a firm of attorneys for three years, getting steadily more and more bored, until she could stand it no longer. On a whim she applied to join the FBI as a trainee special agent, encouraged by her sister Janet, who was already established as a special agent. To Vicki's surprise, she was accepted, and after her initial training in basic skills such as firearms (and to her amazement, she discovered that she was actually an excellent marks-woman. Wow! Just watch out you mother-fuckers!), she progressed within the organisation. Eventually she finished up at the FBI office in Philadelphia, Pennsylvania. However, she was largely office-based, and her experience of field work was rather limited. She hoped that she would soon be able to receive further training and then she could start playing a more active role. And kill a few baddies!

At the same time as Vicki joined the FBI office in Philadelphia, her sister was posted as a legal attaché to the US embassy in London. That was the last time that Vicki had seen her sister alive. Six months later, Janet's body arrived back in America in a casket. She had been investigating the links between an American crime syndicate, which was selling guns and drugs to members of the British criminal underworld, and their 'clients'.

The FBI had investigated Janet's murder fully, the investigation was still ongoing, but no-one had yet been brought to book. Frustrated by the slow speed of the investigation, Vicki had taken an indefinite leave of absence from the FBI and had come to London to pursue the investigation for herself, unofficially. None of her colleagues in the FBI knew who was involved in the guns and drugs business from the British end, but she had the name of a club in London where the illegal transactions had taken place. The name of this club – 'The Tarantula' – had been passed to the British police, but to everyone's frustration, they had taken no apparent action. After this, the FBI had kept any leads to themselves, and had continued investigating the crime without involving the Brits.

Vicki fiercely rubbed away the tears which had sprung unbidden into her eyes, as she remembered Janet. She saw her principal role as extracting revenge for her sisters death – if that involved identifying the perpetrator, and handing them over to the FBI to be punished according to the due process of the law, then all well and good – but she was perfectly willing to do things in a more extreme way if necessary. In fact she decided that she would probably prefer to do it that way. She glanced at her watch; it was nearly ten o'clock and she felt totally weary. She decided that retribution would have to wait until the next day, so she drained her beer, and made her way back to the hotel. And bed.

***

The next morning, Vicki woke early, and lay in bed thinking. Most mornings she went for a run first thing, but she thought that she really couldn't be bothered today. She was feeling very hungry and decided to have breakfast instead. So she got dressed and went down to the dining room. Although not up to the standards of American breakfasts, what was on offer was quite acceptable, and the coffee that was served was excellent.

After eating, she went for a walk, exploring the neighbouring streets. At a small shop, she bought an 'A to Z' street atlas of London, and a 'Time Out' guide to what was currently going on. After walking in Hyde Park to get rid of the cobwebs in her brain, she found a small café, and over a coffee, examined the guide book. She found an entry for 'The Tarantula', and managed to locate it in the street atlas. She also found a telephone number for it, and although she thought that it was ridiculously early for a night club, nevertheless she called it on her cell-phone. To her surprise she was answered.

A woman's voice. *"Hello."*

"Is that The Tarantula?" she replied.

"It certainly is. What can we do for you?"

Thinking quickly, she said "I'm looking for a job. Do you have anything?"

"You sound like an American. Do you have a work permit?"

"No," she admitted.

"Well, in that case we may have something as a dancer."

"A dancer?"

"Yes. Can you come around to see us about one o'clock this afternoon? Ask for Simon. He's the assistant manager. The manager's out of the country at the moment, and not due back for a couple of days."

"OK"

"What's your name?"

"Linda Parks," she said, glancing across at Hyde Park.

"OK. See you at one o'clock, Linda. Remember. Ask for Simon."

There was a click as the person at the other end rang off. *"A dancer,"* she thought. She wondered just what sort of dancing that they had in mind. She suspected that it wouldn't be the sound of music chorus line, although it was possible that she might have to dress up as a nun. Or a policewoman. Or a nurse. And maybe she'd get to carry a whip. She smiled to herself.

***

At one o'clock she stood outside the staff entrance of 'The Tarantula'. She tentatively pushed at the door. It was unlocked, and she entered the club. "Hello. Is anyone there?" She waited, but there was no reply, so she climbed the flight of stairs that faced her. At the top, she entered the night club proper. There were a number of small tables, with chairs, scattered around the floor. At one end there was a raised stage. And there was a bar at the other end of the room, with two guys sitting on bar stools having a conversation. They stopped talking as she entered the room, and watched her suspiciously as she walked across the room towards them.

"Hello. I'm looking for Simon," she said.

"My name's Simon," replied the older of the two. He was in his fifties, balding and overweight, with an ugly face, and thick, fleshy lips. He smiled at her, though it was closer to a leer than a smile. "You must be Linda."

"That's right." Vicki offered her hand. Simon held out his hand, and Vicki shook hands with him. She found the sensation rather like shaking hands with a rubber glove filled with cold jelly. Simon's hand held onto hers for a few seconds too long, in a slightly nauseating sort of way. Vicki gave a mental shudder.

"So I believe that you want a job as a dancer?"

"Well, actually, dancing is not really my scene," she admitted. "I was more hoping for a job behind the bar, or something like that."

Simon glanced towards the other man. "This is Eric, he's in charge of the bar staff. But I don't know whether he needs anyone at the moment. That right, Eric?"

"That's true at the moment," the younger guy said. "But once Mike gets back from Amsterdam, I think he wants to move a couple of girls to The Crazy Horse and set them to working there. So we might very well have a spot then."

Vicki's ears pricked up, and she started making mental notes. 'Mike. Amsterdam. The Crazy Horse.' "So, Mike's the boss, is he? When is he due back?"

"None of your business," Simon replied coolly. "Leave us a phone number, and we'll contact you if we need another barmaid. Sure you don't want to try dancing? Looks like you've got a nice pair of tits hidden away there. The punters always like a nice pair of tits." They both laughed coarsely.

"Quite sure, thank you," Vicki said, colouring slightly. She wrote a fictional telephone number on a piece of paper, and handed it to Simon. His hand brushed against hers in a very creepy, and very deliberate, sort of way as he took it. She gave another mental shudder.

***

The first thing she did when she arrived back at the hotel was to have a shower. She felt unclean after being in the company of the creeps at the club. Afterwards she felt better and decided to telephone one of her FBI buddies who was based here in London, to see if she could get any information out of him. Unofficially, of course. She used her cellphone, rather than the hotel telephone which charged exorbitant rates. After a few rings, the call was answered.

"Jim. Hi. It's Vicki Delaney," she said.

"Vicki. How are you? I was very sorry to hear about your sister. I partnered her for a while. She was a good agent. We'll surely miss her."

"Thank you Jim."

"Where are you?"

"Here in London."

There was a short silence. *"Officially? Or unofficially?"*

"Unofficially," she admitted. "But I was hoping that you might be able to help me." There was another moment's silence.

"So. Just what do you need?"

"Anything you know about a nightclub called 'The Tarantula'. And another one called 'The Crazy Horse'. The boss of both these is Mike something-or-other. He's in Amsterdam at the moment. I'd like to know where he's staying."

"OK. I'll find out what I can. Give me a phone number that I can contact you on."

She gave him her cellphone number, and then they exchanged a few more pleasantries and terminated the call.

***

Later, Vicki was wandering around Hyde Park. It was warm and sunny – atypical for England, she thought, and she was enjoying being in the open air. She bought some bird food from a street vendor, and spent a pleasant half hour feeding the ducks on the Serpentine. Then she sat on a park bench, soaking up the sun, and people watching.

There were some small boys, sailing remote-controlled boats on the lake. Initially they started off by racing them, but very soon it turned into some sort of gladiatorial contest, with boats being driven at full speed towards each other, playing a sort of game of chicken – the winner being the one who didn't flinch and change course. With some amusement she noted that the winner was a small nerdy-looking boy with glasses. *"Pity real life isn't like that,"* she thought.

There were also several pairs of lovers, walking hand in hand. She felt envious. She couldn't remember the last relationship that she'd been in; it must have been about three years ago, when she had a brief fling with a fellow-agent in the FBI. And it must have been about the same time when she'd last had some good sex, in fact any sort of sex. She started taking stock of her life: she was approaching thirty, good looking (she thought), with a nice body, blond hair, attractive face – and yet it was nearly three years since she'd had sex. Three years. Three fucking years. Feeling slightly desperate, she looked round for a man on his own. Anyone would do, she was starting to think. Anyone! Luckily her phone rang just at that moment.

"Hello."

"Hi Vicki." It was Jim from the FBI ringing back. *"I've found out some information for you."*

"Shoot."

"'The Tarantula' and 'The Crazy Horse' are both owned by a guy called Michael Corrigan. And by the way, 'The Crazy Horse' isn't a night club – it's a brothel."

"What? You mean with hookers?"

"Yes. Why? You haven't applied for a job there have you?"

"Nearly," she thought. "Of course not, I've already got a job," she said.

"It's a real high class place. Apparently MPs – from the British Parliament, not Military Police – go there. There's even suspicions that senior policemen frequent the place as well."

"What can you tell me about Michael Corrigan?"

"He's a nasty piece of work. Used to be involved with the IRA – you know, the terrorists in Ireland."

"Yes, I know," she said, "What else?"

"He's into drugs, and prostitution, and gun-running. And he's also got similar interests in Holland. He's there at the moment, meeting with some people, but we can't find out who. We believe that he's staying at the Hotel Krasnapolsky in Amsterdam. That's quite an expensive hotel that is, beyond the reaches of the likes of you and me, but there's a lot of cheaper hotels nearby, if you're planning on following him there. However, try avoid the ones in the Red Light area. Unless you want to earn a bit of spending money, that is."

"Fuck off."

Jim laughed. "Be seeing you Vicki. Good luck."

CHAPTER 3.

London, June 2004.

The next day Joe arrived at Heathrow some ninety minutes before his KLM flight was due to depart for Amsterdam. Because he was flying business class, the queue for checking-in was short, and since he only had hand-luggage, he was given his boarding pass very quickly. He then joined the fast-track queue for security, passed through quickly, and, although he could have had free drinks in the Business lounge, he rather fancied having a beer in the Wetherspoons bar. And anyway, George was paying. And so, soon after, he was seated in the bar in the departure lounge, enjoying his beer, little more than half an hour after he had arrived at the airport.

As usual, Joe was watching all around him with his usual mistrustful vigilance. He was always alert, anticipating the possibility of enemies. Especially in an airport such as Heathrow, where there were very large numbers of people from all over the world. However, on the plus side, there was very little likelihood that any of them would have been able to bring a gun through airport security. But he wasn't even taking that for granted.

He saw nothing to give him any cause for concern, so he relaxed slightly, and turned his attention to the newspaper that he had bought. As usual, the main news was about turmoil in Israel and Palestine. This time it was Hamas, again, who had been firing home-made rockets from Gaza into Israel, provoking retaliation from the Israeli Defence Force. Joe thought about that, and how it might relate to his current project. He knew very little about Hamas, but he knew from his previous experience that the Palestinians were extremely ingenious, and had the skills to make weaponry such as rockets using the sorts of machinery that would be found in any car repair shop. However, he wondered whether they would be making these home-made rockets if they had access to the sort of weaponry that could be provided by Michael Corrigan. He hadn't yet had an opportunity to speak to any of his contacts in Mossad, but he made a mental note to do so at the first opportunity.

He folded the newspaper, and looked around. As usual, terminal four was a heaving mass of humanity, and he expected that terminals one, two, and three would be also. A young couple with two small children caught his attention. They were pushing a baggage trolley that had a wonky wheel. The trolley appeared to have a mind of its own, and the husband was looking increasingly harassed as it kept lurching in new and random directions, threatening to break ankles, or even do worse damage. He found the sight highly amusing, although he felt a little bit guilty at doing so, but he couldn't help himself. A young, rather attractive, blond girl seemed to be finding it equally amusing, and he exchanged smiles with her, as she dragged her own luggage into the bar, and sat down at a table a couple down from his. He turned his attention back to watching the crowds in the terminal.

***

Vicki had not had quite such an easy time. Since she was flying economy class, she had to join a long queue to check-in, which crawled along at a snails pace. As she malevolently eyed the large family who were currently at the check-in desk – they had two baggage trolleys piled high with luggage, and seemed to be taking an interminable age over the whole business – she once again wished that she had her gun with her. Following this family, there was a pair of students, who didn't even seem to have a reservation, and were also taking forever to be processed. As the harassed check-in girl was making yet another phone call, Vicki experimentally tried to activate her X-ray vision, with the intention of boring holes through the skulls of each of these students, and cause brain haemorrhages. As usual, it didn't work. Maybe she didn't have enough anger. She'd have to practice more. But eventually she made it to the desk.

"Yes, I did pack my bag myself, and no, it hasn't been out of my sight, and no, nobody has asked me to carry anything," she snapped at the girl. "Before you ask." She glared at the poor girl, who hurriedly checked her luggage in, and gave her a boarding pass.

Vicki then joined another queue for security, which crawled along just as slowly. It took her three attempts to get through the metal detector, having first forgotten to remove her keys from her pocket, then her loose change, and finally, a pen. When she finally made it through security, she decided that she needed a drink. A large one. Immediately. She went off in search of a bar. As she approached the only one that she could find, her spirits were lifted by the sight of a harassed young family attempting to push a loaded baggage trolley. The trolley had a faulty wheel and was impossible to steer. As it nearly mowed down a clergyman, she exchanged glances with an attractive-looking older man who was sat at a table in the bar, and also watching the antics of the baggage trolley. They smiled at each other, as she continued into the bar in search of a drink.

The first drink – a large Jack Daniels – went down very quickly, giving her a pleasant warming sensation as it did so. She ordered a second, which she sipped much more slowly. By now she was starting to feel mellow, and regretted her anger at the check-in desk. She was certainly pleased that no-one had actually died – perhaps the prohibition on the carrying of handguns onto planes was actually rather sensible after all.

As she sipped her drink, she pondered over what needed to be done when she arrived in Amsterdam. Number one – find herself a hotel near the Hotel Krasnapolsky. But not too expensive. Number two – locate Michael Corrigan. Number three – follow him and see where he went, and who he met. Simple. As she was sat there thinking about all this, another harassed traveller went past, struggling as he pushed a trolley with a faulty wheel. She was definitely starting to feel more cheerful by the minute.

***

Joe was sat by the boarding gate, waiting to be called for

the flight to Amsterdam. There was a crowd of other people milling around, including the rather attractive blond girl that he had first noticed in the airport bar. He noticed her again – she was definitely noticeable, he thought. But it was a long time since he had done anything other than simply notice a girl – way too long – and in any case, he was now focussed on the job in hand. Track down Michael Corrigan, find out what he was up to, and who he was dealing with, and then kill him. Sounded simple. One, two, three. Bang. As bad a reputation as Michael Corrigan had, Joe didn't anticipate any great difficulties. He'd survived in what he was doing for a long time, dealing with the baddest of the bad. People who were a lot more dangerous than some East End hoodlum. But he knew that nevertheless he had to keep his wits about him, and that he couldn't afford to become complacent.

An announcement came over the tannoy: "Ladies and Gentleman, we are starting to board flight KL1010 to Amsterdam. At this time would first and business class passengers, and families with small children, board the aeroplane. Would all other passengers please remain in the lounge until called. Thank you." Joe stood up and moved through the crowd of people to the boarding gate. He showed his boarding pass, entered the plane, and located his seat.

His was a window seat, and so he spent the journey admiring the tops of clouds. As a business class passenger he was permitted a free drink and a packet of peanuts. *"Well worth the extra cost,"* he thought. He slowly sipped his whisky and thought again about what needed doing. One, two, three. Bang!

The flight took little over an hour, and they were soon descending into Schiphol airport. Once on the ground, the passengers disembarked, and Joe quickly passed through passport control, picked up his luggage, and made his way towards the train for Central Amsterdam.

***

As usual, Vicki had a more frustrating time at the airport. At passport control, she had to join the queue for non-EU passports, which slowly crept along. She kept casting envious glances across at the other queue – the one for EU passports – which moved a great deal faster. Eventually, however, she did actually get through passport control, and made her way to the luggage carousel. This time she was heartened by the fact that her bag was already there when she arrived, and so she didn't have to wait. However, on the downside, it only had one wheel, whereas it had most definitely had two wheels when she checked it in at Heathrow. *"Fuck,"* she thought, as she had to carry it by its handle. *"Fuck, fuck, fuck!"* Never having been to Amsterdam before, she had no idea how to get to the centre of the city, but luckily everyone that she approached spoke perfect English, and she was quickly directed towards the train that would take her to the city centre.

Interestingly, the train had two levels, and she made her way to the upper level, so that she could get a better view on the way into the city. Her fellow passengers were mostly excited young backpackers, though she recognized the middle-aged man that she had seen at the bar in Heathrow airport. He was sat at the far end of the carriage, with his nose buried in a newspaper.

It didn't take long to get into the centre of Amsterdam, which was good because she thought that there wasn't much of a view to be seen, anyway. Once there, she made her way to Hotel Krasnapolsky, briefly admired it, regretfully crossed it off her list of possible hotels, then started wandering around the small streets nearby. As her colleague had said, there were plenty of hotels to choose from, and although the area seemed a little seedy, not particularly threatening but definitely seedy, she soon found one which seemed decent enough. It was conveniently located - only a couple of hundred yards from the hotel where Michael Corrigan was staying.

Once she had checked in, under a false name, and unpacked her few belongings, she went for a walk around, to get her bearings and do a little sightseeing.

CHAPTER 4.

Amsterdam, June 2004.

Joe had already checked in at his rather more upmarket hotel, the Hotel Krasnapolsky. He unpacked, and admired the view across Dam square. Then he went for a walk towards the Red-Light district of Amsterdam. Even though it was early afternoon, there were already a number of scantily-clad girls posing in their windows, trying to attract customers. He pretended to admire some of them, although secretly he found the whole thing rather pathetic. He was also handed a couple of flyers about massage parlours and the like. He carefully pocketed these, returned to the hotel, and went back up to his room.

He took an envelope from the stationery provided in his room, neatly wrote Michael Corrigan's name across the front, and inserted a couple of the flyers he had picked up during his walk. Joe thought that he might be puzzled by these, but that they would be fairly unlikely to raise any suspicions. He then went back down to the lobby and approached the reception desk.

"Please could you give this message to Mr. Corrigan," he asked, and watched carefully as the receptionist glanced at the envelope and placed it in one of the pigeon holes on the wall behind the desk. He noted the room number – twelve twenty-five – and also noticed that there was no room key in the pigeon hole, indicating that Michael Corrigan was probably in his room at the moment. He confirmed this by crossing to one of the phones in the lobby, and dialling the room number. After a few rings, the phone was answered by a man with an Irish accent. Joe adopted a German accent, and apologized for ringing a wrong number. Now he knew that Michael Corrigan was definitely in his room.

He then went back up to his room, which coincidentally

was also on the twelfth floor, although down a different leg of the corridor. He first detoured past Michael Corrigan's room, noting carefully its position relative to the fire exit and the lifts, and the linen closet. Afterwards he returned to his own room, and poured himself a whisky from the mini-bar.

Joe's next step was to obtain a gun, which obviously he hadn't been able to bring on the plane, and one or two other pieces of equipment which he thought might be handy. He used his mobile to make a call to someone that he had dealt with on a number of occasions previously.

Pieter van Rijn was an ex-member of the Dutch special forces – the KCT, or 'Korps Commando Troepen', which was the equivalent to the British SAS. Since leaving the KCT a number of years previously, Pieter had used the many contacts that he had built up, to set up his own security company, providing body-guards to visiting dignitaries, advising companies on industrial espionage, plus a variety of other services. And he also was willing to supply certain items of equipment, to some of his more valued customers.

The phone rang for a while and was eventually answered in Dutch. "Is that Pieter?" Joe asked.

"*Ja.*"

"Hi Pieter, it's Joe Butler. How are you? It's been a long time."

"*Joe, my friend, I'm very well, life is good to me. And I hope life is good for you also. What are you doing in Amsterdam? We must meet for a drink.*"

"I'm in the Hotel Krasnapolsky. Can you meet me in one hour in the lobby bar?"

"*The Hotel Krasnapolsky! I think that perhaps life is indeed good for you! I'll see you there in one hour.*"

***

An hour later, Joe was sat in the hotel bar, nursing a beer, and thinking about nothing in particular. There was no one else there, except for the girl behind the bar, who kept glancing in his direction. Joe caught her eye and smiled. She smiled back.

"It looks like you could be in luck tonight, my friend." Pieter van Rijn gave Joe a hearty slap across his back, and eased himself into a seat at Joe's table. Joe grinned at him.

"Hi Pieter. Fancy a beer?" He caught the eye of the girl behind the bar, pointed to his nearly empty glass, and raised two fingers. She nodded. "So, Pieter, how's business?"

"Business is booming,"replied Pieter. He made an explosive noise with his mouth, and waved his hands theatrically, mimicking an explosion, then laughed uproariously. Pieter was a large man, about six foot six, with broad shoulders. He had blue eyes and short-cropped blond hair, betraying his military background. His facial features were sharp and angular, but he had a ready smile, and the wrinkles in the corners of his eyes were evidence that he smiled a lot. "You could say that I'm rushed off my feet, with more work than I can handle. Do you fancy coming to work with me, perhaps?"

"I'm on a job at the moment, Pieter. But, who knows, maybe in the future? But just now I need your help with something."

They both fell silent as the girl approached with a tray containing two glasses of beer. She placed one in front of each man, and smiled at them. "Put these on my bill, please. Room twelve forty-six." Joe smiled back.

"Certainly, sir," she said, and offered him the bill to sign.

"Remember that, my girl, room twelve forty-six," boomed Pieter, and winked at her. She blushed slightly, and smiled shyly at Joe, then returned to the bar.

"For heaven's sake, leave the poor girl alone," said Joe.

"I tell you, Joe, tonight could very well be your lucky night. Anyway. How can I be of assistance?"

"Well, I need a handgun. Actually, if I could just borrow one it would be best, because I'll be flying out again in a few days, and I won't be able to take it with me, of course."

"No problem. A gun. I can let you have a Heckler & Koch USP, forty-five calibre, plus ammo. What else?"

"Perfect. And I think that maybe a switch-blade will possibly come in useful as well."

Pieter looked steadily at Joe. "So. Is this a private war that you're starting?"

"It's best that you don't know any details."

"Agreed. I definitely think it's best I don't know what you're planning. Anything else?"

"I would like a room bug. Something really discrete. And a receiver to go with it."

"I've got a really nice one just a little bit bigger than a one euro coin, that you'll be able to hide anywhere. It's very sensitive. Or I can let you have one that's disguised as a pen. It looks really very classy."

"Actually, I think I'd like one of each. And a receiver. With a recorder."

"Consider it done. Anything else?"

"I think that's all for now, thanks."

"All right, two thousand euros sound OK?"

Joe agreed, and they shook hands on the deal. "Two hours. There's a coffee shop on Prinsengracht called Tertulia."

"I know it."

"Ask for Johnny. Give him the money. He'll have the things you need. When you've finished with the gun, take it back to him."

"Thanks, Pieter. Just one more thing. Have you heard of a guy called Michael Corrigan?"

Pieter leaned back in his chair and whistled gently. "Michael Corrigan? So is that who you're after. Well, good luck there! Yes, I have heard of him, though thankfully our paths have never crossed. He's a real nasty piece of work. Very dangerous. He runs a couple of brothels here in Amsterdam. One of them is near here in Warmoesstraat called 'The Pink Lady', the other is in Rozenstraat, which is a fair distance away. He's also involved with hard drugs, brings them into here from Russia, and ships them to the UK. And he's thought to have been involved with a murder which happened last year, although the police could never pin anything on him. Most nights he finishes up at the

Holland Casino near Leidesplein."

"Does he now? That's very interesting."

***

Later that day, Joe left the Tertulia coffee shop, clutching a small parcel wrapped in brown paper. All had gone well in his meeting; when he entered the coffee shop and asked for Johnny, he was directed to a young man sitting in a booth at the back of the shop. Joe had slipped into the seat opposite him, and handed over a thin bundle of one hundred euro notes. Johnny was a taciturn young man, who had simply counted the money then nodded and handed him a package without a word. Joe picked up the parcel, nodded back, and left the coffee shop. Once outside, he decided to walk back to his hotel since it was a pleasant evening, and so he set off along the canal side. As always when walking in Amsterdam, he found himself dodging the constant stream of bicycles, and the occasional tram. There were crowds of tourists about, especially as he approached Dam square, but eventually he made it back to his hotel.

On the way through the lobby, he made a diversion past the reception desk, and noted that Michael Corrigan's room key was now back in the pigeon-hole behind reception. So Joe reckoned that now would be a good time to plant the bug in his room. He went back to his own room to think about how he was going to do it. On the way he noticed that the room maid was busy cleaning a room on the same corridor as his, with her trolley parked just outside. He smiled at her and said hello.

As he entered his room, he thought about what he needed to do. First he crossed to the bathroom and gathered all the towels, which he hid at the bottom of the wardrobe. He then deliberately put his room key on the table by the side of the bed and went back out into the corridor. He closed the door behind him, and approached the room maid.

"Excuse me, but I'm afraid that there are no towels in my room," he said.

"I'm very sorry, sir. May I have a look?"

"Of course." He led the way back to the door of his room, reaching in his pocket as he did so. He banged his forehead with his palm and said, "Oh, I'm so stupid, I've left the key in my room, and locked myself out."

"That's not a problem sir." The maid reached into the pocket of her uniform for a master key, which she used to open the room door. She replaced the key in her pocket, and as she did so, Joe reached across in front of her to politely hold the door open. He also very deftly picked her pocket, and transferred the master key to his own pocket. The maid crossed over to the bathroom to check on the towels, pointing out Joe's key on the bedside table as she did so.

Joe smiled at her. "Sometimes I think that I'd forget my own head if it wasn't attached to my neck." He picked up the room key and put that in his pocket as well.

The maid determined that indeed there weren't any towels in the bathroom. "I'm sorry sir, I don't know how that could have happened." She went back into the corridor to collect some towels from her trolley. As she was doing so, Joe politely held his room door open for her. She took a set of towels into the bathroom, and hung them over the towel rail. "Will there be anything else, sir?"

"No, I think that everything's fine now, thank you very much."

"Well then, goodnight, sir."

"Goodnight, and thank you again." Joe passed her a ten euro note as she left the room.

"Thank you, sir."

Joe closed the door behind her, then crossed over to a chair, picked up a newspaper and sat down. And waited. Sure enough, within a couple of minutes, there was a knock on the door. He smiled to himself, and crossed back over to the room door. He opened it to find the maid stood there, looking slightly embarrassed. "Well, hello again," he said, smiling at her, "what can I do for you?"

"I'm very sorry to disturb you sir, but have I left my key in here?"

"No, I don't think so. But do come in and have a look around." The maid entered the room, and Joe made a big show of looking around, trying to help her locate the key which, of course, was in his trouser pocket. Eventually they admitted defeat. "Well, I'm sorry, but it doesn't seem to be here. Is there anywhere else that you may have lost it?"

"I don't know. Well I apologise again for disturbing you. Good night, sir."

"Good night."

Joe closed the door behind her and waited for about half an hour. He then cautiously re-opened the door, and looked out into the corridor. It was now clear. He was ready to break into Michael Corrigan's room. But first, one last check to see if Michael Corrigan was in his room. Joe picked up the phone in his room and dialled room twelve twenty-five. There was no reply – the coast was clear. He left his room and quickly went down the corridor to Michael Corrigan's room, keeping an eye out for the room maid – he didn't want her to see him sneaking into someone else's room with the stolen master key. Fortunately there was no-one else around, and he made it to room twelve twenty-five without incident.

Using the master key, he opened the door, and entered the room. He hung the 'Do Not Disturb' notice on the door as he did so. Then he crossed the room and bent down to look under the desk. He was looking to see if it would be suitable for the small bug that he wished to leave in the room. It looked ideal, so he took a small piece of chewing gum from his pocket, put it in his mouth, and quickly turned it into a soft and sticky state. This he used to secure the small bug to the underside of the table. The pen bug he decided to hang onto for the time being.

Having successfully positioned the bug, Joe then took a

few minutes to do a quick search of the room. There was nothing of interest on any of the surfaces, or in the desk drawers, but in the waste bin he found a screwed-up piece of paper. He retrieved it and smoothed it out. There were some doodles, the sort that you might make whilst answering the phone, together with a date written several times - the 3rd July, which was about ten days away – and the letter 'F', embellished with ornate curls. This was underlined heavily. Joe pocketed the piece of paper then continued his search of the room. The only other thing that he found of interest was an opened packet of condoms in the drawer of the bed-side table, with one missing. He looked at these and smiled, *"Who was the lucky girl?"* he thought, *"Or guy?"* he added, as a mischievous afterthought. There was nothing else to be found in the room, though he noted that the room safe was obviously being used. He decided against trying to break into this – his safe cracking skills were more or less non-existent – so he left the room, taking off the 'Do Not Disturb' sign as he did so.

Joe returned to his own room, and taking the receiver that Pieter van Rijn had given him, he tuned it in to the transmitter that was in Michael Corrigan's room. As expected, it was totally silent. He then switched on the voice-activated recorder attached to the receiver. Having done so he poured himself a large whisky, while he contemplated a fairly satisfying day's work, and decided that it was about time for a meal, followed by a visit to the Holland Casino to finish off the day.

CHAPTER 5.

Amsterdam, June 2004.

A couple of hours earlier, whilst Joe had been at the Tertulia, Vicki had been sat in the lobby of Hotel Krasnapolsky, waiting to see if Michael Corrigan would show up. She had no idea what he looked like, but she had managed to find out his room number, and was now keeping an eye on the reception desk, waiting to see if anyone dropped off the key for room twelve twenty-five.

She had used her own method for obtaining Michael Corrigan's room number. Plan A had simply been to waltz up to reception, and ask for Michael Corrigan's room number. Unfortunately plan A hadn't worked – the receptionist had looked down her nose at her and refused. The look that she gave Vicki carried an unspoken suggestion that she suspected Vicki of being a hooker. Vicki slunk away with her tail between her legs, feeling slightly embarrassed.

Plan B was a bit more subtle. Vicki moved across to one of the pay phones at the other end of the lobby area. Luckily she was hidden from reception, as she dialled the hotel number and asked to be put through to Michael Corrigan. Once she was connected, she pretended that she was calling from the hotel's housekeeping department, checking up on reports that some guests had not had their room towels replaced everyday. She was assured that there was no problem.

"I'm calling a random selection of rooms. Just for the record could I have your room number, please?"

"Room twelve twenty-five."

"Thank you, sir," she said.

She was now sat in the lobby waiting to see if anyone dropped off the key for room twelve twenty five. Luckily the snooty receptionist had left a while ago, so there was no danger of Vicki being recognized. While she was sat there, she amused herself by trying to guess the nationalities of the various guests as they approached the reception area. A young couple who approached the desk arm in arm – she realized that they were actually a bit the worse for wear through drink and were holding each other upright – were clearly English. She was right. Another family who were all rather overweight with big fat arses, were obviously typically American. She was right again. She was so enjoying this game, that she nearly missed Michael Corrigan as he dropped off the key, and the receptionist put it in the pigeon hole that she had been watching.

Michael Corrigan was a fairly burly man with ginger hair, and a hard looking appearance. He was smartly dressed. With him were two other men – both large and well-muscled, with thuggish faces. One had a shaven head, the other had long hair, worn in a pony-tail. Vicki guessed that these were his bodyguards. Both of them looked around the room suspiciously. Then all three went out through the front door of the hotel into Dam square.

Vicki paused, and followed them. Luckily for her they had decided to walk rather than take a taxi, it being such a lovely afternoon. She followed them at a discrete distance. They headed through the throngs of tourists, crossing several of the picturesque canals which criss-cross the centre of the city. They finished up in a street called Rozenstraat. Vicki hung back as the three men went into a rather seedy-looking bar called 'Bang Bang'. Just opposite, on the other side of the street, was a café which she entered, and found a table near the window. She ordered a coffee and sat, watching the bar across the road. The three men had disappeared into the back room, and she assumed that they would be there a while, so she relaxed and turned to her favourite pastime: people-watching. There was certainly plenty of scope for it in Amsterdam.

She found the coffee excellent, and had a second cup, all the time dividing her time between watching the bar across the street, and watching the people around her. She found that she was herself being watched by a smartly dressed, middle-aged, Dutch lady who was sat on the adjoining table. The Dutch lady smiled at her, and then leaned towards her with a conspiratorial look on her face.

"Excuse me, dear, but why are you interested in the place across the street?" she asked.

Vicki blushed slightly. "No, no, I'm not. It's just that I stopped here for a cup of coffee."

"Well, I have to say that 'Bang Bang' is not a very nice place. It's a brothel. And the girls are not treated well. A smart, good-looking girl like you could do so much better. I have a friend who runs a much nicer place, and is always on the look-out for quality..."

Vicki was starting to feel faintly shocked by the turn that the conversation was taking. "No, no, thank you, I have to go now." She abandoned her coffee, and hastily left the café. In the street she nearly collided with a pair of youngsters, who were clearly smoking cannabis. God, this place really was too much. And her an FBI agent. Her natural instinct was to arrest everyone in sight. Only she didn't have a gun. Or a pair of handcuffs. Or indeed any authority to do anything at all. Just then her attention was drawn to a pair of handcuffs in the window display of a sex shop next door to the café that she had just come out of. She started giggling.

Just at that moment, Michael Corrigan and his two companions, came out of the entrance of the bar/brothel, and started walking down the street. She paused for a moment and then started following them. The street was fairly busy, so she didn't feel worried that they would spot her. She hung well back, but made sure that she kept them in sight. They walked down the street a little way, then came to a canal, and turned right into the street which ran alongside the canal.

Vicki followed them, glancing up at the street sign, as she turned the corner. Prinsengracht. The Prince's Canal. She continued following the three men as they strolled down the street. This street was quieter, and so she allowed a greater distance to open up between them, but she didn't feel worried that she would lose them.

She followed them down Prinsengracht for quite a while, until eventually they turned onto a very busy street with trams running down it. Leidsestraat. Within a short distance, they arrived in a large square called Leidsplein, which had many open air cafés and restaurants. And there were a lot of people milling around, together with street entertainers, making it a very lively place. The three men walked through the square, turned into a street nearby, and soon arrived at a casino. The Holland Casino. She guessed that this was their final destination.

The three men had entered the casino, and Vicki decided to follow them in. As she approached the entrance, she could see from the people in front of her that she would be required to show her passport, which luckily she had brought with her. At the entrance, she was pleasantly surprised to discover that it was ladies' night, and that not only did she get free entry, but she was also given a voucher entitling her to a free drink. Who knows, with luck like this, maybe she could risk a gamble.

Once inside, she exchanged her voucher for a vodka and coke, and started wandering around looking for Michael Corrigan and his friends. The inside of the casino was very similar to a casino that she had visited a couple of times back home in Atlantic City, although there were less slot machines, and more tables for roulette, poker, and blackjack. She soon spotted Michael Corrigan sat at a blackjack table. To her surprise, amongst the other players at the same table, there was a man who she thought that she recognized. She thought hard, and then realized that she had seen this man in Heathrow airport, and again when they had first landed in Amsterdam. Coincidence or what? She moved away slightly, so that she could watch both men without being observed herself.

***

Joe was sat at the same table as Michael Corrigan, surreptitiously watching him play. He was making all the correct choices – hitting, standing, doubling, or splitting at exactly the right moments, depending on the dealer's exposed card. Clearly he knew how to play the game, as indeed did Joe. Joe himself was slightly down – the odds are always a little bit in the house's favour anyway – but he suspected from the way that Michael Corrigan was playing, and winning, that he was using some sort of card-counting strategy. By keeping track of the cards that have been played, card-counting allows a player to have a good idea of when the remaining cards in the deck are advantageous to him, and thereby adjust his stakes accordingly. The more that Joe watched Michael Corrigan's play, the more convinced he was that Corrigan was card-counting.

As Joe glanced at the other players, and at the dealer, he realized from the tense expression on the dealer's face, and the way that he watched Michael Corrigan's play, that the dealer himself suspected that Michael Corrigan was card-counting. There was also a bystander nearby, wearing a tuxedo and a serious expression on his face, who was also keenly watching Michael Corrigan. Joe guessed that the man was from the casino security. Now card-counting is quite legal, unless some sort of electronic or mechanical device is used for assistance, but casinos obviously do not like it, and may well use some pretext to eject, or ban, a player who they believe to be card-counting. Joe waited with interest to see what, if anything, would happen. He wondered if Michael Corrigan's unsavoury reputation was known to the casino, in which case they might very well decide to do nothing.

As he glanced around at other bystanders, he caught sight of an attractive blonde girl half-hidden behind a pillar. She was also watching Michael Corrigan intently. With a start, he realised that he had seen her before somewhere. He searched through his memory, and then remembered her from Heathrow, and the baggage trolley with the faulty wheel. He watched her from the corner of his eye, unsure as to whether her presence here was purely coincidence, or what. But her obvious interest in Michael Corrigan, triggered his suspicions, and he made a mental note to keep an eye on her.

Just then, the casino security man approached Michael Corrigan, bent over and whispered something in his ear. Michael Corrigan smiled and nodded, then pushed one of his chips towards the dealer, and pocketed the rest. He stood up and accompanied the security man towards the rear of the casino floor. They entered an office and closed the door behind them. Joe noticed the blond girl watching all this keenly. God, what was going on here? He decided to find out, or at least to have a bit of fun.

He pocketed his own chips, and left the blackjack table. He made a beeline towards the blond girl, who, as she noticed his approach, had an alarmed expression on her face. Joe smiled broadly at her as he drew near. "Excuse me, but I think that we've met somewhere before," he said.

"N-no, I don't think so," replied the girl, a bit flustered.

"Yes, I'm sure that we have," insisted Joe. "Heathrow airport, perhaps?"

"No, I'm certain that we've never met."

"Oh, well, perhaps you're right. But I would be delighted if you would allow me to buy you a drink. Are you on your own here?"

"Thanks for the offer. But I'm waiting for someone. My boyfriend. He's English and he plays rugby," she said. Lying was something that she rather enjoyed, and she considered herself to be very good at it..

"Oh. What position does he play?"

She experienced a brief flash of panic, but managed to

control herself. "Errmm, one of the ones at the front."

"A forward, you mean. In the pack."

"Yes."

"Which position in the pack? Prop, hooker, second row, what?"

"Err, prop."

"Loose head or tight head?"

Her panic grew, but she pressed on. "Yes, one of those."

Joe smiled. "Big lad, is he?"

"Yes."

"What, bigger than me?"

"Yes."

"Well, in that case we certainly wouldn't want him to catch me trying to chat up his girlfriend. I think that I better say 'Bye-bye'. Or maybe 'Au revoir' might be better." He smiled at her genially, then turned and moved away. Once his back was to her, he allowed a grin to spread across his face.

***

Vicki thought that she'd actually managed that rather well. She thought that lying was one of her strong points. Perhaps it was time for her to update her CV and make sure that it emphasised her strengths as a really good liar. Maybe it might even be possible to get an academic qualification in lying. Harvard perhaps? That would certainly stand her in good stead should she were to choose to embark on an alternative career as a politician, if she ever felt that she'd had enough of being in the FBI. A politician! Hmmm, now there's an idea. Who knows, maybe the White House one day? And then – just watch out you mother-fuckers!

She watched the man move away with a touch of regret. He was actually rather good-looking, he seemed a nice, friendly person, and, since it was three years since she'd last had sex, she wondered if he might have been willing to oblige.

She shook her head angrily. She was being stupid - she was here to do a job, and allowing herself to be distracted by ridiculous thoughts like those, was not particularly productive. In any case, what was he doing here in the casino, playing Blackjack at the same table as the man she was here to watch? Was that a coincidence, or was there something more sinister going on? She resolved to keep an eye out for that man.

As he moved away, she glanced towards the back of the casino where Michael Corrigan had disappeared. He had by now emerged from the office that he had previously entered, and was shaking hands with the man that had accompanied him earlier. They were laughing together about something. A third man was stood watching them. That man was smaller and thinner than the others, with a swarthy complexion, quite possibly of Middle Eastern appearance. And, his most notable distinguishing feature was that he only had one eye. His left eye. His right eye socket was simply an empty scar. She glanced around; no-one was watching her, so she quickly took her mobile phone from her handbag, and used it to take a photo of the threesome. She glanced around again, it seemed that no-one had noticed and that she had got away with it. Though she doubted that the photo would be very useful, the distance was rather a bit too far.

Michael Corrigan crossed back across the casino floor, and was joined by the two ugly-looking men who had accompanied him from the hotel. Vicki guessed that they were his bodyguards. She watched the three of them as they left the casino, and went out into the street. Then she moved after them.

CHAPTER 6.

Amsterdam, June 2004.

Vicki was incorrect in her belief that no-one had noticed her when she took the photograph of Michael Corrigan and his companions. Joe had noticed. He watched her take the photograph with interest, and wondered again what was going on. Who was this girl, and why was she interested in Michael Corrigan? And he thought that she had acted rather rashly in taking the photograph the way she had. Whatever she was up to, she was clearly an amateur in cloak-and-dagger activities. He decided that he needed to keep an eye on her, partly for her own protection, but mainly to prevent her totally fucking everything up for him as she blundered around.

One other person had also noticed Vicki's photographic activities. The pony-tailed bodyguard of Michael Corrigan had noticed. The thoughts that went round in his head were very much more unfriendly than Joe's. As he went towards his boss who was crossing the casino floor, he refrained from looking at Vicki, but murmured something to his boss as he joined him. Michael Corrigan stiffened, and gave a slight nod as the three of them left the casino.

Once outside, the three of them stopped, ostensibly for Corrigan to light a cigar. He was facing the casino exit as he did so, watching people who were leaving. As Vicki left the casino, the bodyguard nudged his boss slightly with his elbow. Michael Corrigan glanced at Vicki, taking in her her long blond hair and blue eyes, and her attractive face and figure. He smiled to himself, then turned away and started walking down the street with his two bodyguards. He leaned towards the pony-tailed guy, and muttered something to him in a low voice.

Joe had left the casino at about the same time as Vicki. He observed Michael Corrigan's reactions with alarm, realising that he had recognised Vicki's interest in him, and that now she was quite possibly in danger. The three guys started walking down the street, with Vicki following at a discrete distance, unaware that everyone knew about her. Joe followed behind her, staying well back and well out of sight, watching carefully.

When they reached Leidseplein, Michael Corrigan and his two men stopped to watch one of the street entertainers. This was a young guy who performed a variety of tricks, such as juggling with flaming torches, which he then extinguished in his mouth. He then did some more juggling tricks with bayonets, and axes, and finally with chain saws. The crowd applauded enthusiastically, and Michael Corrigan put some money in the young man's collecting box at the end of the act. As he did so, the pony-tailed guy slipped away from the other two.

Vicki had allowed the juggler to distract her from watching Michael Corrigan and his bodyguards and didn't notice the one who slipped away. Joe did, and he watched carefully what was going on. As Michael Corrigan and his one remaining bodyguard started walking again towards Dam square, Vicki looked around worriedly for the third man, but couldn't see him, and resumed her discrete pursuit of the two that were left.

Joe waited for a few minutes, until, as he expected, the pony-tailed guy slipped out of the shop doorway where he had been lurking, and started following Vicki. Joe then joined in at the end of the increasingly long procession. He was starting to feel grimly amused by the absurdity of it all, and he cast a quick glance over his shoulder to make absolutely certain that there was no-one following him.

Joe could see both pony-tail and Vicki, though he had lost sight of Michael Corrigan and the shaven-headed guy. He assumed that they were still there at the head of the cavalcade, and that the girl had got them in her sights. He closed the distance between himself and pony-tail, so that he could more quickly intervene as soon as it became necessary, and he reached behind, to reassure himself that he was still carrying his gun tucked into the waistband in the small of his back. It would have been useful to have had a silencer for the gun, and he kicked himself that he hadn't thought to ask Pieter for one, though he rather hoped that he wouldn't have to actually use it.

The procession made its way along Leidsestraat, and Spuistraat, heading for Dam square. As they got nearer to the square, the amount of pedestrian traffic lessened, and Joe tensed, expecting the three men to make their move. However, nothing happened, and eventually they all arrived in the square, where there were more tourists crowded around. Michael Corrigan and his companion chatted and smoked another cigar, then made their way into the hotel.

***

It was by now getting quite late and Vicki suspected that the two men were probably going to retire for the night. She contemplated entering the hotel and having a drink in the bar, on the off chance that they would be doing so as well, though she wasn't sure what that would achieve. It would probably be more useful to return to her own hotel, and get in touch with Jim, her FBI contact in London. She was hoping that he would still be willing to help her, and in particular, she hoped that he would be able to identify the Middle Eastern man who had met with Michael Corrigan in the casino.

Before she set off back to her hotel, she looked around Dam square one more time, checking that the coast was clear. As she did so, her feminine intuition kicked in and she started feeling that something was not quite right. Where was that third man, the bodyguard with the pony-tail?

Vicki cautiously started walking towards her hotel, which was not far away, down a poorly lit street called Warmoesstraat. In the light of day, it had seemed like a nice location, only a short distance from Dam square, but at night the street seemed rather more sinister, and she picked up the pace as she carefully made her way towards the hotel. She was followed by pony-tail, who started closing in on her. Joe brought up the rear, and also moved closer, and tensed, realising that something was just about to happen. He glanced around, just to satisfy himself again that he himself wasn't being followed.

Vicki's instincts were now on high alert, and as pony-tail made his final approach, she sensed what was about to happen, and she whirled round and kicked him in the balls. Hard. He screamed, and bent down clutching his groin. As he did so, Vicki's foot came up again and contacted the centre of his face, breaking his nose. He collapsed on the ground, moaning. Vicki kicked him once more in the head, rendering him unconscious.

She stood over him, breathing deeply. *"Well. My training in unarmed combat finally came in useful,"* she thought. She looked down at the man, then bent over and started going through his pockets. She found a British passport, in the name of Peter O'Reilly. She tore it in half and threw it into a nearby litter bin. She also found a wallet containing several hundred euros plus a couple of hundred pounds. She pocketed the money, *"I do believe that means that I will be able to finish off the evening with a very nice nightcap!"*, but found nothing else of interest apart from a couple of credit cards, so she threw the wallet into the litter bin as well.

***

Joe had observed all this with interest. He revised his opinions about Vicki. Clearly she was not such an amateur in cloak-and-dagger activities as he had first thought. Just who was this girl, and what was her interest in Michael Corrigan? Very cautiously he followed her to her hotel. He watched as she entered the hotel, waited for a while, then discretely followed her in. Thankfully, she did not notice him. He watched as she retrieved her room key from the hotel's reception, and carefully took note of her room number as she did so. Vicki headed for the elevator and was clearly heading for her room and so, after a couple of minutes, Joe decided to go back to his own hotel.

As he walked down the street he chanced upon the pony-tailed bodyguard of Michael Corrigan, lying inert in the street. He figured that the bodyguard would probably be OK, and so, after a moment's thought, he gave him a good kick in the head and then happily continued towards his hotel.

***

As Joe approached Hotel Krasnapolsky he encountered a couple of thuggish looking characters walking in the opposite direction. With a start, he realized that one of the two was the second of Michael Corrigan's body-guards that he had seen earlier in the casino. He waited until they had passed him, and then he turned around and started cautiously following them.

They were heading towards Vicki's hotel. As he followed them, Joe reassured himself by patting the gun tucked into his belt in the small of his back. Suddenly they stopped walking, and Joe guessed that they had chanced upon their pony-tailed colleague. He waited to see what their reaction would be.

One of them bent over pony-tail, and attempted to pull him upright. Then the second guy started walking rapidly towards Vicki's hotel. Fuck! It looked like they knew exactly where Vicki was staying! Joe thought that the shit was about to hit the fan and he needed to do something. Fast! He pulled out his gun from his belt then rapidly walked towards the pair. As he approached, the guy who was standing looked towards Joe, and started reaching for his gun. But not quickly enough. Joe raised his own gun and shot him in the head. He fell to the ground, leaving brain-matter splattered all over the wall. Joe then looked down at pony-tail, lying on the ground unconscious, and decided to allow him to live. For now. The gunshot would undoubtedly attract attention, so he had to move. Quickly. He hid his handgun under his jacket then hurried on his way towards Vicki's hotel.

***

Joe cautiously walked down the corridor where Vicki's

room was. He saw that the door to the room was open, so he pulled out his handgun and moved even more stealthily, his senses on high alert. As he got closer to the room he heard Michael Corrigan's goon talking to Vicki.

"OK, bitch, why were you following us? Who are you working for?" He had her by the throat and was slamming her head against the wall for emphasis, with each word. Vicki was seeing stars, and starting to lose consciousness. Joe could see that Vicki was out of her depth this time. She was starting to panic, convinced that she was going to die. The man grabbed her handbag and then released her. She slumped to the ground, and managed to gasp some air into her lungs, but she realised that this was only a temporary respite.

As he started searching her handbag, Joe moved into action. He rapidly approached him from the side, drew his gun and held it about two foot from the side of the man's head. "OK, mother-fucker! Freeze!" he shouted.

The guy slowly turned his head to face Joe, and shouted, "Just who the fuck are you? Do you know who you're fucking messing with? You're fucking dead, man." He looked as though he was about to take a step towards Joe, who shrugged and pulled the trigger. The bullet entered midway between his eyes, right about on the bridge of his nose, and the complete back of his head disappeared in an explosion of gore. The force of the gunshot threw the body backwards several feet.

"No, actually it's you that's fucking dead," corrected Joe mildly, "Sorry." He quickly glanced down the corridor. Luckily, at that moment there was no-one around but Joe knew that the gunshot would have been heard and the shit would be about to hit the fan very, very soon. They had to move quickly. He bent down to Vicki, put his arm round her, and helped her to her feet. "I'm sorry, but we've got to get moving now," he said urgently. "This place is going to be swarming with police very soon, and that's an illegal weapon that I've just used to kill someone. Well two people, actually. There's a second body in the street. I think that we might very well have a bit of a problem. So let's go." He picked up her handbag and handed it to her.

Vicki staggered back against the wall. She looked dreadful; she was gasping for breath, tears were streaming down her face, and she was clutching her stomach where she had been punched. "Wh-wh-wh," she stammered.

"Ssshh. Don't try to talk. I'll take you to my hotel. That'll be the last place that they'll think of looking for you." He supported her as they stealthily crept down the back stairs and into the street, as quickly as they could manage. The street was still deserted, but it could only be a matter of minutes before the police arrived. Someone must surely have heard the shots, and dialled 112. He was practically carrying Vicki as they hurried down the street back towards Dam Square and the hotel. He knew that there was a back entrance to the hotel, so he ducked down a side street, which brought them to a canal just behind the hotel. From there he took a small alley, which brought them to the hotel's back entrance. No-one was about as they sneaked in, and then he used the service lift to take them to the twelfth floor. Very cautiously, he peered out of the lift into the corridor. Luck was still on their side, the corridor was empty, and they cautiously made their way to Joe's room.

CHAPTER 7.

Amsterdam, June 2004.

Once inside his hotel room, and with the 'Do Not Disturb' notice in place, Joe laid Vicki on the bed, and went to the bathroom to get a damp flannel. He gently wiped her face with the flannel. Vicki was starting to recover, the colour was coming back into her cheeks, and she focussed on his face. "You again. Who are you?" she asked.

"Allow me to introduce myself. My name's Joe Butler. And you are?"

"Vicki. Vicki Delaney. But who are you working for? And why did you help me?"

"Actually, I think that I'll ask all the questions for the time being." He regarded Vicki coolly. "I want to know whose life I just saved. So who are you working for? And exactly what is your interest in Michael Corrigan?"

"How do you know about Michael Corrigan?"

"Never mind. Just tell me why you're after him, and why you took that photograph."

"I'm not telling you anything, until you tell me who you work for," she said animatedly.

"Oh, this is getting us nowhere." He grabbed her handbag and stood up.

"Give. That. To. Me." Vicki tried to get up and grab the handbag back.

"No." In one quick movement, he opened the handbag, upended it and tipped all the contents onto the bed. Then he started rummaging through everything on the bed with one hand while he held Vicki at arms length with the other.

"Let. Me. Fucking. Go." Vicki flailed her arms impotently. She was quickly recovering from her ordeal, helped by her anger at her treatment from this very annoying, albeit cute and sexy-looking, man.

"Holy shit." Joe grabbed her FBI ID card and examined it. "You're FBI. A Fed. Shit. I don't believe it."

"You better believe it," she replied spiritedly. "And you're going to be in big trouble, if you don't give that back and let me go."

"Big trouble? What? For saving your life?"

"Yes, well, OK, thank you for that," she said, starting to calm down.

"So why are the Feds interested in Michael Corrigan?" He continued combing through the contents of Vicki's handbag, and picked up her mobile phone. "May I?"

"Feel free. I don't think that I can stop you doing just whatever you want."

"Hmmm. Interesting invitation." He grinned at her and examined the phone. Then he started pressing keys, until eventually, he displayed the photograph that she had taken in the casino. He examined it, then suddenly froze. "This is the man who met Michael Corrigan?" He demanded, and showed her the picture displayed on the phone.

"Yes. Didn't you see him?"

"I didn't get a good look at him," he said.

"Do you know him?"

"Yes."

"Look. Before we go on, I need to who you're working with," Vicki demanded. "Who are you? What is your interest in Michael Corrigan? And who's this man?"

Joe looked at her long and hard without and said, "Are you really a Fed?"

"Yes. Now just who are you?"

"I'm MI5."

"Now that I don't believe. What, MI5 are licensed to kill nowadays? Like James fucking Bond. Who are you, then, double oh seven and a half? Don't give me that crap. I'm asking you again. Who are you?"

"I'm MI5," Joe insisted, "well more accurately, I'm a free-lancer, employed by MI5."

"A freelancer. You mean a fucking mercenary. Now that, I can believe."

"Look, I saved your life, remember. We're both on the same side here. Let's share what we know. OK?"

"OK. You start."

Joe explained MI5's interest in Michael Corrigan. "We believe that he's bringing in drugs – heroin from Afghanistan – which he's exchanging for guns. The guns then go back out to the Middle East, either to Islamic militants, or to Palestinian terrorists. And Michael Corrigan makes a big profit." He told Vicki about his previous involvement with the IRA. And about the range of illegal activities – drugs, protection rackets, prostitution – that Corrigan was currently involved with. He didn't share with Vicki the suspicions about a traitor in MI5. Nor did he inform Vicki of his mandate to kill Corrigan.

In return, Vicki told Joe about her sister's death, whilst on an assignment investigating the connections between American criminals who were selling drugs and guns to people within the British underworld. "Presumably Michael Corrigan. He owns the nightclub – 'The Tarantula' – where all this was happening."

"So are you doing this officially or unofficially?"

"Unofficially," she admitted.

"Hmmm. I guess that explains your blundering around with no back up. You're lucky to still be alive."

"Well, thank you once again. Now tell me. Who's the guy in the photograph that I took in the casino? The Middle Eastern looking guy with only one eye?"

Joe went very quiet. After a long pause, he said, "His name is Abd-al-qadir. He's an Arab. One of the most evil bastards that you can imagine. And I'm going to kill him." His face had the grimmest and coldest expression that Vicki had ever seen, and she thought that she detected a glimmer of tears in his eyes. "I'm going to fucking kill him..."

CHAPTER 8.

Israel, April 1975.

Joe stood by the side of the road just outside Dimona with his thumb stuck out, feeling totally pissed off as the umpteenth car passed him by without stopping. For fuck's sake, surely as a member of Mossad, he should be entitled to better than this...

***

For the last few months he had received training in unarmed combat, firearms, survival techniques, and so on. He had also been taught rudimentary Hebrew and Arabic Joe was reasonably proficient in languages already, speaking good French, some German, and a good understanding of Greek (acquired during his recent travels round the Greek islands). General Shavit was particularly interested in his skills with French, though he didn't say why, and Joe was intrigued to know why this was so. Joe was also encouraged to cultivate his hippy appearance, growing his hair and so on, and Joe was also intrigued by by the reasons for this. Thankfully Leah loved the new, hippy, Joe and started adopting a hippy persona for herself, wearing beads and a caftan. Chaim and the others all found this highly amusing.

"I know, why don't you take me to the Woodstock festival," Leah exclaimed excitedly one day.

Joe burst out laughing. "I'm afraid that we've missed it by a few years. Sorry."

"Oh."

***

Eventually, in early 1975, he had embarked on his first mission with Mossad. And here he was. Stuck at the side of the fucking road...

He had left the kibbutz, and Leah, two days earlier to travel down to Eilat, with the aim of mingling with, and becoming part of, the hippy community of ex-volunteers who had made Eilat their home, centred, it was believed, on a place called the "Peace Café". His assignment was initially to get involved with the drug sub-culture in Eilat, and through that, to infiltrate the Lebanese drug trade. He was after a dangerous Arab terrorist, Ali Hassan Salamel, who was a key figure in the terrorist attack on the Is-raeli team at the Munich Olympics of 1972 and very high on Israel's wanted list. He was also heavily involved with the Leba-nese drug trade, and Joe's mission was to endeavour to track him down through that.

Joe had several hundred Israeli Pounds in his pocket for him to use as required. Buying drugs. Also hidden away in the bottom of his back pack was a handgun – a Beretta – along with a box of 19mm ammunition. Joe hoped that he wouldn't have to use it, but.... better safe than sorry, as the saying goes. He toyed with the idea of using the gun to kill the driver of the next car that approached him, then stealing the car, and thus getting a ride that way.

However, in keeping with his role as a hippy, he also had a finger of cannabis with him, and so he moved away from the road and rolled himself a joint. He smoked it, and then he started feeling much more relaxed; suddenly the desert scenery seemed incredibly beautiful. He enjoyed the sun on his face, and the breeze in his hair. And almost immediately a car stopped to offer him a lift, going all the way to Eilat. Things were definitely look-ing up. Far out!

Once he arrived in Eilat, he soon made himself at home on the beach among a crowd of hippy ex-volunteers. He shared a couple of joints with them, and then, through seemingly in-nocent questions, confirmed his belief that the "Peace Café" was definitely the place that he needed to investigate. All the guys that he was with hung out there. As did the local dope dealer.

Plus various other nefarious characters. For example the woman who ran a black market, money-changing, business.

Also the Peace Café had the cheapest beer in town, and did decent, and cheap, food. And played pretty good music.

And it was also where local employers went to recruit casual, unskilled labour. They turned up every morning at about six o'clock to recruit people for a day's work, for example labouring on a building site. Many of the people that Joe was with frequently went there to earn a bit of cash to spend on dope, beer, and food. Some even slept there; the Peace Café didn't have walls all the way round, so it was possible to doss down inside on the floor, and thus be first in the queue when potential employers arrived in the morning. (The bar, however, was definitely closed overnight with a securely-locked shutter!)

To help gain acceptance with his new friends, Joe went looking for work at the café. Next morning he turned up at six, and was quickly recruited as a casual dock labourer. For the next ten hours or so he first helped load up a barge with a variety of provisions. The barge was then taken out to a freighter moored in the middle of the channel. He then helped unload the barge and transfer the goods onto the freighter. The temperature was well over 40°C, even more than he was used to when he was picking olives on the kibbutz. He started feeling totally pissed off. *"Fucking hell"* he thought, *"I didn't join Mossad for this!"*

After an incredibly hard and boring days work, he got paid sixty-four Israeli pounds, which was about five pounds sterling, and he rushed off back to the Peace Café. He downed three beers in quick succession, accompanied by a meal of falafel and chips, then he sought out Yoav, the local dope dealer. Joe found him to be easygoing and friendly, and bought a finger of Lebanese hash from him. It was believed that the Lebanese hash was brought into Israel, and brought down to Eilat, by Bedouin tribesmen, who apparently could cross the Lebanese border relatively easily. Joe realized that it was important to move carefully, and avoid raising any suspicions, so having paid for the dope (twenty-five

Israeli pounds – nearly half his earnings for the day!) he left Yoav on amicable terms and made his way back to the beach, where he enjoyed a rather stoned session with his new hippy friends there.

After three more days working in Eilat docks, followed by two days spent picking olives (*"not more fucking olives – for fucks sake!"*) Joe decided he'd had enough of this sort of casual work for now, and he felt that he'd done enough to gain acceptance into the community of hippy ex-volunteers.

. By now, he had on several occasions bought dope from Yoav, the dope-dealer, and felt that he was starting to strike up a friendship with him. They found that they had a shared passion for the music of Pink Floyd.

"So which period of Pink Floyd do you prefer, Yoav? The original Syd Barret stuff? Or the more recent work?"

"Oh, definitely the new stuff. I think 'Dark Side of the Moon' is fantastic!"

"Couldn't agree more." They both sat and listened appreciatively to the music that was currently being played in the Peace Café. 'Dark Side of the Moon' of course. (At that time, practically every bar in Eilat was playing 'Dark Side of the Moon'.)

After several such conversations, Joe tentatively raised the subject of dope dealing. Did Yoav have room for a partner? Joe was disappointed, but not greatly surprised, when Yoav turned him down. So Joe decided to move on to the next step, one that he had already worked out in his mind. He had learned from the various people that he had socialized with whilst in Eilat, that a key place for the 'import' of cannabis from Lebanon, was Nueiba, in the Israeli-occupied Sinai desert. Nueiba was a Moshav, which Joe thought of as a little bit like a Kibbutz. And apparently there was also a lot of hippies living on the beach, with a very active drug culture. He decided that he needed to phone Chaim, back at the kibbutz, and bring him up to date.

While he was sitting with Yoav, he decided to ask him if he

could have a discount on a multiple finger purchase. Yoav was rather more amenable on this request.

"Sure Joe. I'll give you twenty five percent discount if you buy four fingers. Buy three get one free." He laughed. "That'll be seventy five pounds for four fingers."

Encouraged, Joe decided that a little haggling would probably not go amiss. "How about sixty pounds for four fingers?"

"Seventy pounds for four fingers!"

"Sixty five pounds for four fingers?"

Yoav laughed. "OK. Deal. But you can buy me a beer. And make it the decent stuff – Goldstar not Nesher."

Joe wandered off to the bar to buy two beers. He rejoined Yoav; handed him his beer together with the money, and received his hash in return. After spending some more time with Yoav, he then went back down to the beach, and spent the next couple of hours with his hippy friends, smoking several joints, getting more and more stoned until he finally fell asleep.

Next morning he woke and made his way to Eilat's post office, taking care to make sure that he was not being followed. Once there he found a public phone, and put in a call to the kibbutz, knowing that it would be picked up by Malka.

"Shalom Malka, it's Joe Butler. How are you?"

"Shalom Joe. I'm good. And how are you? And is your magic wand still working?" She laughed.

"I'm pretty good, Malka, pretty good. And, yes, I think that my magic wand is still working pretty good, though it hasn't had much practice recently."

"So what can I do for you, Joe? Where are you?"

"I'm in Eilat, Malka, and I need to speak to Chaim. It's quite urgent. Please could you get him to phone me on …", he looked at the phone, "… '08 636 3444' as soon as possible."

"OK Joe. I'll do that. Lehitraot Joe."

" Lehitraot Malka."

Joe put the phone down, and then hung around in the phone booth, knowing that at her age, Malka moved quite slowly, and it would probably take her quite a while to get to Chaim. Luckily, there was no-one else wanting to use the phone. And thankfully he didn't have to wait too long, a few minutes later the phone rang. Joe picked it up.

"Shalom, Chaim."

"Shalom, Joe. What have you got to report?"

"Well, Chaim, I've got to the main dope-dealer here in Eilat, but I can't get any further with him. I haven't been able to find out his main supplier in Lebanon. So now I'm planning on heading down to Nueiba in the Sinai desert. One thing that I have found out is that Nueiba is a key location for the cannabis that's being smuggled in from Lebanon. By Bedouin tribesmen, I believe. So I'm going down there to dig around, and see what I can find. And I think that I could maybe do with some help."

"OK Joe, I'll head on down there and meet up with you." He went quiet. Joe sensed that Chaim was smiling. "And I'll bring Leah with me. She's driving us all mad, wanting to go to the bloody Woodstock Festival. Maybe she'll be able to help."

Joe laughed but then went quiet, torn between excitement at seeing Leah again, but at the same time worried at exposing her to possible danger. In the end, his desires won out. "OK, Chaim. I'll see you both in two days at the Nueiba Moshav Café. About noon."

"OK Joe. We'll see you there about noon. The day after tomorrow. Lehitraot Joe."

"Lehitraot Chaim. See you."

CHAPTER 9.

Israel, April 1975.

The next day Joe was stood by the side of the road just outside Eilat, on the road to Nueiba, with his thumb stuck out. Knowing that he would very soon be seeing Leah put him in a really good mood. He was standing across the road from a café, idly taking in life's goings on. He was highly amused by what he saw...

A jeep with two soldiers pulled into the café's car park, near a car that was already parked there. The soldiers went into the café, and shortly after came out, and climbed back into their jeep. They started up the jeep, and quickly reversed – straight into the side of the parked car. They looked back, viewing some quite serious damage to the side of the car, but they simply shrugged their shoulders and drove off. Joe waited, eagerly anticipating the return of the car's owner and his likely reaction. He wasn't disappointed. Just a little while later the guy returned, saw what had happened to his car, started jumping up and down shouting obscenities, and then rushed back into the café.

Joe found all this highly amusing, but just then a car pulled up, offering Joe a lift all the way to Nueiba. He gratefully accepted the lift, relaxed and enjoyed the ride.

***

When he arrived at Nueiba, he wandered around, getting his bearings. He looked in at the Moshav, found the café, and bought falafels wrapped in pitta bread, which he ate as he wandered down to the beach area. He was surprised and delighted to find Bruce and Jane camped there, the Americans he had been with when he first came to Israel. He rushed over and embraced them.

"Hey, you two! When did you leave the kibbutz?"

"Soon after you," Bruce said, "but we haven't really left. We're just taking a short holiday break down here. Chilling out. Getting stoned."

"Far out!" Joe grinned broadly, pulled out his dope and then rolled a joint which they all happily shared. They chatted happily, bringing each other up-to-date about their recent activities. Bruce and Jane had spent some time in Jerusalem, taking in the sights, then headed straight down to Nueiba, not stopping in Eilat. They were amused to hear about Joe's work experiences in Eilat.

"Picking olives?" Bruce started laughing. "What, more olives? Fuck!"

Joe decided to change the subject. "What's the dope scene like down here?"

"Pretty cool. We buy it from an English guy down here in the beach. It costs thirty Israeli pounds per finger."

At this Joe's ears pricked up. "An English guy? And where does he get it from?"

There's some Arabs – Bedouin I think – who are continually passing through. They deal in it. Selling it to anyone who's willing to buy twenty fingers and then act as a middleman to the likes of us. There's the English guy, and there's a couple of others further up the beach. One's an Israeli. Rumour has it that he's a deserter from the Israeli army. Actually the Israeli army is probably a lot better off without him. He spends most of his time stoned out of his head." They all laughed.

Joe's interest grew. "And how much do these Arabs charge?"

"Somewhere between twenty and twenty-five pounds per finger. And it's good stuff. It comes from Lebanon. Apparently these Bedouin have some sort of cosy relationship with the PLO, to cross back and forth over the Israeli-Lebanese border. I don't know why the Israeli army isn't doing anything about it. Probably sitting around with their thumbs stuck up their arses. Getting stoned." They laughed even louder.

Joe's ears pricked up. He started thinking that he was finding some useful information that he could usefully pass on to Chaim. He decided to get to know this Englishman, under the pretext of buying some dope off him. "So what's this English guy's name, and how do I find him?"

"He's called Keith something or other. You can't miss him. He's got ginger hair, and a bushy ginger beard. He's shacked up with a bird called Sue."

Joe happily spent the next couple of hours smoking dope and getting stoned with Bruce and Jane. Another couple who were living on the beach joined them, and they all swapped gossip. Joe found out a bit more information about the Bedouin cannabis smugglers. Apparently there were three of them, but only one spoke any English. However his English was quite good. Joe tried to find out more about where they were crossing the border between Lebanon and Israel. No-one really knew for sure, but someone suggested that it might be near a place called Metula. Some more information for Joe to pass on to Chaim.

***

Joe had dossed down on the beach, fairly close to Bruce and Jane. He slept well, helped, probably, by all the dope he had smoked. He woke up next morning in good spirits, looking forward to seeing Leah. He ate breakfast in the Moshav café, then went back down to the beach to wait for the arrival of Chaim and Leah. He wandered down the beach, looking for Keith, the dope dealer. He soon found him, introduced himself, and then bought a finger of hash. They parted amicably, and he then spent the next couple of hours daydreaming and turning things over in his mind. Lost in thought, he was suddenly awakened by an excited squealing. He looked up and saw Leah running towards him across the beach. He leapt to his feet, and embraced her.

"Christ, Leah, it's great to see you."

"You sure that you don't want to go to the Woodstock Festival?"

Joe burst out laughing. "Quite sure, Leah, quite sure." He looked beyond Leah at Chaim who was grinning broadly. "Good to see you. Chaim. We need to talk." The three of them walked along the beach to get some privacy. "Eilat turned out to be a bit of a non-starter. Except that it's led me to here. And I think that there's a lot more going on down here." He brought Chaim up-to-date about the Bedouin drug smugglers, and the various dealers on the beach.

Chaim was particularly interested to learn about the Israeli army deserter. "I'm going to lean on that fucker," he said, "and he can either help us, or he can spend the next couple of years in a prison cell." He moved away leaving the two of them together. They smiled at each other, leaned forward, then kissed enthusiastically.

"OK. We better leave it at that for now." Joe grinned at Leah. "Later... Our sleeping bags can zip together... But let's help out Chaim for now. He's after the Israeli guy. I'm going to work on the English guy. Keith. And through him find a way to get to these Bedouin Arabs, and into Lebanon that way." He grinned, feeling quite excited. "Let's go! He's called Keith, his girlfriend's called Sue." He jumped up, pulled Leah to her feet, and they started walking down the beach, hand in hand.

They spent a very pleasant couple of hours in the company of Keith and Sue. Smoking dope and finding out about each other. Keith was an ex-teacher, having taught Chemistry at a school in the suburbs of Manchester. Sue was a fully qualified nurse, and intended to go back to nursing when (or if) she returned to the UK. They had met while travelling around Greece, on the island of Paros – an island that Joe knew well, having spent some time there the year before. They happily exchanged reminiscences about the island.

"Please, Joe, will you take me there. Paros sounds lovely," said Leah.

"Sure, Leah. Is this before or after Woodstock?"

Keith looked puzzled. "What, Woodstock near Oxford? What's so special about Woodstock?"

Joe laughed, "Never mind Keith. Private joke." He did successfully find out some useful information about the Bedouin drug smugglers. They were expected back through Nueiba in a couple of days, and would be meeting up with Keith. Their names were Abdul (he was the one who spoke good English), Musharraf and Hussein. Keith believed that they did indeed have some connection to the PLO. And Abdul supported Leeds United! The PLO and Leeds fucking United! Wow!

Some time later, they spotted Chaim coming back down the beach. They excused themselves from Keith and Sue and moved off to meet with him privately.

"Well. Did you find out any useful information?" Joe asked.

"I certainly did," said Chaim, looking pleased with himself. "The cannabis comes from the Bekaa valley in Lebanon as we might have expected. It's the main production region. You may have heard of it?"

"Yes, I think so."

"There's two or three farms in that area that our Bedouin friends deal with. But there's another one that they've started avoiding. Apparently the farmer is somewhat antipathetic to the PLO. He's still operating, still growing cannabis, but there's a feeling that his time on earth might be somewhat limited, if you get my meaning."

"Hmmm..."

"So we need to get to him quickly before anything happens to him. His farm's near a town called Baalbek. And the farmer's name is Rakim. Do you fancy a trip up there?"

Joe hesitated, then shrugged and said, "Yeah, I suppose so.

But I don't want Leah to come with me. I want her to stay safe. OK?"

Leah looked at him questioningly. But Chaim agreed. "There won't be any of us coming with you. Not Leah, not me, not anyone. Not to start with. It's too dangerous for us. But a lot less dangerous for you. Hopefully. And, hopefully, you will be able to find out the information we want. You will have some backup. There's some Lebanese Christians who are more or less on our side. In the near future there may well be problems between the Christians and Muslims in Lebanon. Which will probably tie them even more closely to us. But actually things are fairly quiet at the moment. And in any case we'll be close by, in Cyprus, and with a boat just off the coast of Lebanon. Once you've found useful information we'll be coming in, and then we can take out Ali Hassan Salamel, Anyway, did you learn anything from the English guy?"

"Yes. The PLO support Leeds United."

Chaim stared at him blankly for a moment, then burst out laughing. "Leeds United! Leeds fucking United! Well for sure your time was spent usefully in finding out that information for us." Joe reddened and Chaim laughed even louder. "That's another black mark against them. Not only are they a bunch of murderous fucking bastards, but they support Leeds fucking United. Well thank God they don't support Manchester United, else we'd really be in serious trouble. Leeds United. Ha!"

Joe scowled at him. "OK, OK, you've made your point. What now?"

"Cyprus. Then Lebanon..."

CHAPTER 10.

Lebanon, May 1975.

Joe had left Beirut about an hour earlier, and was riding his motorbike towards Baalbek in the Bekaa valley. He had flown in from Nicosia three days ago and made his way to the Youth Hostel on Rue de Damas. There he had linked up with Chaim's contacts. He was not entirely certain of their usefulness – he felt that they seemed somewhat lacking in discretion – but at least they had loaned him the motorbike that he was currently riding. Tonight he was meeting with them in a bar in Achrafieh in East Beirut, and he would give them the benefits of the doubt till then. But for now he was simply enjoying the sunny weather and the fine views, with the wind blowing his long hair behind him.

There were two reasons for his journey. The 'innocent' reason was to meet up with Rakim, a farmer who grew cannabis, sample his product, and then purchase a couple of kilos of resin, supposedly to smuggle out of the country. He was rather looking forward to this. 'Red Leb' had a great reputation amongst his contemporaries. It was widely available in Israel, being smuggled over the border by Bedouin Arabs. Joe had been selected, and trained, for this mission because he could so easily pass for a dope-smoking hippy smuggler. After he had finished his mission in Lebanon, he would be heading to Cyprus, assisted by Chaim. After Cyprus, back to Israel and Leah.

But the real reason for his journey, and the meeting with the farmer, was to obtain information as to the possible whereabouts of the Black September terrorist Ali Hassan Salamel, the mastermind behind the massacre of Israeli athletes at the Olympic games in Munich, a few years earlier. Mossad had tracked down and executed several of the terrorists involved in the Munich massacre, in operation 'Wrath of God'. But Ali Hassan Salamel had so far evaded them. He was believed to be hiding out in Lebanon, possibly in Beirut. If Joe managed to find out the current location of Ali Hassan Salamel, then Chaim and his Mossad colleagues would be able to take him out and finally complete their mission of revenge.

The farmer that Joe was going to meet supposedly had some information as to his whereabouts. It was believed that he was antipathetic towards the PLO. However, Chaim had warned Joe to be careful as he didn't know just how reliable the farmer was, and consequently, just how accurate any information that he might provide. And in any case, he knew that his neighbours would certainly be hostile towards him. Nevertheless, Joe believed that he could very easily pass as a drug smuggler, and therefore that he would be unlikely to raise any suspicions.

However, there were underlying tensions in Lebanon between the Christian and Muslim factions in the country, and there was a feeling that open hostilities could erupt at any time. Joe wanted this mission to be over and done with so that he could get out of the country and get back to Leah, who he was badly missing. Although he suspected that General Shavit would have another mission lined up for him, and his time with Leah would be limited.

***

Joe slowed down as he approached Baalbek, looking for the turn-off to the farm. Eventually he came upon a dusty side-road, which seemed about right. He stopped the bike and looked at the rough road, which didn't look much fun. He shrugged then started slowly driving along the road. After a couple of miles, he realized that he was riding alongside a field of marijuana plants. He pulled the bike up and gazed in amazement at the sight. *"Well, I guess this is the right place,"* he thought, and set off again. Eventually he came upon a surprising nice-looking house. *"Growing dope must pay well."* Standing outside the house was tall Arabic-looking man dressed, surprisingly, in jeans and tee shirt. He smiled at Joe. Joe stopped his bike and dismounted.

"Salaam alaykum," said Joe, approaching the man.

"Wa alaykum as-salaam," he replied, grinning. "You speak very good Arabic. But let's continue in English. It might be easier."

"Thank fuck for that," thought Joe. "Yes, thank you."

"Come inside and let's drink coffee." He turned and led Joe into the house.

***

Once inside, he prepared the coffee, which he poured into two cups. He handed one cup to Joe.

"My name is Rakim. And you are Joe?"

"Yes," replied Joe, sipping his coffee. "This is excellent coffee, Rakim."

"Thank you. It is a special coffee from Ethiopia. I'm glad you like it. But let's get down to business. I understand that you would like to purchase some 'Red Leb', I believe it is called in England."

"Yes."

"How much would you like to purchase?"

"Well... I would like to buy two kilograms initially. If all goes well, and I successfully smuggle it back to England, and sell it on, then I would like to buy twenty kilos. Regularly."

"OK," said Rakim, "That sounds good. I won't ask how you intend to get it out of our country. That is your problem. But in any case, I am sure that first you would like to sample the merchandise." He smiled at Joe.

"Yes please, Rakim."

Rakim stood and walked across the room to a shelf, picked up an ornate tin, and returned to sit by Joe. He opened the tin. Inside were a couple of pipes and several lumps of hashish. He handed one of the pipes and a lump of hashish to Joe. Joe smelled the hashish. It smelled good. He smiled approvingly at Rakim.

"That smells good."

Rakim handed Joe a lighter. Joe lit it and gently warmed the hash, then crumbled it into the bowl of the pipe. He put the end of the pipe in his mouth, lit the lighter again and played the flame on the hash in the pipe. He inhaled deeply, pulling the smoke into his lungs. He held it there, feeling the buzz hit him. Great,

"Yeah, far out Rakim," he said, reverting to his hippy ego.

"Enjoy!" said Rakim.

Joe took a second hit of the hash, revelling in the feeling. "OK, Rakim, what price are you asking?"

"Five hundred dollars a kilo. And four hundred for the larger amounts that you talked about."

"OK. Two kilos at five hundred dollars a kilo. That's, err..., one thousand dollars."

Rakim laughed. "Your mathematics is very good."

Joe laughed with him. "There's one more thing. Maybe you might have some information that I would be willing to pay for?"

Rakim looked at him quizzically. "Go on."

"I'm looking for Ali Hassan Salamel. Do you know where he is? That will be worth another two thousand dollars."

Rakim looked shocked." Ali Hassan Salamel! Who the hell are you? And are you really interested in buying my cannabis?"

"Errr. I'd rather not say who the hell I am. But rest assured that I really am interested in buying cannabis. But let's up the price and say four thousand dollars for Ali Hassan Salamel and the cannabis."

"For five thousand dollars you can have one kilo of cannabis and the information you want."

"What! Only one kilo of hash? That's only going to last me a couple of weeks, then I'll have to come back for more."

Rakim laughed. "OK two kilos of cannabis, and the information you want for five thousand dollars." He held his hand out.

Joe hesitated, the reached into his pocket and pulled out the bundle of money. At the same time his other hand was touching the handgun in his other pocket. Which had been given to him by his contacts in Beirut. But Rakim smiled reassuringly at Joe, and Joe relaxed somewhat as Rakim reached onto a shelf and passed two large lumps of hashish to Joe. Joe sniffed at it approvingly and than counted out the requisite five thousand dollars, which he passed to Rakim.

"OK Joe, that's good and I hope that we'll be able to do more business in the future. But I rather think that will depend on how you use the information that I'm about to give you. Who knows, you might very well end up dead." He went silent and gave Joe a hard stare. Joe held his breath and stared back at Rakim. After a minute's silence Rakim spoke. "In Beirut there's a street called Moawiya. On that street there's a garage. The garage is where Ali Hassan Salamel and a bunch of very unpleasant people hang out. That's all I can tell you. Good luck."

Joe looked steadily at Rakim. "Thank you, Rakim." He turned to go.

"There is one more thing, Joe." Joe turned back to face Rakim. "Be on the lookout for someone called Abd-al-qadir."

"Why, Rakim?""

"Because he's fucking dangerous, that's why." Rakim turned away from Joe. "Good luck, Joe."

Joe climbed astride his motorbike, kick-stared it and rode slowly away from the cannabis farm. "*Abd-al-qadir, now just who the fuck is he?*" Joe thought.

CHAPTER 11.

Amsterdam, June 2004.

Vicki said nothing. Clearly there was something very personal between these two – Joe and Abd-al-qadir. She didn't dare say anything more to Joe – he had such a savage look on his face.

After a while, his expression softened. "But first, we've got a couple of problems," he said. "There's a dead body just around the corner. And another one in your hotel room. I'm sure that the police will be all over the area now. But you can't go back to your hotel to collect your belongings and check out. And that will obviously cast suspicion onto you. The other problem is Michael Corrigan. He knows your face, and when his man turns up dead, he'll be coming after you. I need to think." He crossed over to the mini-bar. "Fancy a drink? There's wine, beer, vodka, whisky, brandy, you name it, it's here. What would you like?"

Vicki settled for a brandy, which Joe poured into a glass and handed to her. Joe had a whisky. Then he picked up the receiver that he had set up earlier. "Here's one that I bugged earlier. So let's see what's going on." He set the recorder to playback.

Vicki looked astounded. "You bugged his room? Isn't that illegal?"

Joe gave her an amused look. "Yes, I believe that it probably is. Even here in Holland. But I would guess on a scale of one to ten of illegality, bugging someone's room is an awful lot lower than killing them. Now, sshhh, let's listen to what they're talking about."

They heard a door open, some footsteps, and then two men started talking.

"Pour me a drink, Dave, and get one for yourself." There was a

sound of ice tinkling in a glass and drinks being poured.

"Do you think that maybe someone's on to us, boss."

"Yes, Einstein, I think that maybe someone's onto us."

"So what will we do?"

"Once Peter has the girl, he'll take her round to the Pink Lady, and he'll give us a ring. We can meet him there and then we'll find out who she is and what she knows."

"What if she won't talk?"

"Oh, she will, she will. I can guarantee that she'll talk. And we can all have some fun making her talk!"

"And then what?"

"We'll do whatever needs to be done. I don't think that anyone can possibly know anything of the details, but if they do, well then, we'll just have change things. Improvise. No big deal. Nothing's set in concrete, yet."

"And what happens to the girl?"

"We can drown her in one of the canals. You can do that. Do it real slow if you like, and enjoy yourself at the same time. But best make it look like an accident. And then we've got to head back to London."

Joe glanced at Vicki. She looked a bit pale and rather shocked at what she was hearing. He gave her a sympathetic smile, then turned his attention back to the recorder.

"What about the Arab?"

"We're meeting him there. Then we'll all head down to the boat, to get ready for the third. I don't know how he's bringing the drugs in, but if he's with us there'll be little chance of him double-crossing us. Bring a couple of girls from the Crazy Horse. They can help entertain him. Once the deal's done they'll need to be silenced, but with the profit we're going to be making, a couple of dead whores is nothing."

Joe paused the recorder and glanced at Vicki. She was still looking pale. "God, he's rather a ruthless bastard," he said, "I don't think that there's going to be many tears shed if, or should I say when, he ends up dead at the end of all this. Are you ready to listen to more?

"Yes," she said resolutely. Joe switched the recorder, back on.

"If we're down at the boat, we'll miss the match next Saturday."

"What do you think of Chelsea's chances..."

"Jesus," Joe said. "Well I suppose that even psychopaths have other interests. And I suppose that some are interested in football." He fast forwarded the tape.

"Where the fuck's have all the guys got to? We should have heard from them by now."

"Eric's got his mobile with him. Shall I phone him?"

"Yeah."

Joe and Vicki listened to the recording, and heard the bleeping sounds of a phone being dialled. They then heard one side of a conversation.

"Hello, who's that?"

"Why, what's happening?"

"What? When did that happen?"

"No. No. I don't know him very well. I hope you catch whoever did it. Goodbye."

The conversation to Eric's mobile was obviously terminated abruptly, and the conversation resumed between Michael Corrigan and his remaining bodyguard.

"Eric's dead!"

"What?"

"Shot. Back of his head missing. Brains and stuff like that all over the fucking pavement."

"Where did it happen?"

"Just up the road from here. Warmoesstraat. They found his

body near a hotel, right by the Pink Lady. And Peter's been taken to hospital. Badly beaten. What a fuck-up!"

"That fucking bitch. Right. Find her and kill her. Start at the hotel. Maybe that's where she was staying and they followed her there. And Dave's gone missing as well. What the fuck's happened to him? |OK, go to the hotel, turn the place upside down, anyone doesn't cooperate, then give them a good slapping."

"What about the police?"

"Was that who you were talking to?"

"Yes."

"Police. Hmmm. OK, Well in that case I guess that we'll have to be be careful. Go down there, have a look around, see what's happening. Get into the hotel if it's at all possible, but try not to attract attention. If we can't get her now, we'll keep an eye on her and get her later. We'll probably have to be patient. But we'll get the bitch sooner or later. Right. Off you go."

Joe switched off the recorder and looked at Vicki. She was definitely looking a bit pale. "Well, I think we've got a big problem. What did you leave in your room at the hotel. Anything that could identify you."

Vicki thought carefully. "I don't think so. I've got my passport, and my other ID with me. And I've got all my money and credit cards and stuff with me. I think that all that's in the hotel, is change of clothes, dirty knickers, toiletries, that sort of stuff. And I left most of my things in London. So there's nothing personal, nothing that could identify me."

"Did you register under your real name?"

"Well, no I didn't actually. Thankfully. I gave a false name. I was pretending to be a hooker, so they didn't want to see my passport."

Joe smiled approvingly. "Good thinking. So we'll just abandon your stuff in the hotel and head back to England." As he was saying this, the voice activated recorder switched on. Joe reached over and turned up the receiver so that they could listen to it real-time.

"*The place is swarming with fucking police. I can't get near the fucking hotel.*"

"*We'll just have to leave it for now. But that bitch will get what's coming to her. For now we'll head back to London, and meet up with the Arab. You go out to the airport and keep an eye out for the bitch, just on the off-chance that she'll be flying. I'll join you later, and we'll fly out in the morning.*"

"*What do I do if she turns up at the airport?*"

"*Find out where she's heading. Follow her if you can. Keep me posted.*"

"*Right.*"

Joe and Vicki heard the sound of a door slamming, then Joe reached over and turned off the receiver. They looked at each other.

"Right. Let's get moving. Or as your lot would probably say let's 'haul ass'. He grabbed his overnight bag and quickly packed it with the few possessions he had brought with him. He also carefully packed the receiver and the remaining bug that he had bought from Pieter van Rijn. He checked around thoroughly, then went into the bathroom, and collected the little bottles of free shampoo, and bath gel, and the little packets of soap, and put them in his bag with everything else. Vicki looked on in amazement.

"I don't believe it. I do not believe it. You just killed some-one, and now we're on the run from a couple of hoodlums, and yet you're still taking time to rip off the hotel for the free toilet-ries.

"I'm not ripping anyone off," he said indignantly. "I paid for these. Or more precisely my employer paid for these, and, who knows, he might be rather pissed off if I didn't collect them. Now, where's the free pen?" He looked around, saw the hotel pen on the bedside table, and put that in his bag as well. Vicki shook her head despairingly.

"OK, be quiet now, I need to make a phone call." He picked up his mobile, and dialled Pieter van Rijn's number.

"Pieter, hi, it's Joe Butler. Errrm, I've got rather a little problem."

"Joe. I do hope you're not going to tell me that the gun I lent you was used to kill someone in Warmoesstraat, are you?"

"Well, yes, actually I was going to tell you something very much like that."

"Hmmm. That could certainly present a bit of a problem. Well, at least on the positive side, that gun can't be traced back to me. But obviously I don't want it back now. Get rid of it in a canal or something."

"OK"

"And Joe, good luck...."

The phone went dead, and Joe turned to Vicki. "Right, let's go. I'm going to have to check out properly, otherwise, if I just disappear, then that's going to raise suspicions. After all there's a couple of dead bodies just up the road. It'll probably raise suspicions anyway, checking out just now, but it'll have to be done. Though, thankfully, I used a false passport."

They cautiously left the room and walked towards the lift. Each time they came to a bend in the corridor, Joe went first to reconnoitre, then signalled to Vicki. Eventually they reached the vestibule, and pressed the button to summon the lift. They didn't go all the way to the ground floor. Instead Joe stopped the lift on the second floor, and Vicki got out there, to wait until Joe had checked out. Joe continued to the ground floor to check out. As the lift reached the ground floor and the doors opened, Joe was confronted by the sight of several policemen in the lobby. Joe stayed where he was, and pressed the button for the second floor. The lift doors closed, and the lift returned to the second floor; luckily no-one in the lobby had noticed Joe's arrival and instant departure. When the lift arrived at the second floor, Joe got out and met Vicki in the vestibule.

"That didn't take you long," she said, rather surprised by his swift reappearance.

"Change of plan," said Joe. "The place is swarming with police. I couldn't check out. We'll just have to go, and I'll add 'Not paying the bill for a room' to the list of charges against me."

"But the police don't know who you are, surely?"

"No. But I don't want to be seen checking out just now. And I'm still carrying the gun. That'd be a bit of a give-away, don't you think? So let's look for a back entrance."

They cautiously looked around the second floor, and found some stairs which were signed 'For the use of hotel employees only'. Ignoring this notice, they quickly descended the stairs and eventually found a door to the outside; when they exited through this door, they found themselves in a deserted alley. At the end of the alley there was a canal. Joe looked both ways. No-one was looking, so he surreptitiously took the gun out of his pocket and threw it into the canal. They then turned and walked briskly along the path by the side of the canal.

"Where are we going?" Vicki asked.

"The station. From what we've just heard, I don't think Michael Corrigan will be there. The police may well be – but they don't know who they're looking for. We can just pretend to be a normal couple on a night out. If the police are there, I think that they will be more interested in someone suspicious-looking getting on a long-distance train. So we'll just get a local train. And then, when we get to where we're going, we can get a long-distance train to, say, Paris. Does that sound all right?"

"You've obviously run from the police before."

"Err, yes."

They continued along the canal, which eventually brought them to a large open space in front of the station. Joe looked around cautiously, but couldn't see any signs of either Michael Corrigan, or his men, or the police. Sure, there were police, but probably no more than you would normally expect to find late at night. They entered the station, and Joe examined the destination board to see what trains were leaving soon.

"Haarlem. That's local. It only takes about fifteen minutes, then when we arrive there, we'll be able to get a train to Paris. And then one from Paris to London. Right, lets go for it..."

CHAPTER 12.

Beirut, May 1975.

Joe had made it back to the Youth Hostel on Rue de Damas smoothly and without any problems. He had the two kilos of hash, and the gun, safely tucked away in the bottom of his backpack. And the name of the street where Ali Hassan Salamel could be found - Moawiya - and the name of the guy he had been warned about - Abd-al-qadir - both safely tucked away in his mind.

His first task was to locate Moawiya Street on the street map of Beirut. He found it and discovered that it was a mile or so away from the Youth Hostel. He also noted that it seemed to be very close to what appeared to be a Palestinian refugee camp, and so he decided that before he made any decisions about what to do next, he would meet up with his contacts in Achrafieh and pick their brains (*"If they have any!"*) He looked at his watch and decided that he had better get moving; he was meeting up with them at a bar in Sassine square at about eight o'clock – little more than half an hour's walk away – although the plan was to ride there on the motor bike that they had loaned to him, so he could return it. First he secured the two kilos of hashish in his locker; the handgun he decided to hang on to – just in case! He tucked it into the waistband of his jeans at the back, hidden underneath his jacket. Hopefully he wouldn't run into any policemen. He thought that he better drive very carefully and not break any traffic laws. But then he decided that if he did that he'd actually be much more likely to attract police attention, as he'd be the only person on the roads of Beirut who was driving carefully and not breaking traffic laws!

He climbed onto the bike and set off. As always, the roads

of Beirut were a nightmare to navigate, with cars double-parked everywhere, and vehicles jostling for priority at every junction. Thankfully he was on a bike rather than in a car which would have been ten times worse. Eventually he made it to his destination and parked up the bike. He didn't immediately go to the café where he was meeting up with his contacts but hung back at the other side of the square, observing carefully the people sitting in the café and sitting at the tables outside. Better safe than sorry, as they say. He saw his contacts, Yussef and Ibrahim, sitting at a table outside. Thankfully, away from the other occupied tables. Seeing nothing to arouse his suspicions he crossed the square and joined them. They greeted him cautiously. Joe ordered a beer for himself, and for the other two, and they waited until the waiter had brought them to the table before they got down to business.

"So, Joe, did you find out anything useful?" Yussef enquired.

"Yes. There's a garage on Moawiya Street."

Yussef and Ibrahim looked at each other. "Yes, we know of it," Ibrahim said warily, "but it's not a real garage. It's a front for a criminal gang. All sorts of nasty people meet there. They're especially into protection racketeering. But not in this particular part of Beirut. It's more the businesses in and around the refugee camp near Moawiya Street that attract their attention. Hmmm. And you say there's a link with the PLO?"

"That's what the guy in Baalbek told me."

"You're going to need to get close and see what's going on there. We can come with you, but you're going to stand out like a sore finger."

"A sore thumb, you mean."

"Yes, one of those as well. We'll need to disguise you somehow." He looked at Joe, then started smiling. "A keffiyeh to hide your hair, and baggy trousers instead of those jeans. Your skin is dark enough to more or less pass as an Arab. I know that your

French is good, which will be useful. What about Arabic?"

"Finjan qahwa bidun suka, min fadlak."

Yussef and Ibrahim looked at other, then burst out laughing. "A cup of coffee without sugar please," said Yussef. "Yes, that phrase will certainly come in handy when you're dealing with the sort of people that will be in the garage. Especially when spoken in Arabic with an English accent. I think perhaps that you'll have to leave the talking to me and Ibrahim. But if you really do need to say something, say it in French."

They sat around discussing the details of how they best they could approach the garage, with the intention of spying on the goings-on within it, and in particular, to see who was coming and going. Apparently there was a small café nearby which they could visit without, hopefully, attracting attention. They changed their minds about Joe dressing as an Arab.("*Thank fuck for that!*" Joe thought) and decided that it would be better if he just dressed in his normal jeans and tee shirt, and pretended to be a French visitor.

"But do make sure that you only speak French. Be very careful not to accidentally use any English, or you'll land yourself in a heap of trouble."

"And I think it will be a good idea to bring your gun along, but keep it well hidden," added Ibrahim.

They arranged to meet next morning at the city bus station, which was relatively close to Moawiya street. From there they planned to go to the café near the garage, to have breakfast, and then spend some time carefully observing the activities within the garage.

"Now, if we can have our bike back," said Ibrahim, "and then you can walk back to where you're staying."

Joe handed the bike keys back, and pointed to where he'd left their bike. They parted, after agreeing to meet next day at 10 o'clock at the city bus station.

***

As he walked back to the youth hostel, grateful that he wasn't having to negotiate Beirut's traffic, Joe pondered over what had seemed to him a fairly lightweight meeting. He was still not convinced that Yussef and Ibrahim were particularly useful to him, and to his mission any more. Joe felt that he needed to contact Chaim, for advice and maybe to get some sort of backup. Since he was meeting with Yussef and Ibrahim at 10 o'clock in the morning, he decided that he would be able to put in a phone call to Chaim in Cyprus the next morning, before he met up with them.

As he walked, Joe was paying careful attention to his surroundings. He noticed that there seemed to be an awful lot of soldiers about, which concerned him somewhat, as he was aware of the underlying tensions between the Muslims and Christians within Lebanon. In particular, he felt that here in Beirut, this could very well cause a problem with the completion of his mission.

But for now, he decided to switch off and relax a little bit – and search for some inspiration using artificial stimulants. He quite fancied some arak – the Lebanese aniseed-flavoured spirit – and he stopped off at a bar on the way back to the youth hostel. After a couple of glasses of arak he started to relax, although inspiration was not yet happening. *"I know,"* he thought, *"A smoke. That's what I need."*

He made his way back to the youth hostel and went to his locker there. He broke off a lump of hash from the stash in his locker, and then went and sat outside the hostel. He rolled a joint and started smoking it. Two other hostel guests – a couple of Australian backpackers called Matina and Scott – joined him and they spent a pleasant couple of hours together. Matina and Scott were apparently on 'walkabout', having spent several months travelling around Europe. Matina had actually been born in Greece before emigrating to Australia many years earlier, where she met Scott. Joe was intrigued as to why they had come to Lebanon, but found them a little secretive about this. This caused him to be slightly suspicious of them. He thought that maybe the dope was perhaps making him paranoid, but nevertheless decided to be careful about what he said in their presence.

Eventually they said their 'good-nights' and they all went off to bed. Joe made a mental note of which room was Matina and Scott's, and wondered if it would be worthwhile searching it sometime when they were out. Just to check up on them. He had certain rudimentary lock-picking skills – acquired during his Mossad training. But for now a good night's sleep. Up early in the morning to phone Chaim before meeting up with Yussef and Ibrahim.

CHAPTER 13.

Beirut, May 1975.

Next morning, he was outside Beirut's main post office by eight o'clock, waiting for it to open. Then, once inside, he made his way to a phone booth. He emptied his pocket of small change and placed it on the counter by the phone. He didn't have a great deal. Never mind. He dialled Chaim's number in Cyprus. It was answered almost immediately.

"Shalom, Chaim."

"Shalom, Joe."

"OK, Chaim, please can you ring me back. I have very little change. The number is..." He looked at the phone he was using. "...961 1 629 888." He put the phone down and waited. He didn't have to wait very long. The phone soon rang and he picked it up. He brought him up to date with the details of the garage on Moawiya Street, where Ali Hassan Salamel was believed to hang out.

"Hmmm," said Chaim, "I've heard of that garage somewhere else. I'll ask around the guys in Mossad. And what do you think of the Lebanese guys that I put you in contact with? Yussef and Ibrahim?"

"Not sure. They've been a bit help helpful, but I'm not totally impressed. I'm not sure they'll be much use to me any more. But I have arranged to meet up with them this morning to organize surveillance of the garage." Joe laughed. "And then I might kill them."

Chaim laughed. "I do hope that you're joking, Joe." He went quiet for a while. Joe sensed that he was smiling. Chaim then said. "And what do you think of Matina and Scott?"

"What the fuck?" Joe exploded. "Matina and Scott! Who are they? Just what the fuck is going on here, Chaim?"

Chaim started laughing. "I'm sorry, Joe, I really am. But we thought that they might be useful to you. They're CIA trained, but nowadays they work as freelance agents. We've used them a couple of times before. They actually know Beirut fairly well – they've been there before. We really need Ali Hassan Salamel. I do think that they may be very useful to you."

"OK. I'll go along with you on this. But I think that it will complicate matters. I'm supposed to be meeting with Yussef and Ibrahim soon. So what do I tell them about Matina and Scott?"

"Don't tell them anything. Just get rid of them and work with Matina and Scott from now on. Tell Yussef and Ibrahim that you've been instructed to back off for the time being, to keep clear of Ali Hassan Salamel. But reassure them that they'll be getting paid anyway, through the usual channels."

"OK I'll do that and then liaise with the Aussies. We'll have a look at that garage and then I'll get back to you."

"That sounds good."

"Oh, and Chaim..."

"Yes."

"Have you heard of someone called Abd-al-qadir?"

Chaim went silent. Joe waited for his answer. Finally Chaim said quietly, "Yes. Where did you get that name from?"

"From Rakim, the farmer in the Bekaa valley. The one I bought the cannabis from. He warned me about this guy. Who is he?"

Again, Chaim went silent. "We believe him to be responsible for the murders of three of our Mossad people. He seems to get a kick out of murdering them in an extremely brutal way. But he tortures them first, and, we believe, has successfully extracted some seriously heavy-duty information from them. Which has then subsequently caused us operational difficulties.

Because, we think that he passed this information on to, or quite possibly sold it to, the PLO and caused us some serious problems, He's a real nasty piece of work and we'd like him dead. Hmmm. I wonder if he's in Lebanon. The trouble is that we don't really know what he looks like. The only fact that we have about him is that he only has one eye. His left eye. He lost his right eye some years ago in a terrorist action on the Lebanese border, when a home-made bomb exploded prematurely. You need to be careful. Very, very, careful. But just see what you can find out about him."

"OK. I'll liaise with Matina and Scott. And we'll – very, very, carefully of course – put the garage under observation. I've got that picture of Ali Hassan Salamel that you gave me earlier. Though that's rather a bit old. Do the Aussies have a more up-to-date idea of what he looks like?"

"No, sorry, I don't think so."

"OK, We'll do our best. As soon as I confirm that he's in the garage I'll contact you again. But, if practical, shall we take him out, rather than bringing you guys in."

"Be very, very, very careful."

"OK. So that's a go-ahead to take him out, is it?"

After what seemed like an eternity of silence, Chaim quietly said, "Yes. Just kill the bastard."

Joe went silent. Then he said, "I've never killed anyone before."

Chaim laughed grimly. "It's easy. Just point the gun in the right direction and then pull the trigger. And Joe..."

"Yes?"

"Remember. He was responsible for the death of seven of my people. So kill the bastard!"

**

OK. First thing. Get rid of Yussef and Ibrahim. Joe made his way to the bus-station, thinking carefully about what he was going to do, and what he was going to say to Yussef and Ibrahim.

Get rid of Yussef and Ibrahim. Sounded simple enough. OK. Let's do it.

***

"Hey guys," Joe cheerfully greeted Yussef and Ibrahim in the bus station. "Hope you're both OK. I've got news for you. (" *You're fired, you fuckers!* ") I'm heading back to Cyprus for a meeting with my Mossad guys. We're going to leave Ali Hassan Salamel alone for the moment and come back for him at a later date. But don't worry," he added hastily, noting the look of alarm on the faces of Yussef and Ibrahim, "you'll be getting paid just the same. Through the usual channels I am told. And then, when we come back, we'll still be needing your assistance," he added, lying through his teeth.

"OK, Joe. We'll be seeing you," said Yussef. He gave Joe a brief smile, and then they climbed onto their motor bike and rode off, without another word.

"*That went OK, I think,*" thought Joe. He now turned his attention to Matina and Scott. The youth hostel seemed the best place to meet up with them. He made his way back there, stopping on the way for a cup of coffee. "*Finjan qahwa bidun suka, min fadlak.*"

***

When he arrived at the youth hostel he found Matina and Scott sitting outside. They smiled warily at each other, and Joe gestured with his head for them to move to a quieter location in a small park nearby. He looked around cautiously, checking for possible eavesdroppers. Satisfied, he turned to them. "Well, well, well. Chaim's told me all about you two."

"We're sorry that we didn't say anything, but it had to come from Chaim," said Scott.

"Yeah, well, I'm OK with it," Joe reassured them. "So now let's get down to business and decide what we need to do next."

"I think that maybe you have a good idea where Ali Hassan Salamel hangs out."

"Apparently there's a garage on Moawiya Street. On the face of it, it's a front for criminals running a protection racket. But Ali Hassan Salamel has been seen there. And it seems that in addition to the terrorism, he's also heavily involved with drugs. I think that probably that will be to raise money for PLO operations."

"Perhaps you could pose as a drug customer, and get to him that way," suggested Matina. "You do rather look the part."

"Perhaps not," said Joe firmly. "I've played that part far too many times. And this time I think that it might not work. No, we'll just observe the place to start with – very carefully, of course. Apparently there's a café nearby that'll be useful."

"OK. We'll forget about the drug buying persona for now. Maybe we can use it later on."

"Hmmm. Maybe. Or maybe not."

"Anything else we need to know?" asked Scott.

"Yes. I've been warned about a guy called Abd-al-qadir. Do you know anything about him? According to Chaim he's a real nasty piece of work who's been responsible for the torture and murder of a number of Mossad guys."

Matina and Scott looked at each other. "No, we haven't heard of him," said Scott. "But we'll put some feelers out amongst our CIA contacts, and see what they come up with. You got any idea what he looks like?"

"Apparently he only has one eye. His left one. The right eye was lost in a terrorist action."

"Well, we'll have to be extra cautious. Treat every Arab-looking person with suspicion."

"Ha ha. Very funny."

"No, I'm just saying we need to be very careful, and not trust anyone."

"Especially men with only one eye," added Matina, helpfully.

"OK, for now, let's head off to Moawiya Street and suss the place out."

"You two go ahead," said Matina. "I'll see what I can find out about this Abd-al-qadir character. I'll catch up with you later."

***

Joe and Scott steadily made their way from the youth hostel towards Moawiya Street, keeping a watchful eye on their surroundings as they walked. On the lookout for suspicious-looking characters. Both had handguns tucked into their belts, hidden by their shirts. Unfortunately, everybody that they passed looked suspicious, and Joe had to suppress a demoniacal desire to pull out his gun and then shoot everyone that they passed. However he successfully managed to resist the temptation, and decided to keep the bullets for Ali Hassan Salamel, and also for Abd-al-qadir should they encounter him as well. Joe had shown the picture of Ali Hassan Salamel to Scott and they both kept an especially careful eye on their surroundings, and the people that they were passing in the street, as they got closer to their destination. He had brought a small spy camera with him, hidden inside a cigarette lighter, in case he felt the need to photograph any suspects. Earlier he had proudly shown this off to Matina and Scott, who had been (or had pretended to be) suitably impressed.

As they turned into Moawiya Street they were especially wary, but they saw nothing that alarmed them. They identified the garage where Ali Hassan Salamel was supposedly to be found. It seemed deserted. They also found the café nearby and settled themselves at a table which gave them a clear view of the garage. They both ordered arak, which the waiter brought to them, along with a jug of water. They added water to their arak, and then sat there, sipping the aniseed-flavoured drink, but at the same time keeping a careful eye on the garage. Joe took a packet of cigarettes from his pocket, put one in his mouth, and lit it with his special cigarette lighter, surreptitiously taking a photograph of the garage as he did so.

"So, Scott, whereabouts in Australia are you from?"

"Sydney. You ever been there?"

"No. Never actually been to Australia."

"We've got a nice place out there. Maybe you could come visit after this is all over."

Joe smiled grimly. "This is never going to be over. Let's change the subject. How did you two get involved with the CIA and Chaim?"

"Long story."

"Well, we've got plenty of time."

Scott suddenly stiffened. "Careful. Don't look now. Something's happening."

Joe very casually glanced towards the garage. Two cars had pulled up. Suspicious-looking cars. Both had tinted windows, obscuring his view of the people within. He looked away, lifted his glass of arak, and took a sip. He found himself distracted by the activities at the garage, and didn't notice the aniseed flavour. As he watched the garage, he saw several men leaving the cars. All of them suspicious-looking. He looked back at Scott, picked up his cigarette lighter, and furtively took a couple of photos.

"Recognize anyone, Scott?"

"Nope."

Joe looked back at the garage. Suddenly he did recognize a face. Ali Hassan Salamel. "That's Ali Hassan Salamel! Holy shit! What should we do?"

Scott looked at the garage. "Nothing. We'll just watch him for now." He smiled grimly. "It would be nice to take him out. But we can't. We'll just have to watch and wait."

They both sat tensely, sipping their drinks, continually glancing towards the garage. However, there was nothing much to see as all the men had disappeared inside. Apart from one of the drivers, who was leaning against a car, smoking a cigarette, seemingly on watch.

"Hmmm. Maybe it's a dodgy area round here for car thieves," said Joe. "Or maybe he's just on the lookout for the likes of you and me."

"The latter I suspect. I don't think car thieves are likely to target the cars of people like that." They sat quietly, sipping their arak. All of a sudden, several men left the garage, climbed into one of the cars, and drove off. Joe and Scott watched them carefully.

"I don't think that any of those guys was Ali Hassan Salamel," said Joe, "I think that he's still in there and, by my reckoning, I think that there's only three guys still in there with him. I vote that we move in and take a closer look."

"OK. Lets do it." They signalled to the waiter and paid for their drinks, then stood up, ready to move off.

"Got your gun?" said Joe, patting his, still tucked in his belt at his back, to reassure himself.

"Yeah. Let's go." They started walking towards the garage.

***

Whilst they were getting ready to leave, one of the other customers in the café had been observing their activities with considerable interest. His eyes were hidden behind dark sunglasses, but as Joe and Scott started walking away from him, he removed his glasses to watch them more closely. He was fairly inconspicuous apart from one distinguishing feature. He only had one eye. His left eye.

Abd-al-qadir.

As Joe and Scott moved away he stood up, replaced his sunglasses, and started following them. All three of them walked slowly towards the garage, with Abd-al-qadir some thirty yards behind the other two.

Joe and Scott grew tense as they got nearer to the garage, and slowed down. They kept looking around as they proceeded but failed to notice Abd-al-qadir who was following them and watching them intently. They did notice another man, an older man, leaning against the wall on the opposite side of the street, but considered him to be harmless. A big mistake. As Abd-al-qadir grew level with this man he silently gestured towards Joe and Scott. The man nodded, and joined the procession. Joe and Scott in the lead with Abd-al-qadir and the fourth man both following.

Suddenly a white van came racing down the street towards them. It screeched to a halt alongside them. The door opened. "Get in the car," Matina shouted at them. "Quick. Get in the car!"

Joe and Scott exchanged shocked expressions. "Why? What's going on?" said Scott.

"Just get in the fucking car! NOW!"

They both hurriedly climbed into the van. Joe and Scott looked at each other. "OK, I can see who wears the trousers in your house, Scott." They both laughed nervously. "But what's this all about, Matina?"

"Just shut the fuck up. Those two blokes we just passed. One of them was Abd-al-qadir. I've just found out that there's a hit squad after you, Joe. So I'm taking you to the harbour. There's a speedboat waiting there to pick you up and take you out to liaise with Chaim in Cyprus."

"Hold on. Hold on. What the fuck is this all about? And what are we going to do about Ali Hassan Salamel? Are we going to let him get away? And what about all my stuff at the youth hostel? I've got a load of dope stashed in my locker. I could surely do with a smoke right now."

Matina smiled at him, reached into her pocket, and pulled out a ready-rolled joint. She silently handed it to to Joe, who nervously smiled back at her as he took it. "Have you come across a farmer called Rakim, who lives near Baalbek in the Bekaa valley?" she asked.

"Well yes, actually. I bought my cannabis from him. And he gave me some useful information. In fact he's the one who gave me the info about this garage. But how do you know about him?"

"He's dead. Murdered."

"Oh, shit. What happened?"

" We believe that he was tortured by some Palestinian terror group. Who now know all about you. And your interest in the garage. And were, in fact, planning to ambush you from that very garage that you were walking towards. That's the hit squad that I was talking about." She smiled sweetly at Joe. "I think that a 'thank you' might be in order."

"Yes, thank you Matina," said Joe hurriedly. "But you know, there's only three guys plus Ali Hassan Salamel in there at the moment. The three of us could take them out, if we could surprise them. They must have seen us drive away. Let's circle round the block, and then sneak up on them, and then we can take them by surprise."

Matina smiled patronizingly at Joe. "Just smoke your fucking joint Joe. Then perhaps maybe your brain will start working properly. Have you forgotten Abd-al-qadir? And I rather think that he'll have some more backup. No. We're going to the harbour. And then you're out of here." She turned towards Scott. "Actually, all three of us are out of here. Ali Hassan Salamel will have to wait for another day."

Scott shrugged. "Fair enough. Now pass that joint to me, Joe."

Joe inhaled deeply, then passed the joint to Scott. "OK. Let's get down to the harbour, then let's hit the road."

CHAPTER 14.

Limassol, May 1975.

Joe, Matina, Scott, and Chaim were sat outside a bar in Limassol slowly drinking beer. "This is not your fault, Joe," said Chaim. "I don't know how they found out about Rakim." He shrugged. "Collateral damage."

Joe exploded. "Collateral damage! Collateral fucking damage! I liked Rakim. I thought that he was a good guy."

Everyone went quiet, and watched Joe. Gradually he calmed down. "OK. So, what now? And how are we going to get at Ali Hassan Salamel?" he said.

"I don't know," admitted Chaim. "But I don't think that we'll be able to get at him in Beirut. I think that the whole place is just about to blow up. The PLO and the Christian militia are squaring up to each other. No-one knows what's going to happen. I think that for now it would be better for us all to head back to the kibbutz. " He grinned at Joe. "And Leah."

Joe immediately brightened up. "Yes. I do rather like that idea."

Matina and Scott looked intrigued. "Who's Leah?" asked Matina.

"Oh, just a friend," said Joe, beaming at Matina and Scott. "A good friend. A very good friend, A very, very good friend." Matina and Scott both laughed.

"And I think that all three of you can go to the kibbutz with me," said Chaim, "then we can decide what to do next. We still want that bastard Ali Hassan Salamel. But we aren't going to be able to get at him in Lebanon. So we're going to have a good think about what to do next. So. Next stop Ashdot Yaakov

Meuhad."

"Great!" said Joe. "You ever done any olive-picking, Scott?"

"What? Picked them out of a jar with a cocktail stick? Yeah, I rather think that I'm really pretty good at that. Bloody bonzer, as we Aussies would say." Everyone laughed.

"Right. Another round of drinks then we're off to the harbour. There's a speedboat waiting to take us to to Haifa. And then it's only a couple of hours drive to the kibbutz. He winked at Joe. "And Leah."

CHAPTER 15.

Kibbutz Ashdot Yaakov Meuhad, May 1975.

The four of them climbed wearily out of the jeep which had brought them from Haifa and stretched their tired limbs. Suddenly they heard a high-pitched, joyful squeal and turned to see Leah run towards them and throw herself into Joe's arms. They kissed passionately.

"Aha. I guess that this is Leah," said Scott with a broad grin on his face.

Joe turned towards Matina and Scott, smiling happily. "Allow me to make the introductions: Leah, meet Matina and Scott. Matina and Scott meet Leah. And,"catching sight of an old lady out of the corner of his eye, "this is Malka. Malka, meet Matina and Scott."

"Shalom Matina, shalom Scott. And Joe." She reached out and pulled Joe towards her, and hugged him. "It's wonderful to see you again." There was a glimmer of tears in her eyes,

"Shalom Malka." Joe hugged her back. "It's good to be back."

"Yes. There are lots and lots of olives just waiting to be picked. And now, Matina and Scott, let me show you to your room. Joe, I think you know where your room is." Her eyes twinkled at him. "And I guess that you will have brought your magic wand with you..."

**

The next morning Chaim, Matina and Scott were sitting together at a table in the kibbutz dining room, relaxing, enjoying their breakfast.

"Everything OK, Scott?" said Chaim.

"Yeah, great, thanks Chaim. But... you got any vegemite here on the kibbutz?"

They all started laughing. "No, but I think we can rustle up some crude oil. Will that be OK? I think that you'll find that it will look and taste just about the same." Chaim laughed even louder, Scott and Matina rather less so."

"OK. Now let's start thinking about our next step. We want to get Ali Hassan Salamel. Who knows, maybe that bastard Abd-al-qadir will be with him and we can get to him at the same time. But our top priority is Ali Hassan Salamel!"

"Shouldn't we wait for Joe before we have this discussion?"

Chaim looked thoughtful. "I want to bounce an idea or two off you first. Before Joe gets here."

"OK."

"Here's my idea. We know that Ali Hassan Salamel and his guys know about Joe, and that they were after him in Beirut. Principally, to shut his mouth, after he collected some useful information from that farmer, Rakim. So, I guess as far as they're concerned, Joe is unfinished business. The bastards probably believe that he's likely to present an obstacle to their future plans. I don't actually think that Joe knows very much, but they don't know that. Now, we can't go back in to Beirut; the whole of Lebanon is a powder keg, about to explode, with the Christians and the Muslims at each others throats. And us Jews definitely aren't welcome. So we need to draw them out. And," he paused, "we'll use Joe as bait."

Matina and Scott exchanged shocked expressions. "Strewth. I'm not sure about that idea, Chaim. I do rather like Joe," said Matina. "I think that him and Leah are a real sweet couple. Don't you think that he's been used quite a lot. Maybe he could do with a rest?"

"Hear me out. It'll be up to Joe whether he agrees. But we could do this in a neutral country – obviously not here, or the

Lebanon. Maybe back to Cyprus, or maybe somewhere else, we need to think about that. Though perhaps not in Cyprus, because that's not totally stable at the moment after what happened last year. I'm just tossing ideas around in my head, thinking on my feet, I think you Americans, sorry Australians, would say. In any case I think that Leah will definitely stay here. We'll keep her safely out of the way. And we'll have Joe closely watched. Somehow we'll get word to those two bastards where he is. I've got a couple of guys in Lebanon – called Yussef and Ibrahim – and we'll use them. I know that Joe thinks that they're a bit useless, and I tend to agree with him, but I think that we'll be able to use them to help us with this. Joe's principal gripe against them is that he believes that they're somewhat indiscrete. If he's correct with that, then we can feed them some info, and wait for their big mouths to do their fucking worst. Then we'll be waiting for Ali Hassan Salamel and whoever's with him, and we can take them out when they move against Joe. What do you think?"

Matina and Scott both looked a bit doubtful. "I think that we'll see what Joe says about all this. But I do think that you should let him have a bit of time with his sheila first."

"Sheila?"

"No worries. Here's Joe and Leah coming now. Let's see what they have to say about your great idea."

Leah and Joe, carrying trays with a selection of breakfast items, came towards the table where the other three were sitting.

"OK if we join you?"

"Please do. Enjoy your breakfast."

"Thank you. We will. Although disappointingly, there didn't seem to be any vegemite in the breakfast buffet." Joe started laughing.

Scott scowled at him. "You taking the piss, Joe?"

"Now would I do that, Scott? Vegemite? Nectar of the gods."

"Enough, enough!" They all started laughing.

"OK. OK." Chaim adopted a serious expression. "We need to talk."

They all went quiet. Matina and Scott knew what was coming next. Joe and Leah looked expectantly at Chaim.

"Joe." said Chaim, "We urgently need to take out Ali Hassan Salamel. Maybe Abd-al-qadir will be with him so we can get both of them at the same time." He went quiet. "And, Joe, we know that they know about you. And they're after you." He looked directly at Joe. "So... We need to use you as bait. Draw them out. Then kill them. Are you OK with it so far?"

Joe looked directly at Chaim. "Hmmm, possibly. What exactly do you have in mind, Chaim?"

Chaim looked back at Joe. "We find somewhere suitable. We put you there. Closely but discretely watched. We somehow get word to those two fuckers of where you are. Then we wait for them to come after you."

"So how do you propose we get word to them?"

"One possibility is through Yussef and Ibrahim."

"Hmmm... Maybe that might work. I think that perhaps all we need to do is tell them where I am, tell them to keep their lips buttoned tight. I believe that they're actually rather loose-lipped, and so we can just wait for them to do their worst."

"And where do you think might be a good place to set all this up?" Chaim went quiet and waited for Joe's response.

"Cyprus is maybe an obvious choice, convenient for both here and Lebanon, but I'm not sure, I think Cyprus is rather wobbly at the moment after last year." He went quiet. The others all waited, Suddenly Joe grinned. "Crete. I know it well, at least the east of the island." He went quiet, thinking hard. "Maybe we could perhaps organize some sort of ambush in the mountains. The mountains between Agios Nikolaos in the north and Ierapetra in the south. I know that road quite well – I've hitch-hiked up and down it lots of times."

"OK, that sounds good. But we'll have to go out separately, otherwise I think it could look suspicious. So how are we going to manage this? What are your ideas?" Chaim waited expectantly.

"There's a place called Mirtos on the south coast. Fairly quiet and remote. Not very far from Ierapetra, so relatively close to where we're going to take out those two. I know it well. There's just one road in and one road out.. I spent a few weeks there a couple of years back, camping on the beach, with a bunch of hippies. And it's nice. We could meet up there initially." He grinned at Leah. "You'll love it there."

She grinned back. "That sounds great."

"Errr... We weren't thinking of taking Leah with us. It's probably going to be rather dangerous. And that's putting it mildly."

Joe went quiet. "OK, Chaim, fair enough, I think that maybe you're probably right." He looked at Leah. "At least we'll be together for a few days here before we go."

Leah looked stubbornly at them. "No. If Matina's going, so am I!"

"Matina's CIA-trained in self-defence, that sort of thing."

"And I can use firearms. We're all trained in their use, here on the kibbutz. No. I'm going with you. No more discussion about this!" She stuck her tongue out.

Joe looked helplessly at the others. "I think that I'm probably going to lose this argument."

"OK," said Chaim in a resigned tone. "I'll pair Leah and Matina together while we're out there. You two can keep an eye on each other."

Matina smiled at Leah. "Us two can do girly things together. A bit of sunbathing. Drinking cocktails. Leave the menfolk to do all the killing."

Leah smiled back.

"Enough!" said Chaim. "This isn't a fucking holiday! We do all need to remember that!"

"Except," said Joe, "that maybe we need to move in to Crete carefully. Play the role of hippy holiday-makers to start with. Merge in, and look like we're simply having a good time.. And so on. Gradually build up to the main event. Which is, of course, to kill Ali Hassan Salamel and, possibly, Abd-al-qadir."

After further discussions, it was decided that they would travel to Crete in two separate parties. Joe, Leah, Matina, and Scott would fly to Athens, then catch a ferry from Piraeus to Sitia in eastern Crete, then travel down from there to Mirtos. Joe got excited at the thought of hitch-hiking down through Crete, but, sadly, all the others squashed that idea.

"We'll get a bus."

"But hitch-hiking's great fun."

"No. We'll get a bus."

It was decided that Chaim, together with three colleagues from Mossad, would wait until the others were well established in Mirtos, then set in motion the plan to feed the information to the Palestinians. And then they would travel in secrecy to Sitia in the East of Crete, on an Israeli navy speedboat. Going in that way, they would be able to smuggle suitable weaponry in with them, Once in Crete they would get a hire car, and head for Mirtos. Chaim would drop the three Mossad guys in the hills overlooking Mirtos, in the foothills of the Kripti mountains. They would set up camp there, overlooking the main road between Agios Nikolaos and Ierapetra, and then pick a suitable location for an ambush. Meanwhile Chaim would meet up with the others in Mirtos. In Vassili's Taverna, which Joe knew well. They would prepare for the possible arrival of Ali Hassan Salamel and whoever might be with him, hopefully Abd-al-qadir. (Just in case they evaded the ambush set up for them.)

It all sounded relatively straight forward, but at the same time they all felt slightly uneasy at the potential for things to go wrong.

"Chaim," said Joe. "How on earth will your guys know which car on the road into Mirtos contains the guys we want to take out? It's not a particularly busy road but there's enough traffic to make the choice of who to kill just a little bit problematical. Know what I mean?"

"Don't worry. They know who they're looking for. Believe me, they won't take out the wrong guys. If there's any doubt they'll leave it for us to pick them up in Mirtos. Don't worry. OK, lets go!"

"But, surely those two won't be alone. How on earth will your guys manage if there's, like, two car loads of nasties?"

"My guys are good at what they do. OK? And if they can't get them on the road, they'll leave them for us. Just don't worry."

"Hmmm..."

CHAPTER 16.

Mirtos, Crete. June 1975.

Joe, Leah, Matina, and Scott were sat around a table in Vassili's Taverna. They were tired but happy. Their journey had been long, but now they had finally arrived safely at their destination they were starting to feel relaxed. The flight from Tel Aviv to Athens by El Al had gone smoothly, and it had proved surprisingly easy to bring handguns with them in their checked-in luggage. The ferry journey from Piraeus to Sitia had been especially enjoyable: relaxing on the deck in the sun, drinking beer. The bus ride from Sitia to Mirtos had been rather less fun. Long, hot, and bumpy. But now here they were.

"We need to let Chaim know that we've arrived safely so that he can put the next phase of the plan in action."

"Yeah, I suppose we do. But let's leave it for a couple of days. Let's get properly settled in here first," said Matina. "let's enjoy the sun and have another round of drinks." They all happily agreed with her.

After their arrival in Mirtos they had got two rooms at a small pension called Nikos house, and had reserved a third room awaiting the arrival of Chaim. And since then they had enjoyed themselves exploring, wandering along the beach, and drinking in the various tavernas.

Joe, especially, was delighted to be back in Mirtos, having been here not much more than a year before. Unexpectedly, even, he had run into someone that he remembered from his previous visit – an English guy called Brian Wilkins – who had spent the previous twelve months in Mirtos, living on the beach. Excitedly, they exchanged details of their lives over the previous year. Necessarily, Joe gave a somewhat censored version of his adventures. And he wasn't sure how much he felt envious of Brian's rather more uncomplicated, even boring, life. Nevertheless, they happily spent many hours playing backgammon, drinking ouzo and beer, and reminiscing.

Eventually, Matina, who seemed to have taken charge of the whole project, (Joe had secretly nicknamed her 'Bossy boots'), decided that it was time to move on to the next phase. Time to contact Chaim to let him know that they were settled in Mirtos, so that he could set in motion his plans to start dropping hints to the Palestinian terrorists. Hints about Joe's current location. And then he could start moving his Mossad comrades into their ambush position.

***

A few days later the four of them were again sat at a table in Vassili's Taverna, drinking beer, waiting for Chaim's arrival. Joe was still feeling uneasy about the possibility for Chaim's plans to go wrong and over the last couple of days he and Leah had been exploring the surrounding hills checking out potential ambush sites. Despite the potential seriousness of what they could be facing, they nevertheless, on more than one occasion, took time out to make love on the hillside. Definitely more than once.

"OK. So are we sure that this is all going to work? Chaim's bringing, what, three guys from Mossad? What if Ali Hassan Salamel and Abd-al-qadir bring several others with them? What if they don't even come? What if they simply send a bunch of foot-soldiers? And, anyway, there's more than one way to get to Mirtos. Chaim hasn't thought this out properly. I think that maybe we could be fucked!"

Scott and Matina both smiled at him. "What you're short of is PMA. Positive Mental Attitude. Relax. Have another beer. And then we'll wait for Chaim. See what he has to say."

***

Several beers and a couple of ouzos later, Joe, and all the others, were definitely feeling rather more relaxed. Their tranquillity was short-lived. Joe's friend, Brian Wilkins, came wandering up the street towards them.

"Hey Joe, how's it going, man?"

"Far out, Brian, far out." Joe grinned at Brian. "How's things with you?"

"Pretty cool, man, pretty cool. But, anyway, I came looking for you to let you know that there's a couple of guys looking for you. I told them you might be here. Have you seen them?"

"No. What guys are these?"

"I've never seen them before. But, I think that they looked and sounded like Arabs. You expecting anyone like that?"

"*Oh shit!*" thought Joe. He glanced towards the others. They all desperately tried not to look too alarmed at what Brian had just come out with.

"Well actually, Brian, I can't think of anyone that even knows that I'm here." He looked at Matina. "But, I think that we need to go now." He stood up. "Brian. I think that you'd best forget that you've seen us. Understand?"

Brian looked somewhat alarmed at what Joe was saying. "Hey, what's going on, Joe? What's this about?"

"Brian. I suggest that you head back to your lodgings. Get your head down. And if you hear any gunfire, just ignore it."

Brian's alarmed look turned into a look of horror. He turned on his heels and scurried away, with a backward glance towards the other four.

"First thing, let's go back to our digs. Tool up." He grinned. "This is starting to get exciting. I think we'll call it a day on the ouzos for now. We better settle our tab."

***

A little while later the four of them got together in Joe and Leah's room in Nikos.

"So what do we do now?" said Matina.

"I vote that we wait for Chaim," said Scott.

"No. Let's just do it. We'll head down to the main square. I'll be the bait. You three keep a close eye on me from a distance. Not a very big distance, of course. Anyone suspicious-looking, take them out."

The others looked doubtful. "I don't know," said Matina. "We need to be careful. If we start killing people here in Greece, we could get into a lot of trouble with the Greek police. Let's wait for Chaim and see what he thinks."

"When Chaim arrives we're going to be faced with exactly the same problem. It'll be better to sort it out as quickly as possible. And, of course, we'll be bloody careful if we do need to take out these guys. We'll need to be certain of who they are, for one thing. Come on. Let's just do it."

Matina sighed deeply. "OK. Here's how we do it, I think. Scott, you go first. Joe, you follow. Fifty yards or so behind. Then me and Leah. You OK with that, Joe?"

"Yeah."

"Leah, you OK?"

Leah smiled sweetly at them all. "Let's just do it. Now!"

***

They all slowly wandered down the street, looking carefully around. Scott in the lead. Joe, some distance behind, especially alert, knowing that he was the actual intended target of the two terrorists. Matina and Leah bringing up the rear.

Joe grew increasingly nervous as they progressed, a sixth sense telling him that something bad, something really bad, was just about to happen. But nothing did. They reached the main square without any complications arising. They all relaxed.

Mistake.

A big mistake.

A very, very big mistake.

Suddenly, there was a burst of gunfire. Joe threw himself flat on the ground. Behind him loud screams rang out. Joe whipped his head round. He was horrified to see both Leah and Matina down on the ground. He jumped onto his feet and ran towards them. Scott shouted, "No Joe, stay down," as he started shooting towards the far corner of the main square. A car came hurtling into the square and screeched to a halt. Chaim leaped out of the car, drew his gun, and also started shooting in the same direction as Scott.

Joe kept running towards Leah and Matina. Matina sat up, clutching her shoulder, looking shocked as blood seeped between her fingers. Leah was motionless. A bullet hole in the centre of her forehead. Joe looked into her lifeless eyes, and gave an anguished cry. He looked towards the far corner of the square, pulled out his gun, and started running towards it, shouting frenziedly, "You fucker, you fucker, you fucker!"

"Careful Joe, take care," Scott shouted, also running towards the shooter. They arrived together, with Chaim a few seconds later. They looked down at at a dead, Arabic-looking individual, clutching his chest, blood oozing between his fingers. "You fucker, you fucker," Joe shouted, and emptied his gun into him.

"Enough Joe," Chaim said, and gently placed his hand over Joe's. "He's not a problem any more." He glanced back towards Matina, who was leaning over Leah's lifeless body. "This is Ali Hassan Salamel." He looked further up the street. Another Arabic-looking guy, wearing an eyepatch over his right eye, looked back, made an obscene gesture towards them, and disappeared round the next corner.

"Fuck, that's Abd-al-qadir," Chaim shouted, and all three of them started running up the street. Joe was yelling obscenities and brandishing his gun. Scott and Chaim were both horrified at what was happening, and were feeling very anxious that Joe's reaction – although understandable – could very well lead to an even greater disaster. They passed a couple of shocked-looking local Greeks who hurried back into their houses.

"Joe! Stop!" shouted Scott. "We must go back to the square, and Matina and Leah."

Joe ignored him, and kept running. The others stayed with him, until they reached the corner that Abd-al-qadir had just disappeared round. There was no sign of him.

"Fuck, fuck, fuck!" yelled Joe.

Chaim and Scott exchanged worried looks. Chaim gently put his hand on Joe's shoulder. "I'm sorry Joe, but we need to go now. There's going to be big trouble. We've got to go. We'll have to forget about Abd-al-qadir for now. We need to go back to Leah and Matina."

***

Back in the main square, Joe knelt by Leah's lifeless body, tears streaming down his face. Matina, Scott, and Chaim stood by feeling helpless. Chaim broke the silence. "We've got to go. Now. We'll put Leah's body in the car and take her with us. We'll take her back to the kibbutz and bury her there. But we need to go. The shit's going to hit the fan any moment now!"

Joe exchanged anguished looks with Chaim. "I'm going to kill that bastard. I'm going to kill him! That's all I want from now on. I'm going to kill Abd-al-qadir!"

CHAPTER 17.

London, June 2004.

The train from Amsterdam finally pulled in to Paris Gare du Nord just after nine o'clock the next morning. They had been travelling for over ten hours and Joe and Vicki were both tired and just a little bit irritable. Their first action was to buy single tickets for the Eurostar train to London, leaving at just after eleven o'clock. They then found a small café nearby, and bought a coffee and croissant each. They were each lost in their own thoughts.

Joe's thoughts went along the lines of: get back to London, ditch Vicki, locate Michael Corrigan and Abd-al-qadir, kill them both, job done. Especially Abd-al-qadir. Killing that bastard would mean that he would finally get relief from his lifelong demons. Though actually, he thought, before killing the two of them he ought to get the information that George desired, who was, after all, paying him a great deal of money. He needed to find out where the meeting was taking place between the two men; it seemed to be on July third – the day before Independence Day, was that significant? - and on a boat somewhere. The letter 'F'? Folkestone maybe? He sighed and glanced towards Vicki.

Vicki was thinking that maybe she ought to pass what information she had, over to the FBI. She had names – Michael Corrigan and Abd-al-qadir – which was more than she had started with. But she didn't really know who was responsible for her sister Janet's death – it might be Michael Corrigan, she supposed – but she had neither seen nor heard anything to suggest this. For all she knew, it could have been Corrigan's man Eric, who was now dead. Whether or not he was to blame for Janet's death, she nevertheless felt grim satisfaction at his death, and glanced towards Joe. Although she was grateful towards him for saving her life, and was impressed by his competence, she sensed that there was a deep and dangerous hunger within him, and a single-minded thirst for revenge that could destroy anyone who got in his way.

Joe caught her eye and smiled. "Come on, time to go."

***

On arrival at Waterloo station Joe decided to head for his hotel. He tried to say goodbye to Vicki, but instantly relented on seeing a momentary flash of disappointment in her eyes. Instead he arranged to take her out for dinner that evening.

"Only don't get dressed up. Do you like Indian food?"

"As long as it's not too spicy."

"Rubbish. Indian food's supposed to be spicy!"

They agreed that he would meet her at her hotel, just off the Bayswater Road, at seven thirty that evening, and then he headed back to The Dorchester. The moment that he walked into his suite the phone rang. He answered it, and found George at the other end of the line.

"George. How nice to hear from you."

"There's a dead body in Amsterdam just off Dam square. And another one was found in a hotel nearby. Are either of them anything to do with you by any chance?"

"No. I don't think so. No, I'm pretty confident that it's nothing to do with me. Definitely not anything to do with me."

"Hmmm. Have you anything to report?"

"One or two things are starting to come together, but I can't commit myself to anything yet."

"That tells me precisely nothing. Can't you do better than that?"

"Something's happening on July third."

"What?"

"I think it may be a ship coming in with either arms or drugs. What ports can you thing of starting with 'F"?"

"Folkestone. Felixstowe. Falmouth."

"Well, they're fairly well spread around the country. I can't cover all of those. I guess that I'll just have keep digging. When I've got something more positive to go on. I'll get back to you."

"Keep in touch. Oh, and Joe…"

"Yes?"

"Don't allow yourself to get too distracted by attractive, blond, FBI agents."

George rang off then. Joe stared at the phone in his hand, then thoughtfully replaced the handset. Just what the hell was going on here? Was he under observation by one of George's men? Was Vicki more than she seemed? Was his room bugged? He decided to tread even more carefully in his dealings with George. As for Vicki, he liked her and was starting to trust her, and he didn't think that her apparent ingenuousness was hiding anything deeper. And finally, he decided to purchase a bug detecting device, and check his room out.

It was a pleasant day, and although he was short on sleep, he thought that it would be nice to go for a walk in the park. There was an electronics shop that he knew of in Edgeware Road, where he would be able to purchase a bug detector, or, to give it its correct technical name, a Radio Frequency detector. So he left his hotel, crossed the road using the pedestrian underpass, and entered the park. Halfway through the underpass, he stopped to tie his shoelaces, and checked carefully that he wasn't being followed. As far as he could tell, there was no-one, but he checked again as he entered Hyde Park, and after walking towards Marble Arch for a couple of hundred yards, sat on a park bench, and watched the other pedestrians around him for ten minutes or so. Finally satisfied that he wasn't being followed, he continued on his way to Marble Arch, and from there crossed to Edgeware Road. He quickly located the electronics supply shop, and purchased a suitable bug detector – pocket-sized but very powerful, and covering an extremely wide range of frequencies.

Back at his hotel, he spent several minutes sweeping his room for bugs and found nothing. To prove the device he had just purchased actually worked, he took the pen transmitter that he had got from Pieter in Amsterdam and switched it on. The bug detector instantly emitted a squealing noise. OK, so the detector was working, and therefore it looked like there weren't any bugs in his room. He switched off the detector and put it away, and put the pen in his pocket.

***

Vicki had decided that it would be a good idea to adopt a disguise. Michael Corrigan now knew what she looked like, and since he had designs on her life, it would be prudent to keep out of his way as far as possible, and to disguise herself for the occasions when their paths might cross in the future. Consequently, she went to a hairdresser's shop just around the corner from her hotel, and had her hair cut quite short. She also visited a chemist's shop, where she bought some red hair dye, and also some photo chromatic sunglasses – she thought that she would wear these as ordinary glasses to hide the shape of her face. Next door to the chemists was a lingerie shop where, on the spur of the moment, she bought a push-up bra.

Back at her hotel Vicki read the instructions on the hair dye, then turned herself into a spiky-haired redhead, with considerably more cleavage than that with which she had started in the morning. She thought that if she wore a fairly low-cut top, then very few men would actually be looking at her face – they'd all be waiting for one of her boobs to fall out. With the sunglasses altering the shape of her face, and the change of hair, she thought that there would be little chance of being recognized. She admired herself in the mirror, and decided that she was satisfied with the end result. She couldn't wait to meet up with Joe, and see what he thought. Perhaps they ought to visit 'The Tarantula', just to prove that she was now invisible to Michael

Corrigan and his henchmen.

In the meantime she decided to go for a run around Hyde Park, as it was such a lovely day, and it had been quite a while since she had last done any serious exercise. She changed into her running gear, left her hotel, and crossed Bayswater Road into the Park. She failed to notice the West Indian man loitering near the entrance to the park, who watched her closely as she ran by. He then took out his mobile phone, and made a call.

"George, she's just gone for a run in the park, by the look of it."

"Don't try following her. I don't want you to have a heart attack. Hang about where you are, and wait till she gets back."

"OK. Oh, and George, she's changed her appearance."

"Has she? Clever girl. What's she look like now?"

"Short red-hair. It'll probably keep her safe from Corrigan, but I guess that Joe will see through it in an instant."

George chuckled. *"Well, give me a ring when she gets back to the hotel. I think it's likely that Joe will be meeting up with her tonight. So stay where you are until Joe turns up, then phone me again, and leave it up to Joe at that point. Don't let Joe see you, and don't try follow them. Joe will spot you for sure."*

"But Joe has never met me and doesn't know me from Adam."

"He'll still spot you for sure if you try to follow him. Just keep away from Joe. He's got an itchy trigger finger, and I'd hate to lose an agent to friendly, or rather, not-so-friendly, fire."

CHAPTER 18.

London, June 2004.

At seven thirty on the dot, Joe arrived in the foyer at Vicki's hotel. The receptionist placed a call to her room, and Joe waited downstairs for her to appear. A few minutes later the lift door opened, and Vicki appeared. Joe suppressed a smile at the sight of the spiky-haired redhead, wearing sunglasses, and sporting an impressing cleavage. He kept a totally neutral expression on his face as Vicki walked towards him.

As she got close and smiled at him, he smiled back vaguely and said, "Sorry love, but I'm supposed to be meeting someone."

"It's me, Joe," Vicki replied.

Joe gaped at her. "Vicki! Is that really you? My god, have your boobs grown, or has your hair shrunk, or what?"

Vicki punched him on the arm playfully. "Yes, it's me. Honestly, you didn't recognize me, did you?"

"No. I'd never be able to recognize you in a million years. You look so totally different, that I bet your own mother wouldn't be able to recognize you."

"OK, that's enough, I think."

"It's truly amazing."

"Enough!"

Joe laughed and held out his arm. "Honestly, it looks all right, Vicki. Now let's go eat. I'm famished. There's a good Indian restaurant just around the corner."

"Not too spicy, I hope."

Joe laughed again. "Yes. Exceptionally spicy. But not to worry, they do food that's suitable for wimps and women, as well as for us real men." She smiled at him and took his arm as they left the hotel.

Across the road, the West Indian guy phoned George. "They've just left the hotel together."

"*Good. Leave them to it. Like I said, don't try to follow them. Go home now, then get back in the morning, and keep an eye on her, and watch just what she does tomorrow.*"

"Goodnight George."

George rang off without saying a word.

***

Joe and Vicki left the 'Taj Mahal' a couple of hours later, feeling pleasantly full. "Well, I agree, that was a very nice meal," said Vicki.

"Not too spicy?"

"No, not too spicy. Just right. So what shall we do now?"

"I thought that we might go to 'The Tarantula', and have a look around. Maybe Michael Corrigan will be there."

Vicki felt a flash of trepidation, which she suppressed. "Are you sure that my disguise is good enough?" she said.

Joe regarded her solemnly. "Well, it certainly fooled me."

Vicki punched him on the arm again. "Come on, I want the truth."

"Ow. All right then, it didn't really fool me. But I rather think that it's good enough to fool Michael Corrigan, who only saw you for a short time, and in poor light. Come on, let's go." Joe hailed a taxi, and they both climbed in the back.

***

They stood outside watching a constant stream of people entering the nightclub. Vicki recognized a minor American film star, in the company of a famous super model. Joe recognized a TV weather-girl and a footballer from a premiership football club. There was the drummer from a well-known rock group, and several other celebrities. Vicki suddenly forgot about all her misgivings, and got excited about the prospect of going into the club, and mingling with celebrities. Joe regarded her excitement with amusement. He was disinterested in the celebrities entering the club, he was watching keenly for less wholesome clubbers – in particular he was rather hoping that he would see Abd-al-qadir. Then that would be the end of it. Abd-al-qadir would die tonight. And Joe's long wait for revenge would finally be over.

After several minutes spent watching people enter the club, Joe started getting restless. "Let's go, time to have a look around inside and see who we can see. Keep a look out for anything of interest. Don't be too inquisitive, and start asking questions, that sort of thing. We don't want to attract attention. We'll just mingle in with all the so-called celebrities. And I'll be an ageing rocker – the singer in a long-defunct band that nobody's ever heard of - 'The Flying Lobsters'."

"The Flying Lobsters?"

"Yeah. That sound cool?"

"No. It sounds ridiculous."

"Well, it'll have to do."

"And who am I?"

"You're my rock chick girl friend."

"I thought I might be." She suddenly went quiet, and looked serious. "Joe?"

"Yes."

"It's not possible for us to ever become involved. We have to keep work and, you know, other stuff, separate. And besides you know that I already have a boyfriend. He's English and he plays rugby. We're planning on getting married sometime soon."

"Oh." She thought that a disappointed look flashed briefly across his face as she lied to him. "Don't worry, your virtue is safe with me."

"I want you to promise, never to try to get into my pants."

"I promise never, ever, to try to get into your pants, or even think about getting into your pants. Actually the not thinking part will be rather difficult, but I'll try do my best. Satisfied?"

"Yes. Thank you." Vicki felt a pang of disappointment as she said this.

"OK, so now let's go into the club. Remember, I'm the lead singer of the Flying Lobsters, and you're my rock chick girl friend."

***

They were both sat at a small table in the nightclub, each nursing a drink. They were listening to a reasonable good jazz band, and carefully watching the other patrons. Vicki had an exotic cocktail, and Joe a pint of lager.

"So what's that called, then?"

"A 'Screaming Orgasm'," replied Vicki, blushing slightly.

Joe grinned, and raised an eyebrow. "Considering what it cost, one of those ought to be guaranteed. Better make it last." He started looking round at the other people in the nightclub. There were some famous faces that he recognised, and although he tried to be blasé, he couldn't help being impressed. "There's a big lad over there. Looks like a rugby player. That your fiancé?"

Vicki sighed and looked round. She was beginning to regret inventing a boyfriend. "No, I can't see him here. Anyway this isn't his sort of place. He's teetotal."

"Teetotal? A teetotal rugby player?" Joe said incredulously. "He must be having you on!"

"Leave it Joe. Just fuck off will you!"

"Sorry." After a few minutes of strained silence, he said contritely "I'm sorry Vicki. I really am. I promise not to mention your boyfriend again. Can we be friends once more?"

She smiled warmly at him. "Yes of course. Just try not to be such a dickhead."

"I'll try. But not being a dickhead is really rather difficult for me. Everyone that I know thinks that I'm a total fucking dickhead. But I'll do my best. OK?" They both started people-watching again. After a while he said, "I think that we need to concentrate on people who aren't celebrities. Remember that we're actually here to work. Vicki... Vicki... VICKI..." He tried to attract her attention, while she gawked at yet another minor celebrity nonentity. "VICKI..."

"Sorry. What were you saying?"

"I was saying that we're not here to enjoy ourselves. We're here to work. We're supposed to be ..." He suddenly broke off as a ginger-haired man walked into the bar, accompanied by a vacuous-looking girl with long, cascading, curly blond hair, breasts that seemed almost unfeasibly large, and long, shapely legs. She wore an extremely short skirt to show off her legs, and tottered along on impossibly high heels. The ginger-haired man was also accompanied by another man, well-muscled and shaven-headed with a brutish face.

Vicki noticed his reaction and glanced around to see what he was looking at. She tut-tutted, and said, "Those breasts can't possible be real. And she's so top-heavy, she's going to come a cropper wearing those heels. And I doubt that she's a natural blond. Tramp."

Joe gave her an irritated glance, and then looked back at the ginger-haired man. "It's not her that I'm interested in..."

"Yeah, sure!"

"Vicki. Shut up. The bloke with her is Michael Corrigan, I think." Vicki started to turn round again. "Don't turn around to look at him. Just be a bit more discreet."

Vicki opened her handbag, and took out lipstick, and a small mirror. She pretended to repair her lipstick, whilst angling the mirror so that she could look at the ginger-haired man. Very deftly done, thought Joe.

"Are you sure?" she said. "It's very dark where he's sat."

"I'm pretty sure. I'll go to the toilet. And I'll pass by his table to get a closer look. You stay here, don't go anywhere, just keep an eye on him. And don't let anyone pinch my beer. Or else someone will die!"

***

He didn't really need to urinate, but he managed to force out a trickle. On his way to the toilet, he had passed near the table where Michael Corrigan was sitting, and confirmed that it really was him. He needed to get back to Vicki, to tell her. As he was washing his hands, another person entered the toilets. Joe glanced up at the mirror, to meet the gaze of the shaven-headed man who was with Michael Corrigan. The bodyguard. He gave the man a polite nod, then finished washing his hands, and dried them in the hand-dryer. While he was doing so, he gazed at the hand-dryer, thinking carefully. It was called a 'Hurricane' he noticed. All the time that he was staring at the hand-dryer, he was acutely aware of the other man watching him. He tensed, not knowing what was going to happen. He finished drying his hands, and moved towards the door. As he did so, the other man spoke up.

"You. Don't I know you?" he demanded brusquely.

"*Oh, shit.*" thought Joe. "Maybe you remember me from the band I was in," he said. "I used to be lead singer in 'The Flying Lobsters'."

The other man's face slowly broke into a broad grin. "That's it. Yes, of course. The Flying Lobsters. You were great! Say, please can I have your autograph?" He pulled out an autograph book.

"Yeah, sure," Joe replied, feeling relieved. He pulled out his pen, and took the autograph book. "Who should I dedicate it to?"

"Frank Boyle."

Joe wrote with a flourish, 'Best wishes to my good friend Frank Boyle.' He glanced again at the hand-dryer, and then signed it 'Joe Hurricane'. He handed the book back.

The other man looked at the book. "That's great. Thank

you. Of course - Joe Hurricane. Yes, I remember you. Good to meet you, Joe."

"And good to meet you, Frank." They shook hands. "Here, please have this pen as a souvenir." He handed him the pen containing the hidden microphone and transmitter.

"Well, thank you Joe." He gave him a delighted slap on the back as they both left the toilet.

***

"You're looking very pleased with yourself," Vicki remarked, as he returned to the table.

"Do you think it's possible that there might actually have been a band called 'The Flying Lobsters'?" Joe asked.

"What?" Vicki said, confused. "No, I don't think so. Why?"

"Oh. No particular reason."

Just then one of the waitresses came across with a tray containing another of Vicki's Screaming Orgasms, and another pint of beer for Joe. "Compliments of Mr. Corrigan," she said, as she placed the drinks in front of them.

"Who's Mr. Corrigan?" Joe asked innocently.

"He owns this club. He's sitting over there." She indicated the table at the far end of the bar where Michael Corrigan was sitting with his girlfriend, and his bodyguard. Joe and Vicki both turned to look. His new friend, Frank Boyle, the bodyguard, was smiling and waving at them. Michael Corrigan gave them a brief nod. Joe raised his glass in salute and smiled, Michael Corrigan returned the gesture, then turned and resumed his conversation with his companions.

"Is there something that you haven't told me?" Vicki asked.

"It's just that the bloke with a shaved head, seems to be a leading member of 'The Flying Lobsters' fan club. He's called Frank Boyle."

"They're all very deep in conversation about something."

"Probably talking about the Flying Lobsters. We were a one-hit wonder and reached the lower reaches of the charts with a song called 'Highway to Hell'. It was a cover of the classic by the rock band AC/DC. They're an Australian band and I believe that the Aussies know them as Akka Dakka. But after that one hit we had musical differences, and finally split up. Douggie, the drummer, became a vegetarian and went off to live in a Buddhist monastery in the Himalayas. He's still there, I believe. Jimmy, the lead guitar, is in jail for possession and supply of class A drugs. I don't know what happened to Alex, the bass guitar. And here I am. Lead singer of the Flying Lobsters! Would you like my autograph?"

Vicki shook her head despairingly. "I don't think that they're talking about the Flying Lobsters," she said faintly.

"Neither do I. So let's find out what they're actually talking about."

"What? How do we do that?" Vicki gave Joe a rather surprised look.

"We'll finish our drinks, then we'll head back to my hotel, which luckily isn't far away, and tune my receiver to pick up the conversation that will be being transmitted by the bug that Frank Boyle has got in his pocket." He grinned triumphantly, and leaned back in his chair.

Vicki's jaw dropped in astonishment.

CHAPTER 19.

London, June 2004.

They both went straight back to Joe's room in The Dorchester hotel, which was just around the corner from the nightclub. "I don't know what the range is for the transmitter. But hopefully we'll pick up the signal OK," said Joe. He got the receiver out of his bag and switched it on, then started fiddling with the controls.

"Are you sure that you know what you're doing?" asked Vicki. "Are you tuned in to the right channel? Have you got an instruction book?"

"Yes, I know exactly what I'm doing. Yes, I'm tuned in to the right channel. And no, I don't need the instruction book." Joe continued fiddling with the controls, getting nothing but a hiss of static.

"*... the Flying Lobsters.*"

Joe grinned jubilantly at Vicki.

"*Will you shut up about the fucking Flying Lobsters. I've never fucking heard of them. We need to concentrate on what's happening next week. Tracy, this isn't for your ears. Take a walk will you. We've got important stuff we need to talk about. Man's stuff. Go to the bar. Have a talk with Sarah the barmaid. She's had a boob job as well – you can tell her all about yours.*"

It was Vicki's turn to grin triumphantly at Joe.

"*... load coming in next week ... two hundred ....*"

The reception on the radio deteriorated. Joe started frantically fiddling with the various controls. Vicki rolled her eyes in exasperation. "Are you sure you know what you're doing?"

"Yes. Now please shut up."

"... what day ..."

"He hasn't told me yet ... Falmouth ..."

"... what about the other ..."

"... not the ... perhaps ... definitely next week ..."

Joe was getting frustrated with the meaningless fragments of conversation that they were hearing, and kept continually fiddling with the controls.

"... MI5 agent ..."

Joe and Vicki looked at each other in alarm.

"... two ... need to kill them both ... Falmouth ... first ..."

Joe was fiddling with the controls even more urgently.

"... contact on the inside ...let us know who ... after ... Falmouth ... eight million pounds ..."

At that point the reception deteriorated totally, into nothing more than a hiss of static. Joe fiddled with the radio, but in vain, and in the end gave up and leant back in his seat. "OK. So what have we got?"

"Something's happening in Falmouth. That's the letter 'F'. Probably next week, but they don't know which day, yet. Could be the drugs coming in. Or maybe it's the guns coming in. Whichever it is, it's big. Eight million pounds worth."

"Yes. Whatever it is that's coming in, there's two hundred of them. Now what could that be, do you think?"

"Two hundred kilos of heroin? Would that be worth eight million pounds do you think?"

"I have no idea. Perhaps. Or maybe it's two hundred boxes of guns. That would be forty thousand pounds per box. Sounds rather a lot to me. I think that it must be the drugs."

"I agree."

They both fell silent. Then Joe turned to look at Vicki, with a concerned look on his face. "And there's the other thing that they were talking about. I rather think that we need to have a discussion about it."

Vicki gave him a worried look. "You mean the fact that they know about us."

"Yes. To be accurate, they know about me – the MI5 agent – but they didn't mention the FBI. Though they do seem to know that there's two of us. How on earth do they know that? We're only together by accident, and we've only been together for little over twenty-four hours. I find that very mysterious. But, even though they know about MI5 agents after them, they can't know that it's us, otherwise they wouldn't have bought us those drinks. I rather think that they'd have killed us instead."

Joe said this in such a matter-of-fact tone of voice, that Vicki suddenly started giggling. After a moment, Joe joined in and started laughing as well, but eventually they calmed down.

"They want to kill us, but it seems to me that they want to meet the boat at Falmouth, and collect the contraband, whatever it is, first."

"So what are we going to do?" Vicki asked.

Joe looked thoughtful and said to Vicki, "Are you armed, Vicki?"

"No. I couldn't have brought a gun with me on the aeroplane."

Joe crossed over to the room safe, entered in the security code, and opened the door. He pulled out a pair of handguns, and passed one to Vicki. She examined it. "A Beretta nine millimetre." She checked the magazine, noted that it was fully loaded, and squinted along the sights. "Nice. Are you giving this to me?"

"Loaning it to you. Assuming we're both alive when this is over, I'll want it back." He was holding a similar weapon himself. He checked the magazine in his own gun then pocketed it. "We're going to have to be bloody careful from now on. I'm still puzzled as to how they know about us."

"Do you think that there may be someone on the inside feeding them information?"

Joe thought carefully. He knew that George had suspicions that there was, indeed, someone on the inside who was acting as a traitor, and maybe this confirmed those suspicions, but he wanted to keep this information from Vicki for the time being. "I suppose that it's possible," he said.

"But how do they know about me?"

Joe was aware that George knew about Vicki. It crossed his mind that it might be George himself who was the traitor in MI5. But, no, that was just too bizarre. If that were so, then why on earth would George have employed him to track down the traitor. However, if George knew about Vicki, then it was quite likely that others in MI5 did. Including the traitor. "I don't know," he said. Which was largely true, as he still had no idea how George knew about Vicki. Unless Vicki herself, was more than what she seemed. He briefly considered that idea, then dismissed it. She seemed too ingenuous, and she had come close to losing her life in Amsterdam. He smiled at her. "I just don't know," he said again. "Come on, it's time to get you back to your hotel. Considering the promise I made, it wouldn't be a good idea for you to stay here."

She smiled back. "OK, thanks Joe."

**

Joe said goodnight to Vicki outside her hotel, and arranged to meet her next morning. He waited until she was safely inside, then started walking towards Bayswater Road. As he did so, he was observed by another man standing on the opposite side of the road, half-hidden in a shop doorway. This was not George's man – the West Indian – but another man, of Middle Eastern appearance. He watched Joe with interest, then began to follow him. He waited until Joe was a considerable distance down the street, then levered himself off the wall he was leaning against, and started walking down the street in the same direction as Joe, but a good hundred yards or more behind him.

As Joe reached Bayswater Road, he contemplated hailing a

taxi, but since it was a pleasant evening, and it was probably little more than a mile to his hotel, he decided to walk, and to think while he was doing so.

He revisited the thoughts that he had been mulling over earlier. It was fairly clear to him that there was indeed a traitor in MI5; the fact that Michael Corrigan knew about him, and probably Vicki, seemed clear enough. He had even talked about a contact on the inside. So as far as Joe was concerned, that was good enough. But he had no idea who the traitor could be. He wondered again about George - after all, George definitely knew that Vicki was teamed up with him. But it still seemed absurd that George would have hired him to track down the traitor in MI5, if George himself was the traitor.

And at such an inflated rate of pay. Four hundred thousand pounds. Far more than George had ever paid him for any job he'd done before. And he had agreed to it so readily, had in fact doubled his original offer without resistance. What on earth was going on there? It really was quite curious. He thought about this for a while, and could think of no reason for this huge amount of money, so he shrugged his shoulders and mentally moved on.

Next his thoughts turned to Vicki. He had to admit to himself that he did find her rather attractive, but fully agreed with her reasoning that they had to keep work and pleasure separate. From a practical point of view, although she seemed calm and composed under pressure, he felt that her field-craft skills were rather lacking – as born out by her misguided actions in Amsterdam, when she had taken Michael Corrigan's photo.

And Abd-al-qadir. Where on earth did he come into the picture? As he reflected on Abd-al-qadir, inevitably his thoughts turned to Leah, and to the need for revenge that had been burning in his heart for thirty years. Well, hopefully the final chapter of that story was going to be written very soon.

As he approached Marble Arch, intuitively he knew that something was not quite right. He walked more slowly and focussed all his senses on his surroundings. Although he couldn't see or hear anything out of the ordinary, a sixth sense told him that he was being followed. He suddenly stopped, put his foot up on a low wall, then leant forward and pretended to tie his shoe lace. As he did so he risked a quick glance back down the street that he had just walked down. He saw a shadowy figure about a hundred yards back. It was by no means obvious that he was following Joe, but Joe's instincts told him that he was. He resumed walking along Bayswater Road, but rather more briskly, and tensed, ready to act.

He approached a poorly-lit alleyway, leading into a row of mews cottages, and as he got level with it, he spun on his heel and stepped off the main road into the entrance. A hundred yards behind him, the follower saw him suddenly disappear. In consternation, he broke into a run, to try to catch up. As he approached the alley entrance, he slowed down, and looked cautiously around, wondering where Joe had disappeared to. Suddenly, something slammed into the back of his head, and he went down like a stone, falling onto his face on the pavement.

Joe stood over him, and rolled him onto his back. He gazed at him thoughtfully. It was no-one that he had ever seen before, though he was clearly an Arab, and therefore quite possibly one of Abd-al-Qadir's men. The fall onto the pavement had smashed his nose, and his face was all bloody. Joe searched the man's pockets, finding a handgun – a nine millimetre Walther P99 – which he transferred to his own pocket. In another pocket he found a Kuwaiti passport in the name of Abdullah Mubarak, and a wallet containing an American Express Credit card, several hundred US dollars, and about one hundred pounds sterling. He pocketed the passport and the money, but threw the wallet containing the credit card into a nearby litter bin. He found nothing else of interest in the man's pockets.

Joe stood up and looked at the man. He thought about killing him, but decided that it was not really necessary, and the police interest that would undoubtedly be raised by the finding of a dead body, would be very likely to cause problems. So he simply stamped hard on the man's right hand, crushing his fingers. That should put him out of action for a long, long time. He then weighed up in his mind the likelihood that he might actually be left-handed, and so he did the same to the man's left hand as well.

Then he calmly resumed his journey back to the Dorchester Hotel.

CHAPTER 20.

London, June 2004.

The next day Vicki woke just after seven o'clock. It was the best night's sleep that she had had since she had come to Europe, and she felt totally refreshed, and eager for whatever the day might have in store for her. Her worries of the previous evening, when they had discovered that Michael Corrigan knew of their activities, seemed distant, and she had started to feel confident about Joe's ability to cope with whatever might be in store. She wondered what his next step might be.

Since it was a nice sunny day, she decided to go for a run in Hyde Park to wake her up fully, so she pulled on a sweat-shirt, tracksuit trousers, and running shoes, tied her room key to her shoelaces, and headed downstairs. As she passed through the hotel lobby, the man behind the reception desk greeted her. "Morning, miss."

"Good morning."

"Nasty affair last night. A mugging just up the road. Not half a mile away."

She slowed down and approached the desk, looking concerned. *"Joe,"* she thought immediately. "What happened?" she asked.

"An Arab gentleman, a tourist they reckon, got mugged. Had his passport and all his money stolen, and got badly beaten up. He's in hospital, but he's not in any danger, thank god. Still it's not a very nice thing to happen, is it? This is normally such a pleasant part of London."

"That's terrible," said Vick. Her worries about Joe had partially receded - at least Joe wasn't the victim – but she wondered if Joe might have been involved in some other way.

"If they catch them, they'll just get a slap on the wrist, and be told that they've got to be good boys in the future. They should bring back hanging and flogging." The receptionist was starting to get into his stride. "It was a sorry day when they did away with National Service. That's what they need – discipline."

"Yes, well, I better be off on my run," said Vicki, moving towards the front door.

"You be careful, miss. There's no knowing what sorts of riff-raff are out there, just waiting for a nice girl like you to come along." By now, his eyes had taken on a manic gleam, which was starting to alarm Vicki slightly. She contemplated going back to her room, getting the gun which Joe had loaned her the previous night, and using it to put a bullet through the centre of the receptionist's forehead. Centrally, equidistant between both his eyes. She squinted at his face, calculating the exact spot where a bullet should go. Easy. That ought to shut him up. She managed to resist the temptation, smiled at him instead, and continued on her way towards the front door.

"Goodbye. See you later."

"Yes, well, I sincerely hope so," said the receptionist gloomily.

***

Joe woke at about the same time as Vicki, but didn't even consider the idea of exercise. Instead, he ordered a room service breakfast – fresh orange juice, cereal, scrambled egg with smoked salmon, toast and marmalade, and a pot of coffee. Then he had a shower. He had just finished dressing, when a knock on his door announced the arrival of room service. The waiter wheeled in the trolley containing his breakfast, and also brought him a newspaper – 'The Times'. Joe gave him a generous tip, then settled down to eat his breakfast, and read the paper.

As he was reading, the phone rang. He debated with himself whether to bother answering it, but concluded that there could conceivably be someone at the other end with whom he might actually want to communicate. To his surprise there was.

"Joe?"

Joe instantly recognised the voice at the other end of the line. Chaim, his close friend in Mossad. "Chaim," he said, rather surprised. "It's great to hear you. How are you? And how on earth did you know where I was staying? Are you in London? And if so, do you want to meet for a beer?"

"Very well, thank you Joe, and yes, I really do think that we need to meet for a beer," Chaim replied. Somewhat tersely, Joe thought.

"Is everything all right, Chaim?" Joe asked warily.

"Of course. Why would anything not be all right? When and where would you like to meet up for the beer?"

"How about noon at the 'Red Lion' near Oxford Circus. You know it?"

"Yes, I know it well. I'll see you there."

"That's great, Chaim."

"Oh, and Joe?"

"Yes, Chaim?"

"One of my agents was attacked and badly injured last night. Close to your hotel, I think. Have you heard anything about this?"

Joe was momentarily silent. *"Oh, shit,"* he thought. "No," he said, "I've not heard anything. Why, what was he doing in this part of London?"

"Following you, Joe. Following you. I'll see you at noon."

Chaim abruptly terminated the conversation. Joe stared at the phone in his hand. *"Fuck..."* he thought. What had he done? He replayed the events of the previous evening in his mind, trying to think if the man he had 'neutralized' could have seen his face. He decided that he hadn't – clearly if he had been following Joe, then that put things in a very bad light as far as Joe was concerned. But, nevertheless, if he hadn't actually seen the face of the man who had 'neutralized' him, then Joe might be able to bluff his way out of this. Nevertheless, he wasn't looking forward to meeting up with his friend Chaim.

Next, he turned his thoughts as to why Chaim actually had an agent following him. And an Arab at that. He could only guess that it was related in some way to his current activities vis-a-vis Michael Corrigan, and Abd-al-Qadir. But how did Chaim know about what was going on? Was he in contact with George? Was there something else going on, about which he was being kept in the dark? Joe tossed these questions around in his mind, then sighed, and concluded that he wasn't going to get any answers until he actually met up with Chaim.

He glanced at his watch, and saw that it was getting near the time that he had arranged to meet with Vicki. He switched his thoughts off, and decided to take advantage of a beautiful morning – who knows, it might even be his last if Chaim turned out to be seriously pissed off with him – and walk to Vicki's hotel through Hyde Park.

***

An hour later Joe walked in through the front entrance of Vicki's hotel. The receptionist greeted him as he approached the front desk. "Good morning, sir. It's the American lady that you've come to meet, I think. She's just been for a run, but fortunately she's still alive and in one piece. I'll just ring her room and tell her that you're here, and that it's safe to come down to meet you."

"Thank you," Joe replied, slightly puzzled by the receptionist's strange ramblings. He moved across to an easy chair in the lobby and sat down to wait for Vicki. He watched the receptionist warily.

Across the road, the West Indian guy watched as Joe entered the hotel. He took out his mobile and phoned George. "He's just entered the hotel."

"*I want you to keep a close eye on him. Wherever he goes stick with him. Don't get too close, for fuck's sake don't let him see you, but stick with him. I want to know every time he blows his nose, every time he takes a piss, and above all, I want to know every time he looks like he's just about to kill someone. And in particular, I want to know if he's just killed someone! Understand?"*

"I understand. Don't worry, he's not going anywhere without me. But what should I do if he looks about to kill someone?"

"Nothing. Just let him get on with it. Then tell me about it afterwards."

The West Indian sighed, and leaned against the wall. He resigned himself to a long, and boring day. As it turned out, he was proved wrong.

In the foyer of the hotel, Joe stood up to greet Vicki as she came out of the lift, and walked towards him, smiling brightly. He decided to put aside all his misgivings, forget about George, and Michael Corrigan, and Abd-al-Qadir, and Chaim, and enjoy himself in the company of a beautiful woman. He smiled back at her and said, "Let's forget about all the shit that's happening in the world, and do a little sightseeing for a couple of hours. Is there anywhere that you'd like to see in London?"

"Buckingham Palace, and Westminster Abbey, and Big Ben, and Tower Bridge, and the Houses of Parliament, and Madame Tussauds, and Trafalgar Square, and London Bridge, and St. Paul's Cathedral, and the Tower of London."

He grimaced, and shook his head amiably. "OK, let's go."

Three hours later, after trekking from one tourist attraction to the next, they were both starting to feel rather weary. "I've had a great morning, Joe," said Vicki, "Thank you. You'd make a fantastic tourist guide."

"Thank you for being an excellent tourist, and thank you for believing everything that I've told you. But it's time for lunch now, I think. There's a good pub that I know which is not too far away from here. 'The Red Lion'. It's a very common name for pubs in England. They're named after James the first, or something like that. This one's near Oxford Circus – it's only about ten minutes walk away."

***

Ten minutes later they walked into 'The Red Lion'. Joe looked around warily for Chaim, as he found a table for the two of them. After a bit of discussion, Vicki decided on a pint of bitter, and Joe walked up to the bar to buy a couple of pints. There was still no sign of Chaim. Joe wasn't sure that he had done the right thing by bringing Vicki to his meeting, but he felt that her presence would inhibit Chaim from doing anything too drastic. Hopefully. Like killing him.

As he was waiting at the bar to be served, there was a group of businessmen who had already been served, and he idly listened in to their conversation. They were discussing the Middle East, and the latest attacks by Hamas on Israeli civilians. Two of the men blamed Israel for all the problems - "The Arabs were there first, then the Zionists came along and took their lands off them and pushed them into refugee camps. The Israelis deserve all they get." The other three men were less certain, and a mildly heated discussion was taking place.

All of a sudden, a loud voice boomed out "You're all talking shit. None of you knows the first fucking thing about the Middle East. Have any of you been there? I think not. If you don't know what you're talking about then you should shut the fuck up."

Joe quickly turned to see a very angry-looking Chaim addressing the group. He hastily stepped in front of him. "Shalom, Chaim. Good to see you. Do you want a drink? Come and join me. I'm at a table over there. There's someone I'd like you to meet." He managed to divert Chaim away from the annoyed-looking businessmen. Smiling reassuringly at them, he shepherded Chaim towards the table where Vicki was sat. He introduced them to each other, and then went back to the bar in another attempt to get drinks – the two beers for himself and Vicki, plus a large gin and tonic for Chaim. When at home in Israel, Chaim normally drank arak – the strong, aniseed-flavoured spirit popular in countries of the Eastern Mediterranean. But he loved gin and tonic, and regarded it as one of England's main contributions to civilisation – or indeed, England's only contribution to civilisation.

As Joe sat down at the table, Chaim turned and scowled at him and demanded, "Why did you attack one of my agents?"

Joe stared back at him defiantly and replied, "Why was I being followed?" The two men glared at each other.

Vicki tried to defuse the situation. "Cheers," she said, raising her glass of beer and taking a drink.

Chaim turned to her with a look of incredulity, then started laughing. "Cheers," he replied. Turning back to Joe, he said. "And the next time you do something like that to one of my men, I'll have you killed. Understand?"

"Yeah? You and whose army?" said Joe. Then all three of them started laughing. Gradually they calmed down. "Sorry, mate,"said Joe, "but I really didn't know it was one of your men, otherwise I wouldn't have done it. How was I to know? He was carrying a Kuwaiti passport. But please tell me exactly why I was being followed."

Chaim looked at him steadily, then glanced questioningly towards Vicki.

"You can talk freely in front of Vicki. So once again. Why was I being followed?"

Chaim sighed and said, "Abd-al-Qadir. That bastard has crawled out from under a stone again. And we want him. Rumour has it that he's heading for London, and we know that if that's the case, then for sure you will be after him. You have unfinished business from the past! Perhaps we can work together on this?"

"Perhaps. But this is London. This is my territory, not yours. And I want Abd-al-Qadir at least as much as you do, if not more. So what benefit will I get out of working with you?"

"We'll find him. Between us. Then you will get to kill him.

All I want is to get my hands on him for twenty-four hours to ask him a few questions."

Joe thought hard about that. He knew that Chaim's questioning of Abd-al-Qadir would be very brutal. But he didn't care about that, just as long as he got to actually pull the trigger, and bring the fucker's life to an end. And with Chaim's resources, tracking down Abd-al-Qadir would be so much easier. Although he rather liked Vicki, he wasn't entirely convinced that her field craft skills were up to the standards required to go up against Abd-al-Qadir. He wondered again if he ought to ditch her as soon as an opportunity presented itself, but relented when he glanced towards her, and was rewarded with a tentative smile. OK, so he would keep her on the team for the time being. However, he was still worried by her ill-conceived actions in Amsterdam, by the fact that Michael Corrigan knew of her, and by the possible repercussions that could arise from all of this.

"OK. I'm with you. Let's get the bastard," he said to Chaim. They smiled at each other, then shook hands on their new partnership. "So. Where do we start?"

"Falmouth," piped up Vicki, brightly. Joe gave her a stern look, suddenly starting to feel that he had possibly made a mistake after all, by not ditching her.

"Falmouth?" echoed Chaim. "In Cornwall? Why, what's happening there?"

"Something. But we don't know what, yet." He tried to change the subject. "What do you know of Abd-al-Qadir's accomplices?" said Joe.

"There's a man called Michael Corrigan."

"We know of him."

"And we believe that there are two or three Palestinians working with him. But we don't know if they are in this country, or if their involvement with the 'project' is going to be somewhere else. We think that they are members of a group called 'Hamas'. You have heard of them?"

"Yes."

"Those idiots at the bar were talking about them." He cast a disdainful look towards the businessmen that he had argued with earlier. "They have recently undertaken a number of terrorist attacks within Israel. They are committed to our destruction. But Abd-al-Qadir is not of Hamas. He is simply a mercenary – out to make as much money as possible."

"Can you let me have whatever information you have on the Palestinians."

"Yes. Now what is this about Falmouth?"

Joe sighed and shot Vicki an irritated glance. "We think that a shipment of drugs is being brought in on a ship, probably heroin from Afghanistan. Eight million pounds worth. The drugs will then be sold to buy guns which will be shipped back to the Middle East. Probably to Hamas, I guess."

"Who is meeting this shipment?"

"Michael Corrigan and his gang. And probably Abd-al-Qadir. And us."

"Us?"

"Me and Vicki." A look of surprise crossed Vicki's face at this, but she said nothing.

"What do you want us to do?" asked Chaim.

"Do you know where these Palestinians are?"

"No."

"What about Abd-al-Qadir?"

"No, though from what you say, he'll be heading to Falmouth."

Joe sat back and thought carefully about all of this. Vicki gave him a quizzical look, but he ignored her for the time being. A plan was starting to take shape in his mind. Where is the best place to maintain surveillance on shipping coming to and from a port? Why, from a boat, of course. There were two boats that he needed to identify – the one bringing in the drugs, and the one meeting it which had Michael Corrigan, and probably Abd-al-qadir, on board. Having identified them, then he, and Chaim's men, and Vicki of course, could take appropriate action. He needed access to a boat, to carry out this sea-based surveillance. And as he thought about it, he realized that he knew just the man who could help. A broad grin spread across his face.

Vicki and Chaim both looked at him questioningly. He smiled reassuringly at them and started to explain. "OK, here's the plan. Me and Vicki, we're going to be on a boat, watching all the boats entering and leaving Falmouth."

"On a boat?" said Vicki, with an alarmed expression. Joe ignored her.

"And you and your men, Chaim, will be on land, outside Falmouth docks, waiting to pounce, when I identify the required boat and give you the go-ahead."

"On a boat?" repeated Vicki.

"Yes, on a boat. And Chaim will be on land. Waiting to pounce."

"That's a plan?" asked Chaim, incredulously. "What happens if the drugs are passed from one boat to the other at sea? Surely that's what is likely to happen?"

"We don't have to actually catch them in the act. Once me and Vicki identify one or other of the boats, then you guys can come storming in. You can pinch a speedboat or something. There'll be plenty of time."

"Pinch a speedboat?" repeated Chaim, "Just so long as it's not on the Sabbath. Some of my guys are going to mutiny if I ask them to steal a speedboat on the Sabbath." He winked at Vicki.

"On a boat?" repeated Vicki for the third time. "What sort of boat?"

"I haven't decided yet. Right, are there any more questions?" Vicki and Chaim shook their heads. "OK, Chaim, get me the information on those Palestinians, then you and your men poke around and see if you can unearth them. Check out the likely restaurants, hotels, that sort of thing. Me and Vicki will see if we can uncover anything more about Michael Corrigan and Falmouth. We think it's happening on the third of July, that's four days from now, so we'll head on down to Cornwall tomorrow afternoon, to get ready. Keep in touch." They exchanged mobile phone numbers, then shook hands and Chaim left them.

***

After Chaim had gone, Vicki looked into Joe's eyes with a serious expression. "Joe, I think that you need to tell me what is going on with this Abd-al-qadir. Why do you want to kill him? Just what has happened between the two of you? Please tell me."

Joe sighed. "OK." He sat back in his seat, took a swig of his beer, and thought back to the last time that he had crossed paths with Abd-al-qadir ...

CHAPTER 21.

Kuwait City, February 1991.

Joe stepped off the USAF helicopter onto the ground near the ruins which until fairly recently had been Kuwait City airport. He was relieved to be standing on terra firma as he always felt uneasy travelling on a helicopter, and the Bell Iroquois – which had been nicknamed "Huey" in an earlier conflict in a very different part of the world – had seemed especially shaky.

He looked around interestedly at the surrounding devastation. The sky was dark with black smoke, and the air he was breathing stank, as a result of the burning oil wells left by the Iraqis when they retreated back to Iraq. *"What a fucking mess,"* he was thinking. *"And just why the fuck am I here?"*

After a few minutes, he saw an army jeep coming towards him. It pulled up alongside. A couple of soldiers sitting in the front inspected him. "Joe Butler?" the driver asked.

"Yeah, that's me."

"Get in," the man sitting in the rear seats said. Joe looked at him. He saw a nondescript looking individual, wearing a light-coloured suit, no tie, and very dark glasses, which didn't allow Joe to see his eyes. He instantly labelled the guy as a spook, and, from his American accent, guessed that he was CIA. He picked up his kitbag and climbed in the back of the jeep alongside him.

"So. Why the fuck am I here?" Joe asked,.

"Straight to the point," the man alongside him said. He smiled, but unable to see his eyes, Joe found him a bit sinister. "We've got a problem, a big problem. But first, we're going to take you on a guided tour of down-town Kuwait. Just relax and enjoy the sights." He gave an even more sinister smile.

Joe mentally shrugged his shoulders, and started looking around at their surroundings as they entered Kuwait city. His attention was drawn to an important looking building that they were passing. Noting his interest, the man beside him started to tell him about what they were seeing. "That's what's left of the National Museum. The Iraqis looted it, then, having cleaned the place out of anything important, smashed everything else and set what was left on fire." He smiled grimly.

As they drove along, Joe saw a group of about twenty men, he assumed were Kuwaitis, chasing two other men along the road. "What's happening there?" he asked.

"I would guess that those two are Palestinians," the other man replied. "After we kicked out the Iraqis and liberated the country, some of the Kuwaitis have turned their fury on the Palestinians in the country. They think that Yasser Arafat supported Saddam Hussein and they treat all the Palestinians here as collaborators. Some were, but most weren't." He smiled at Joe. "However, that leads us to the reason as to why you're here."

"Oh," said Joe, rather intrigued, and waited for more information. But the other man said nothing. Joe turned his attention back to their surroundings; building after building was badly damaged, and he found the place rather depressing.

Eventually they came to a halt in front of a fairly anonymous looking building. "Follow me," the other man said, climbing out of the jeep. Joe picked up his kitbag and followed, and after he stepped down onto the road, the jeep pulled away. The two of them entered the building. Joe was both intrigued and apprehensive as to what this was all about. He stayed silent. He was led into a room in which there was a large table with six chairs around it. One of the chairs was occupied, by a slightly older man, wearing a suit, shirt and tie, and a friendly expression. He waved at one of the other chairs.

Joe sat down in the chair indicated, and waited expectantly. The older man smiled at him. Then. "We have a problem. A very big problem." This one had an English accent, Joe noted.

"So I gather."

"You know that there's problems here with the Palestinian exiles. Most are harmless but some ..." he paused.

"Yes?" said Joe.

"Well there are some who definitely collaborated with the Iraqis during the occupation. But we're not interested in them – the restored Kuwaiti government will sort them out. Or perhaps ..." he shrugged, "Kuwaiti vigilante groups will dispense their own brand of justice. We don't care either way. However ..." he paused again.

Joe waited expectantly.

"However, there is a group of Palestinian terrorists who are way off the main stream. Far more extremist than even Yasser Arafat's PLO – which in any case, we believe, is starting to make noises about initiating some sort of peace deal. No, this group is far more dangerous. Their demands are so outrageous and, quite frankly, impossible to meet, that we do not understand just what their ultimate intentions could possibly be." He hesitated.

"And just where do I come into this?" asked Joe.

The other man looked steadily at Joe. "They have taken a pair of hostages who they are threatening to execute – by beheading – unless the West withdraws all its troops from Kuwait. Which of course can not possibly happen."

Joe waited expectantly.

"The hostage's names ..." He paused. "Scott and Matina."

Joe gasped. "Shit!"

"We're well aware that you know them. We're putting together a rescue operation. And we'd like it if you could help us out."

"I don't just <u>know</u> them. They are my friends. But how certain are you that it actually is Matina and Scott who have been taken? And that they are still alive?"

Wearing a grim expression the man stood up and crossed

the room to a bookcase. He picked something up, carried it back, and showed it to Joe. Joe stared in horror at a human finger in a plastic bag. "The answer to your first question: that is Scott's index finger off his right hand – the CIA have verified the fingerprint. It was sent to us along with the demands that they have made. The answer to your second question: we do not know for sure that they are still alive, but we are planning our operation on the assumption that they are."

"Of course I'll do everything that I can to help. You can certainly count on me."

"That's good. And one more thing that may well be of interest to you..." He paused again. "We believe that one of the key members of this terrorist group that took your friends hostage is an Arab called Abd-al-qadir. We understand that your paths may have crossed in the past."

Joe's blood ran cold. His mind was suddenly filled with images of Leah, as he remembered her. Picking olives. Kissing her. Her red hair and freckles. Walking hand in hand. Laughing. Making love on the beach. He stared grimly at the man in front of him. "OK. So now you've definitely hooked me. Tell me just who the fuck you are? And how you know about my relationship to Matina and Scott. And that bastard Abd-al-qadir?"

"The answer to your second question: we have a mutual acquaintance, a contact in Mossad – the Israeli intelligence service – called Chaim." He smiled at the surprised look on Joe's face. "And the answer to your first question: just think of me as a representative of the British government here in Kuwait. You can call me George..."

***

Next day, Joe was sitting in the back of a jeep alongside George. In the front sat Steve, the CIA agent who Joe had originally met when he first entered Kuwait. Despite his initial antipathy towards Steve, Joe had come to the conclusion that actually Steve was OK. But he still hadn't seen his eyes! The jeep was being driven by an American soldier.

The jeep came to a halt at a small military encampment just outside of Kuwait city. Joe looked around interestedly. There were maybe a dozen tents, some jeeps and three Ferret armoured scout cars. Several soldiers standing around observed the new arrivals with equal interest. They were all wearing nondescript looking gear, camouflage combat trousers and shirts. Typical desert gear, Joe thought. He was wearing similar gear himself. A couple of the soldiers had automatic guns slung over their shoulders.

Joe guessed that they were special forces, though at first sight he couldn't tell whether they were British SAS, or American Delta force. At least not until one of them, presumably the officer in charge, casually wandered over and greeted George. He was wearing a fairly serious expression as he shook George's hand. Clearly he already knew George, and Joe concluded that these guys were probably SAS.

"Good morning Lieutenant," said George. "Let me introduce my two colleagues. Firstly Steve. CIA, and here pretty much as an observer only, but I believe that he can handle a firearm OK if push comes to shove." The soldier nodded at Steve. "And this is Joe. He's going to be alongside you in any fight. Joe is Mossad-trained, although he is a Brit, and he knows the hostages well. And, he has crossed swords with the terrorist leader, Abd-al-qadir, on a previous occasion." At this the soldier looked surprised. He nodded at Joe.

"You can call me Max," he said. "And, Joe, I need to pick your brains about the three of them – the two hostages, and the terrorist guy. Everything you know – exactly what they look like, whether they're left or right-handed – everything." Joe nodded. "You need a gun?"

"Yeah, I think that would be useful."

"Hey Jack, get a gun for Joe here," Max shouted to one of the other soldiers.

"OK, boss," the other replied. He disappeared briefly, then reappeared with a sub-machine gun, which he handed to Joe. An Uzi, Joe noted approvingly. He looked over the gun, ejected the magazine, examined it and replaced it.

"That'll do nicely, thank you," he said.

"I figured that since you've worked with Mossad, you'll be happy with an Uzi."

"You figured right. So. Let's get started."

Max led Joe, Steve, and George to a nearby tent. They sat around a foldaway table. Jack joined them. "OK, so what can you tell us about Scott and Matina?"

Joe cast his mind back to the last time he had seen them. "First, Matina. She's the dominant one in their relationship. Even bossy at times. About five foot eight or so. Extremely attractive, good figure, dark haired, wears glasses. I guess she may have changed a bit – it's several years since I last saw them both. Very Australian, though originally from Greece, I believe, as she speaks Greek fluently. Right-handed. I think that the last time I saw her – maybe fifteen years ago – she was holding her gun in her right hand!"

"And Scott?"

"Scott's the more intellectual of the two. He's also about five foot eight, but rather more wiry and muscular. When I last saw him, his hair was starting to recede a bit. We teased him about going bald – 'baldilocks', we used to call him – so he may well have lost rather more by now. He's also right-handed, I think. I remember him picking his nose using the index finger of his right hand. Though I don't think that he'll be doing that any more," he added with a grim smile.

"And Abd-al-qadir?"

"Well. The one distinguishing feature that sets him apart is that he only has one eye - his left eye. I believe that he lost his right eye in a bungled terrorist attack when a home-made bomb exploded in his face. Some times he wears an eye patch, sometimes he simply wears sunglasses. That's his main distinguishing feature."

Max and Jack looked at each other. "That's something we didn't know. OK, you got anything else about him?"

"Yes. He's a fucking murderous bastard. He killed the woman that I loved, and I want to see him dead!"

Max looked steadily at Joe. "Well, we're certainly going to do our best to help you out with that."

"And I want to be the one that pulls the trigger!"

"You've got it. Deal." He unrolled a map on the table between them. "OK, so this is where we are." He placed his finger on the map. "We're pretty certain that the terrorists have your friends about here. We've had a lot of feedback from a spy satellite." He pointed to another position on the map. "That's about fifteen miles, just over the border into Iraq. We'll have to do it on foot. We need to move in silently. But when we've got them, and wiped out all the terrorists – hopefully – we can then radio for the helicopters to come and pick us up."

Joe nodded. "Yeah, fair enough. When do we go?"

"We'll move out tonight about midnight. There'll be clear skies and the full moon will give us plenty of illumination. We'll get in position and then we'll attack at dawn. Hopefully they'll be distracted saying their early morning prayers – salat al-fajr, I believe they call it. And if we kill them, then I guess they'll be guaranteed a place in paradise with seventy two virgins." He grinned at Joe. "Seventy-two virgins! Me, I'd prefer the Red-light district of Amsterdam, and seventy-two prostitutes." Joe laughed. "In the meantime why don't you mingle and talk to some of the guys. We're all on your side, Joe. We want the bastards, and we want to get the hostages freed."

George had been listening to the discussion that had just taken place with considerable interest. He now stood up. "Well, by the sounds of it, you've got everything organized and under control. So, I'll be leaving you now. But I just want to wish you all good luck." He shook hands with Joe, Steve, Max, and Jack. "Good luck. Let's hope that by this time tomorrow, we'll have Scott and Matina back here safe. And that Abd-al-qadir is dead!"

With that, he turned and climbed into the jeep, which set off back towards Kuwait city. The others all watched him go.

"Right," said Max. "Let's get ready..."

CHAPTER 22.

Somewhere in the Iraqi desert, February 1991.

The moon illuminated the sand dunes as Joe and Steve, together with Max and Jack and their fellow soldiers, steadily made their way towards their destination, the terrorist camp where they believed that Scott and Matina were being held hostage. Occasionally they heard distant gunfire. As they progressed, Joe, ever alert to his surroundings, was on edge and constantly looking around, although his mind kept wandering to Leah, remembering their time together. As always, he burned with a cold hatred towards Abd-al-qadir. All he wanted from his life was to see him dead. To look into his lifeless eyes. To know that he was going to hell. Without his seventy-two fucking virgins.

Eventually Max, who was leading the way, stopped and held up his arm, and they all silently dropped to their knees. Joe slowly crept forward and drew alongside Max. They looked down from the top of a sand dune into a small encampment. There were about a dozen sleeping Arabs, with a couple more on watch. There was no sign of Scott and Matina. And no sign of Abd-al-qadir either. Joe looked at Max. Max shrugged and whispered, "I think that we may have a problem. I think that maybe our information is out of date, and that your friends are actually somewhere else. But hopefully those bastards down there will know where they are. We'll go in anyway, and we'll kill most of them, though we do need to keep at least a couple of them alive, so we can question them. We'll wait till dawn like I said earlier. Let's just wait and watch."

Joe was worried. "But when we question them, will they give us the information we need?"

Max smiled grimly. "Yes. Definitely. I can guarantee it."

For the next hour or so, Joe, and the rest of the group, lay on the sand, watching. Nothing much seemed to be happening, except that there was a change of the guards. Eventually, round about six o'clock, as the sky grew lighter in the east, the camp started stirring. Joe and Max watched carefully as the Arabs all unrolled prayer mats, and readied themselves for their early morning prayers. Max slowly raised his arm, waited until all the Arabs in the encampment had positioned themselves facing towards Mecca, which, luckily, meant that they were all facing away from Joe and the boys. Max dropped his arm, and they all started slowly moving towards their target, keeping low as they did so. They had got about half-way, when one of the Arabs leaped to his feet and started shouting and pointing at them. He was rewarded by a burst of gunfire which more or less took his head off.

"I hope that you enjoy your seventy-two virgins," muttered Max.

There was a fairly short skirmish, and the Arabs were quickly overcome. One of the soldiers had received a minor gunshot wound to his upper arm, but everyone else was unharmed. Most of the Arabs were dead; six of them were restrained, lying on their backs, their wrists fastened together with zip ties.

Max stood in front of the captives. He looked down on them with a cold, contemptuous look. "OK, guys, Now, I want to know where the Australians are."

Alongside him, one of the other soldiers, with a certain level of skills in the Arabic language, translated. "*Ayn hi al'usturaliiyn?*"

The captives all stared at him with bitter expressions. "*Aibtaead!*" one of them spat at Max.

"What did he say?" asked Max.

The translator coughed. "Well, actually boss, he told you to fuck off."

"Did he indeed?" said Max. "I think that is very impolite. And not particularly sensible since I'm the one with the gun." He stepped up to the Arab, and thrust the muzzle of his gun into the man's groin. "Right. Now ask him again."

"*Ayn hi al'usturaliiyn?*"

"*Aibtaead!*"

Max looked coldly into the man's eyes for several seconds, then pressed the trigger on his gun. There was a burst of automatic fire, an explosion of blood from the Arab's groin, and he started screaming. "I don't think that the seventy-two virgins are going to get much pleasure out of you," Max muttered. He moved on to the next man in the line, and thrust his gun into his groin. "Now ask him!" he said.

"*Ayn hi al'usturaliiyn?*"

The second man started crying. "*Ana la 'aerif*" he screamed.

"What did he say?"

"He said that he doesn't know."

Max pressed the trigger, and blew away the second man's private parts as well. "Well, if you really don't know, you're not much fucking use either. Not now, anyway." He moved on to the third man, and thrust the muzzle of his gun into this man's groin.

"OK. *Ayn hi al'usturaliiyn?* he demanded. "Where are the Australians? Just fucking tell me! Or do you want to meet your seventy-two virgins without a dick!"

The man screamed, "I know where they are, I know. Please. Show me a map, and I can tell you. Please don't hurt me." He started crying.

"OK. Good lad." Max reached forward and patted the man's cheek. "Right, get me a map, please," he asked the soldier nearest to him. He was handed a map which he unfolded and laid flat on the ground. He pulled the Arab to his knees and used his knife to cut through the zip tie holding his wrists together. "So. Show me where they are."

The Arab pointed a trembling finger to a place on the map. "There."

Max, Joe, and the nearest soldier peered at where he was pointing. "Jarbisi," said Max. "That's about another ten kilometres. The other side of the main road from Basrah to Baghdad, though I don't think that's too much of a problem." He looked at the Arab and put the muzzle of his gun on his forehead. "I hope that you're telling me the truth."

The Arab looked terrified, and burst into tears. "Please. Yes it is true."

"OK. You can live. For now," he added, ominously. "But you will come with us." He turned to to the soldier next to him. "OK. Kill all the others."

He smiled grimly, then nodded towards his colleagues. They all quickly went from man to man, killing each one with a single bullet to the head. The job was finished within less than thirty seconds. Fairly efficiently, Joe thought, He looked on indifferently to what was happening. *Good fucking riddance!* he thought. He made eye contact with Steve, who smiled and shrugged.

"OK," said Max. "We need to move out." He stared at the map. "Look, there's an oil installation – a refinery or something – less than a kilometre from Jarbisi, our target." He looked thoughtful. "OK. This is how we'll do it." He turned towards one of the other soldiers. "Sam, you'll take three men and hit the oil refinery. That should create a diversion for the rest of us,." He grew thoughtful again. "We'll move out now and get to the other side of the highway before we split into two groups. You come with us," he said to the Arab, jerking him to his feet, and fastening his hands together behind his back with a new zip tie. He patted him on the cheek. "If you're a good boy you'll get to live. But if not..." he added ominously, "you'll get to meet your seventy-two virgins. Without a dick. OK, now let's go," he said to the rest of his squad. " And remember: we need to be very careful, we'll be moving in daylight."

***

Some time later, they were all laid on their stomachs on the sand dunes, overlooking the main road from Basrah to Baghdad. There was a steady stream of vehicles, both military and civilian. Max turned to Joe. "We need to get across that road. We can't wait till dark, because the longer we wait, the more time for something to go wrong for your Australian friends. We can't fight our way across, because that'll probably alert the terrorists holding them." He had a thoughtful expression on his face as he considered the possible courses of action.

Steve, the American, now spoke up. He looked at Joe and Max. "Can I make a suggestion? What we need is some sort of diversion that will seem kind of 'normal' and won't alert the terrorists to the likelihood of an attempt to rescue the hostages. How about an air raid, cutting the road, and thereby halting the flow of traffic? Kind of a 'normal' hostile activity. And it would make it a lot easier for us to cross the road. Does that sound plausible?"

Max grinned at him. "Yeah, that's a good idea, Steve. We can contact the base by radio, and then get it under way." He examined the map closely, and put his finger on a particular spot. Joe and Steve leaned forward to see.

"That looks OK. On the road just to the east of where we want to cross over."

Max muttered to himself as he jotted down the map co-ordinates in his notebook. "That's approximately thirty degrees, thirty seven and a half minutes north, and forty seven degrees, two minutes east. Good enough. They can fly there, find the road, and let rip." He grinned. "OK. Let's get on the radio to base." His fellow soldier handed him the radio and Max established a connection to the base. He passed on the essential information regarding the required target area, and a decision about an air strike was quickly reached. He ended the communication, then sat back looking pleased. "OK, they'll be here in less than an hour. We'll wait here; we don't want to get too close to the bombs going off. But we'll get ready to move off as soon as the road gets disrupted. And then we'll all of us go straight to Jarbisi in one group. We no longer need to hit the oil refinery as a diversion – the attack on the road will be diversion enough. Everyone agree with that?"

His fellow soldiers all nodded.

"OK. Let's grab a little rest. But everyone keep alert and be ready to move out as soon as the shit hits the fan."

Joe rolled onto his back and let his mind wander. As always he found himself thinking of Leah. Her red hair. Her freckles. Her lovely smile. He sighed, then turned towards Max. "You married, Max?"

"I was. But I'm divorced now. She couldn't take the endless stress of not hearing from me for weeks at a time, not knowing where I was, and whether I was still alive. In the end we just drifted apart."

"Any children?"

"Thankfully no. And you? You said that Abd-al-qadir killed the woman that you loved. Do you want to talk about it, or is it too painful?"

"No, it's OK for me to talk. Her name was Leah. We met on a kibbutz in Israel. She was a sabra. A native-born Israeli," he added, noticing the quizzical expression on Max's face. "We were only together for about a year. The best year of my life."

"How did she die?"

"I was working for Mossad. Some fifteen years ago. We were after some Palestinian terrorists. But it all went badly wrong." He sighed heavily. "And ever since then I've been after Abd-al-qadir. The one that got away."

"And just how do Scott and Matina figure in all of this? The hostages that we're, hopefully, going to rescue."

"They're actually ex-CIA, but they were also working for Mossad. On that same mission. Matina got shot as well, but it was only a flesh wound in the shoulder. I think of them as good friends, though it's quite a while since I saw them. Fifteen years actually."

"So what have you been doing for the last fifteen years?"

"Oh, this and that," replied Joe, vaguely. "But if I told you, then I'd have to kill you."

"Yeah? You and whose fucking army?"

They both started laughing, then quickly quietened down. "OK. Let's keep an eye on what's happening on the road down there," Max said. "We need to be ready to move at short notice." For the next half-hour they all watched the activity on the Basrah to Baghdad road. There was a fairly steady stream of vehicles heading north towards Baghdad, most were military, but there were quite a few civilian vehicles as well. There were far fewer vehicles heading south.

"I think that it looks good," said Max. "If they hit the road where we want them to, it'll stop the vehicles heading north, and we should be able to get across. Hopefully we shouldn't have to wait too much longer." In fact, they didn't have to wait at all. While they were talking, two planes came in fast from behind them. They each fired several missiles at the vehicles on the road, causing multiple explosions and total chaos, and then they both dropped a bomb into the middle of all of this. Max and Joe watched transfixed by the havoc that ensued, and the fleeing Iraqi vehicles.

Max turned to his men. "OK, guys. Start moving. Steady and low. Get ready to cross that road. We need to take advantage of any gap in the traffic, before they start coming back to investigate. Are we all ready to go?" He looked at Joe and Steve, who both nodded. "OK, let's go. And bring that guy with us." He gestured towards their Arab prisoner.

Taking advantage of the smoke from the burning vehicles on the highway, they all quickly crept forwards. As they got near to the road, there were no vehicles in sight and they ran across to the safety of the sand dunes on the far side. There they regrouped, and waited for instructions from Max. "It's about three miles to Jarbisi. We need to go very carefully from now on." He nodded at Joe and the others, and they all started walking.

***

Nearly two hours later they were all laid flat out on the sand, overlooking Jarbisi. Max was observing closely, through a pair of binoculars, the movements within the village. He handed the binoculars to Joe. "See that building on the far left. There's two armed guards stood outside. If I was a betting man, then I'd wager a week's wages that the hostages are being held there. What do you think?"

Joe looked at the building that Max had identified. He watched the actions of the two men that Max had highlighted. It was very clear that they were closely guarding someone or something. "Yes. I agree with you. I think that's probably where Matina and Scott are being held. So what do we do now?"

"We'll just watch and get a feel for things for now. But when the time comes we'll move in. Very fast. Anyone gets in our way, they're dead. You OK with that?"

"Yeah."

They lay there, carefully observing the activities within the village. Suddenly, Joe tensed. "Oh, shit!" He was dismayed to see a group of several small children come into the main village square and start playing, kicking a football around.

Max sighed and looked at Joe. "OK, Joe, I know what's going on in your head. And I agree with you. We don't want any collateral damage. And definitely not kids." He grew thoughtful. "OK. So, we'll have to be very careful and we'll wait till after dark before we move in." For the next few hours they stayed in position. Eventually, as darkness fell, fairly rapidly, the village became quiet., Max signalled that it was now time to move. They kept a close eye on the two guards as they advanced. Max held up his arm, and they all halted. He looked at two of his men, pointed towards the guards, and drew his hand across his throat. They nodded, and melted into thin air. Max and Joe carefully watched the guards as they walked up and down.

Then, two figures emerged from the darkness. Each guard was grabbed and had a knife pulled across his throat. Their two bodies slumped on the ground, and Max's two soldiers signalled to the rest. Max and his men rose to their feet and started moving steadily forwards. They encountered no opposition as they got closer to the objective. Eventually, they reached the building that they believed Matina and Scott were being held in. Max raised his hand, waited, then let it drop. Three of his soldiers burst in through the door. The rest waited. After a tense couple of minutes, one of the soldiers came back out and signalled 'All Clear'. Max and Joe, together with Jack, cautiously entered. There they found Matina and Scott, sitting in one corner. They had been bound hand and foot, but were currently being released by the soldiers. Amazingly, they seemed unharmed, and were clearly excited to see their rescuers. As soon as she was free, Matina leapt to her feet and rushed to Joe, grabbing him in and hugging him.

"Joe! Thank you, thank you, thank you!" There were tears in her eyes. And in Joe's also.

Scott approached a little more hesitatingly. He embraced Joe and shook his hand. Joe was acutely aware of his bandaged hand. "I'm sorry about everything that's happened, Scott," he said. "But I've brought you both a present." He took his back pack off, reached into it and brought out two packages, one of which he handed to Scott, and the other to Matina. "Vegemite sandwiches!" he announced triumphantly. There was a moment's stunned silence, then they all started laughing.

"OK. Now we need to move out as quickly as possible, said Max. "And quietly. We're surrounded by hostiles. Let's go. Save your vegemite sandwiches for later. And take these." He gave a handgun to each of Matina and Scott. "But don't use them unless absolutely necessary. Remember. We need to move as silently as possible. And that guy." He gestured towards their Arab prisoner. "Just gag him, tie him up, and leave him here. He's fulfilled his part of the bargain so we can let him live."

Joe interrupted. "Before we go, I'd like to ask a question." He turned to Matina and Scott. "Have either of you seen Abd-al-qadir? That fucker with one eye?"

They both nodded. "He was leading the group that took us," said Scott. "He was the bastard that took my finger off. We haven't seen him since, but I think that he's probably still in the village. A couple of times I've overheard some of the others talk about him, and they mentioned a house adjacent to the mosque."

"Well," said Joe, looking steadily at Max."You know what I'm going to ask. How about it? Do you think that we can do it?"

Max shrugged resignedly. "Yes, OK. We'll give it a try." He sighed. "But if we run into too much opposition then we're out of here fast and you'll have to save him for another day. Agreed?"

Joe nodded. "Agreed."

"So, do you know where this mosque is?" Max asked Scott.

"I think that it's about a hundred yards or so north of here."

"OK. We'll split into two groups and go down the opposite sides of the road. You two," he gestured at two of his men, "Go outside and bring those two dead guards in, so they won't be found too soon."

The two men nodded and quickly did what was asked of them.

"Right," said Max. "Joe, Scott, and Matina, and you five guys, in one group. Go down the east side of the road. The rest of you are with me down the west side. Let's go."

They all quickly and quietly left and split into groups. Moving as discreetly as possible, Joe and his group moved stealthily along the east side of the road leading to the mosque. Luckily they didn't encounter any opposition. All was quiet. As they advanced up the road, keeping in visual contact with Max's group opposite, all seemed to go go well. As they gradually got nearer to their final destination, the mosque, they tensed, anticipating potential opposition. But they still encountered no problems. However, when they got almost to their goal, there was a loud shout. An Arab was standing in a doorway watching them, and had raised the alarm. He was immediately silenced by a burst of gunfire from Max. But the shit had hit the fan, and now all hell broke loose.

A firefight broke out. Joe and his companions threw themselves on the ground and started exchanging fire with a significant opposing force who had emerged from the nearby houses and started shooting at them.

"Oh, shit!" thought Joe *"This isn't going to work."*

"We need to get out of here," shouted Max from across the street. "Follow me." He ran down a side street. The others all followed him. Joe hesitated, but decided that there was no alternative. As he stood up, about to start running after Max, he glanced towards the mosque. There he saw Abd-al-qadir standing under a street light. Abd-al-qadir with an eye patch over his right eye. Joe opened fire with his Uzi, but Abd-al-qadir threw himself on the ground and fired back. Joe tensed, ready to run after him but was restrained by Scott.

"You'll have to leave him. We need to go," said Scott urgently. "We've got to go. Now!" Reluctantly, Joe followed Scott and the rest of the group down the side street and into the desert. He looked back towards the mosque as he reached the entrance to the side street and saw Abd-al-qadir make an obscene gesture towards him.

"Bastard," muttered Joe under his breath, as he ran down the alley. Thankfully they were not pursued. The whole group gathered together some distance from the village. A couple of

the guys had received minor flesh wounds, but otherwise everyone was safe and accounted for. Max radioed for assistance and
in a short space of time two helicopters arrived on the scene and
successfully evacuated everyone.

Max looked at Joe with a degree of apprehension. "It
was actually a successful operation. Joe. We rescued Scott and
Matina."

"Yes. But. That bastard Abd-al-qadir got away again ..."

CHAPTER 23.

London, June 2004.

"Joe. You need to tell me just what is going on with this Abd-al-qadir. What happened between the two of you? Please tell me."

Joe put his beer down on the table and took hold of both of Vicki's hands. He gave a deep sigh, then poured his heart out to her. He told her about the kibbutz, about picking olives, about falling in love with Leah. He told her about his involvement with Mossad. He told her about the rather messy business in Lebanon, and the total disaster in Crete. And Leah's death. And Abd-al-qadir.

He stopped talking and looked at Vicki. Her eyes were filled with tears. "Oh, Joe, I'm so sorry. Please will you let me help you kill the bastard!"

Joe smiled at her, leant forward, and gently kissed her on the lips. He sat back. "Thank you. Yes, let's kill the bastard. And Michael Corrigan as well. Do you think that he's the one who killed your sister?"

"Yes. I think that he is. Or at the very least, he was responsible, and gave the order to kill her."

"Well, actually there's a contract out on Michael Corrigan. And I'm being paid to kill him. Being paid rather a lot of money in fact." Vicki looked a little taken aback by this. "By MI5. But we can work together on this, and I'm perfectly happy to let you be the one that actually pulls the trigger, and kills the fucker."

"Thank you."

"Now let's have another drink. And then you can tell me all about your rugby-playing boyfriend."

Vicki looked a little embarrassed. "Well, actually, I don't have a rugby-playing boyfriend."

"What? Do you mean that you've broken up with him? Oh dear, what a shame. So. Does that mean that now I'm in with a chance?"

She looked at him and gave him a warm smile. There was a twinkle in her eyes. "Yes. You're most definitely in with a chance."

Joe smiled back at her. "That's great. But first..."

Vicki looked at him excitedly, her eyes sparkling, "Yes?"

"...we've got some people to kill."

"Why, you old romantic, you!"

***

Joe and Vicki were walking up Oxford Street towards their respective hotels. Feeling relaxed and quite happy. Window shopping.

"My god! Look at the price of those shoes!"

"Actually, I think that they look rather nice."

"But, three hundred pounds for a pair of shoes! Three hundred pounds! Three hundred fucking pounds!"

Vicki laughed and slipped her arm through Joe's. Then got serious. "OK. So what happens next?"

"Well. We're going to be heading down to Falmouth. Tomorrow, I think. Quite honestly, I'm not sure exactly how we're going to handle it once we're down there. First we need to find out as much as we can about the plans of Corrigan and Abd-al-qadir. Hopefully Chaim will be able to come up with a few more details. But I think that we should also get involved, and see if we can discover some useful information about what's going on. Perhaps tonight we'll head to 'Tarantula' and have another look around. But first, how about a curry?"

"Not too spicy, I hope."

"Of course it'll be spicy. That's the whole point of Indian

food!"

Vicki laughed. They decided to head back to their own hotels and get changed, ready for an evening out.

"But don't wear anything too sexy, or I don't think that I'll be able to keep my hands off you!"

"Yes, sir." She curtsied and giggled.

***

Joe started walking towards the Dorchester. On the way he kept continually looking into shop windows, looking at the reflection, observing his surroundings. While he had been walking up Oxford street with Vicki, he had become aware of a possible tail. A West Indian guy who appeared to be taking an interest in them. And whenever Joe turned around to look behind, the West Indian guy would stop and look into a shop window, seemingly taking an interest in its contents.

Joe decided to carry out an experiment. He turned back and entered Marble Arch tube station. After buying a ticket, he went down the escalator onto the westbound platform. There he sat on a seat and pretended to be daydreaming, looking at nothing in particular. He was, however, secretly observing the other passengers on the platform. A skill that he had perfected over the years. Out of the corner of his eye, he observed the West Indian guy whom he believed was tailing him.

The destination board showed that a train to Ealing Broadway was due into the station in two minutes.

Joe waited on his seat when the train came in, seemingly showing no interest in it, to all intents and purposes waiting for the following train, which was going to West Ruislip. However when the train's warning beeps indicated the doors were about to close he jumped to his feet and ran onto the train. He sensed that the West Indian guy was doing the same, but at the very last minute Joe doubled back and jumped back off the train. Leaving the West Indian guy on the train.

Elementary my dear Watson!

The train pulled away, and Joe, grinning broadly, gave the embarrassed-looking West Indian guy a V-sign as the train pulled away. He then went back up the escalator to the street and continued towards his hotel, whistling happily.

He wondered who the West Indian guy was working for. Definitely not Chaim. And Corrigan and Abd-al-qadir didn't really know who he was, so it was highly unlikely to be either of them. That left George. He thought that George was the most probable. But the West Indian guy hadn't been very good at tailing him, and so probably wouldn't be MI5. Unless he was a trainee. But most likely he was yet another freelancer that George was using. A rather inefficient freelancer. He wondered just what the fuck George was up to.

***

Joe and Vicki had agreed on seven o'clock as a meeting time, and on the dot of seven, Joe was sitting in the foyer of Vicki's hotel, feeling quite excited about their forthcoming 'date'. As he waited for Vicki, Joe was, as always, paying close attention to his surroundings, and to the other people around him. But without being at all obvious about it. He saw nothing to concern him, although he thought that the receptionist was watching him with a rather manic expression on his face.

His mobile phone rang. Joe glanced at the display and saw that the caller was Chaim. He moved to a quieter, more private, part of the foyer and then answered it,

"Shalom, Chaim."

"*Shalom, Joe.*"

"Anything to report?"

"*Maybe. We believe that the drugs are probably on a freighter which just yesterday passed through the Suez canal and is right now sailing through the Mediterranean. The boat is Pakistani registered, and set sail from Karachi nearly a week ago. We have spies based in the Sinai peninsula who observed the boat, and think that they identified a couple of members of Hamas on the deck, though they*" *are not one hundred percent certain. The name of the ship is 'Islamabad'. Its destination is Rotterdam, so it will be passing through the English Channel. At some point in the West of the Channel, we anticipate that Michael Corrigan will liaise with the freighter, and the drugs will be transferred to a smaller motor launch to be taken on shore. I must stress that I used the word 'believe'. We do not know any of this for certain. However, through contacts in the Israeli embassy here, we've been able to arrange access to a fast motor boat in Falmouth. It does rather seem that Falmouth is going to be the centre of the action."*

"Your guys have done well, Chaim. What are you up to now?"

"We're going to 'The Tarantula' to have a look around and see who's there."

"Yeah? So are Vicki and I."

"Do you think that's a good idea?"

"No." replied Joe, cheerfully. "But does anything about this job make sense?"

"Good point. But if we encounter each other, then not the slightest hint of recognition between us."

"Agreed."

"And take good care of that Vicki. She's real cute."

"Piss off, Chaim." Joe laughed and terminated the call.

Just then, the lift door opened and Vicki stepped out into the foyer. Joe stood up to greet her. He found himself slightly disappointed that she had actually followed his instructions not to dress too sexily. Nevertheless he thought that she looked incredibly attractive. She was simply wearing jeans and a tee shirt, with her handbag slung over her shoulder. Vicki looked towards the receptionist who was still staring manically at Joe. She made a finger gun gesture at the back of his head, pulled the imaginary trigger, then put the imaginary muzzle to her lips and blew across it. She winked at Joe. He nodded and smiled back at her.

"Right. The Taj Mahal...."

"Now just you be careful, miss, you never know who's out there," the receptionist added gloomily.

***

A couple of hours later they were leaving the Indian restaurant, feeling pleasantly full. "Not too spicy, I hope?"

"No. Just perfect. I think that I'm getting used to this Indian food."

"I think that next time you might like to try a Vindaloo. You will definitely love it! OK. Now let's head to 'The Tarantula'. And afterwards ...?"

Vicki took hold of Joe's hand. She squeezed it and smiled at him. "Not tonight, OK?"

Joe felt a slight pang of disappointment, but grinned at Vicki. "Yes. You're right, of course. We need to be bright and sharp and ready for tomorrow. So let's see if we can find out anything of interest in 'The Tarantula'."

They headed down the street towards 'The Tarantula'. Vicki was holding Joe's hand as they ambled along, both feeling happy, although Joe, especially, was staying very alert to their surroundings and the possibility of a tail. He was especially watchful for the possibility of a West Indian tail. He saw nothing to alarm him, and relaxed somewhat.

As they approached 'The Tarantula' the bouncer on the door saw them and waved them to the front of the queue. "Are you Joe Hurricane from the Flying Lobsters?"

"Yes," Joe spoke quietly, "but I'm here incognito."

The bouncer also dropped his voice to little more than a whisper. "I understand sir. Go right on in. I'll let them know that you're here. All drinks will be on the house for you tonight."

Vicki was desperately trying not to laugh as they went through the door. Once inside they found a table and made themselves comfortable. A waitress came across with an opened bottle of champagne in an ice bucket, and a pair of glasses.

"Why, thank you," said Joe, and tipped the waitress with a five pound note. He winked at Vicki, and poured the champagne into the two glasses. "Cheers." They clinked glasses.

Joe furtively looked around the room. He noticed Chaim sat at a table with a couple of, presumably Mossad, guys. They briefly exchanged glances. And, sat at the same table as yesterday, he saw Michael Corrigan. Sitting with him was Abd-al-qadir. Joe desperately tried to suppress the cold fury that he felt; Abd-al-qadir was most certainly going to die. Very, very soon.

At the same table he saw Frank Boyle, his 'friend' from the previous night. Frank saw Joe, and gave him a friendly wave. Joe smiled broadly at Frank, then murmured to Vicki, "There's my contact. Let's see if he's got any useful knowledge." He waved at Frank, and held up the bottle of champagne. Frank looked at Michael Corrigan, who gave a small nod. Frank stood up and made his way towards Joe and Vicki.

"Surprisingly, I rather think that this might work," muttered Joe to Vicki. As Frank drew closer, Joe stood and greeted him. "Frank. My number one fan! Good to see you again. Have a drink." He waved at the waitress who nodded and brought across another glass. Joe filled it with champagne and handed it to Frank.

"Cheers, Frank."

"Cheers, Joe. If I'd known that you would be here again, I would have brought my 'Flying Lobsters' album for you to autograph. But when I searched through my record collection I couldn't find it. I think that I may have lent it to someone, and not got it back."

"Oh well. I'm sure that I'll be in here again sometime soon. If you can find your 'Flying Lobsters' record, bring it in and I'll definitely autograph it for you next time I'm in here."

"Thanks, Joe."

"We're going to be out of town for a few days. Sailing. But I guess I'll see you when we come back."

"Sailing, eh? What sort of boat you got?"

"It's a thirty-four foot sail boat. A Bavaria thirty-four. Six berth. ' The Holly Golightly'."

"Named after the role that Audrey Hepburn played in 'Breakfast at Tiffany's'", Vicki added, helpfully.

"My boss has got a boat, as well. It's a motor cruiser, called 'Doris'. So where are you going sailing, then?"

"Down in Cornwall. A place called Falmouth. You heard of it, Frank?"

"Falmouth! That's a coinci...." Frank suddenly clammed up, looking slightly embarrassed. "Well thanks for the drink, Joe. I better be getting back to my boss. Be seeing you around." He hurriedly left Joe and Vicki and crossed the room to rejoin the group at Michael Corrigan's table.

"Well, well, that was interesting," said Joe. "But I don't know which 'Flying Lobsters' album he was talking about. We made four, and they all sold a million copies."

"I thought you said that you were a one-hit wonder."

"Oh. Did I? I was just being modest. Anyway, forget about the 'Flying Lobsters', we've now managed to find out some useful information. We don't want to bring attention to ourselves by rushing out, so we'll hang around a bit longer. And then we'll pass what we've just discovered onto Chaim. Let's finish this champagne, and then we can have a Screaming Orgasm each." They both started laughing.

"So we're going to head down to Falmouth, I guess. How far is it?"

"Two hundred and something miles. It's a full days journey. But we're not going all the way there by car. The sailing boat that I mentioned, the 'Holly Golightly', is actually in a place called Foy. It's actually spelt F-O-W-E-Y, but pronounced 'Foy'." He grinned at Vicki. "That's us English for you."

"And how do we get from Foy to Falmouth?"

"We sail. Don't worry," he said quickly, seeing the somewhat alarmed expression on Vicki's face. "I'm actually a fully qualified skipper – what's called a 'Coastal Skipper' – and I'll get you there safely. It'll be about a day's sailing. You'll enjoy it. The weather forecast looks fine so I don't think that it will be rough. Anyway, let's finish our drinks and head off back to our hotels."

***

As they stood outside the 'Tarantula' Joe phoned Chaim on his mobile. He reported everything that he had learned from Frank, especially the key bit of information; the name of Corrigan's boat – the 'Doris'. And final confirmation that Falmouth was where it was all going to happen.

"We're heading down there tomorrow, Vicki and I, although we won't arrive till the day after. We don't know the exact timing of the drugs coming in, though from what you told me about the ship called the 'Islamabad' it's going to be two or three days away. Anyway, we'll be on a sailboat called the 'Holly Golightly'. "

"OK. We'll see you there."

"The 'Holly Golightly' is actually six berth, but I think we should keep our distance when we're down there. We don't want to risk raising suspicions."

"Agreed. We'll find a hotel to check into. We've sorted out a boat for ourselves. Now you take that cute girl back to her hotel and tuck her into her bed for the night."

"Piss off'."

Chaim laughed and terminated the call.

***

Joe and Vicki wandered along towards Vicki's hotel. A some point Vicki took hold of Joe's hand. Joe smiled at her. "But that's as far as it goes for now," she said as she smiled at Joe.

"I agree. We have to focus fully on the job in hand. But

after ..."

Vicki squeezed his hand.

Eventually, they arrived at Vicki's hotel. "Do you want me to see you in safely past that receptionist?"

She laughed. "No. I think that I'll be OK. But I'm not so sure about him. I find myself continually having to resist the temptation to put a bullet into the centre of his forehead. Midway between his eyes."

Joe laughed with her. "OK. For now just try to resist the temptation. It might very well cause a problem with the police, and screw up our mission. But in the meantime I'll sort out a hire car and then I'll pick you up here tomorrow morning about eleven o'clock." He gently kissed her goodnight then turned away and started off towards the Dorchester.

Vicki almost called him back, but thought better of it. Joe was right. They needed to fully concentrate on the job in hand. For now. But later ...

CHAPTER 24.

Fowey, Cornwall, July 2004.

Joe had been driving for nearly five hours, with only a brief stop at a service station to visit the loo and grab a coffee. He had picked up his hire car, a Mazda MX5, early that morning, then he had collected Vicki from her hotel. They were both keeping their rooms at their respective hotels, and each had only a small bag with little more than toiletries and a change of clothes. And a gun.

They had enjoyed each others company for the journey. Vicki had learned much more detail about Joe's relationship with Leah. She found herself desperately wanting to do all she could to help him avenge Leah's death. And then move on. Hopefully with her... She also enjoyed hearing about his escapades with Matina and Scott. "So. I guess that he finds it a bit more difficult picking his nose now?"

For his part, Joe was interested to learn of Vicki's career in the FBI. And saddened to hear of her sister's death. Probably at the hands of Michael Corrigan, who, of course, he was going to earn a very large sum of money – four hundred thousand pounds precisely - by killing.

He finally pulled the car to a halt just outside the house of his friend, Chris, owner of the yacht 'Holly Golightly'. Chris came out to greet them.

"I won't ask what you're up to this time. It's probably best that I don't know. But anyway, the boat's all stocked up. The fuel tank's full, so's the water, and I've checked the engine over. There's all the charts for this part of the channel, the Channel islands, and the north coast of France. Hopefully they'll cover everywhere that you intend to sail. Plenty of food. Including ginger biscuits; good for seasickness," he added for Vicki's benefit. "Some beer, some wine, and a bottle of gin together with a couple of bottles of tonic water. There's wet-weather gear, and the life jackets are all checked and up-to-date. And there's a pair of sleeping bags. Which can be zipped together." He winked at Joe.

"And last, but not least, there's a couple of Uzi machine guns. Wrapped in polythene and tucked away in the bilge. I think that perhaps you might find them useful. There's also a sniper rifle, with a silencer, hidden in the skipper's cabin underneath the bunk. You might very well find a use for that as well. And there's two types of ammo for the sniper rifle – regular Winchester Magnum cartridges, plus a box of cartridges with explosive tips. Be careful. And do try bring the boat back in one piece. Preferably without any bullet holes." He tossed a key to Joe. "She's at the usual berth near the Yacht Club."

"Thanks Chris. Yes, I'll bring her back in one piece. Well, I'll certainly try to bring her back in one piece. And I'll do my very best to bring her back without any bullet holes. So. Au revoir. We'll be seeing you in a few days." He tossed the car keys to him. "Feel free to take that out for a run. But try not to get caught speeding. I've lost count of how many points I've got on my licence."

"Thanks. Now piss off."

***

Joe led Vicki down to the boat, and helped her climb aboard. She was feeling quite nervous. Joe smiled reassuringly at her. "You'll be quite safe with me skippering the boat. I'm an expert. Come, let me take you down below and show you round."

"OK, this is the main saloon." Vicki looked around, quite impressed by the compact cosiness of it. "The kitchen area. And this is the bathroom." He showed her a very small room with a wash basin, a toilet, and a shower-head on the ceiling at one end.

"We don't ever use the shower; it would empty the water tanks in one go. And it's OK to have a wee in there anytime. But if you need a..." he coughed discretely, "a poo when we're moored in a harbour, just as we are now, then you should go ashore and use the facilities there. Like in the yacht club we just passed. But it's OK to poo when we're at sea."

Vicki started giggling.

"These are the sleeping cabins. You can have the main one, and I'll sleep in the smaller skipper's cabin. For now," he added, noticing a flash of disappointment cross Vicki's face. "Remember that we really do need to stay focussed on the job in hand. For now," he repeated, smiling at her.

"One last thing. Very important." He went to a locker and took out a pair of life jackets. He gave one to Vicki, and showed her how to adjust the straps so that it fitted snugly. "OK, so we'll wear these whenever we're sailing. If you go into the water it'll automatically inflate. They're very clever these things are. But for now let's have a nightcap, then get to bed. We need to be up and away by nine tomorrow morning to catch the tide."

***

The next morning. Joe had fired up the engine, and after taking Vicki through the steps of casting off, had motored out of the harbour. Once they were in open sea they had raised the sails and switched off the engine. They were now sailing purely by the wind. Joe patiently took Vicki through the various activities involved in sailing, and eventually let her take control of the wheel. To her surprise, Vicki found that she was actually rather enjoying herself. Loving the wind blowing through her hair, and the sun on her face. She smiled happily at Joe. "How long will it going to take us to get to Falmouth?"

"Maybe six hours. The wind and the tide are both with us. And when we arrive, hopefully Chaim will have more information for us about the course that the 'Islamabad' is taking. So we can guess as to when the meet-up is. Also when we get to Falmouth, we'll have a good look round to see if we can see 'Doris'".

On the way, Joe retrieved the Uzis from the bilge and checked them over. They were standard Uzis with a ten inch barrel. And Chris had provided plenty of 9mm ammunition. Enough to kill quite a few bad people, he thought approvingly. He wasn't sure that he'd actually need the sniper rifle, but he checked that over as well. And they both had handguns already. So now they were definitely ready for all eventualities.

By late afternoon they were pulling into the marina at Falmouth. First Joe took Vicki through the manoeuvres to moor the boat. Then they relaxed on deck.

"That was great, Joe. I really loved it."

"The weather was just perfect. Sometimes the weather's not so good. And then it's not always as much fun. Anyway, it's Gin and Tonic time now. Just sit back and enjoy yourself." He went down below, and shortly came back with two glasses. "It's a naval tradition that we always round off a day's sailing with a Gin and Tonic."

They sat quietly sipping their drinks, just relaxing, enjoying the evening sun.

"So now we'll have a wander around, and see if we can spot 'Doris'." They climbed onto the quayside and started walking down the road. Vicki held Joe's hand, just simply enjoying the moment. Joe, on the other hand, stayed alert, carefully looking around, watching the people around them and also checking out the boats which were moored in the harbour. At first he saw nothing to concern him, but he suddenly sensed that he was being watched, and looked around to see the West Indian guy who had been shadowing him in London. They briefly locked eyes, then the West Indian gave him a V-sign and disappeared round a corner.

"*Shit,*" thought Joe, "*Now, just what the fuck is going on here?*" He said nothing to Vicki. But simply kept on walking along the road, holding her hand, thinking furiously. "*What the fuck is*

George playing at?" He was so distracted that he almost missed seeing the boat that they were looking for. He suddenly froze. "Look, there's 'Doris'," he murmured to\Vicki, nodding towards a boat moored in the harbour. She looked in the direction he was indicating and saw a powerful looking motor cruiser. They saw a single person on deck, busy doing some sort of maintenance activities. Probably a professional crew member, and therefore probably unlikely to be privy to Michael Corrigan's plans.

Joe immediately phoned Chaim. "We've found Corrigan's boat 'Doris' here in Falmouth harbour. There's no signs of Michael Corrigan or Abd-al-qadir. There's just a single crew member on board."

"Corrigan and Abd-al-qadir are still in London. Or they were last night. We saw them in the Tarantula again yesterday. Along with that buddy of yours, Frank Boyle. But we think that they'll probably be heading down to Falmouth right now. From the current position of that ship – the 'Islamabad' – the rendezvous will most likely be scheduled for the day after tomorrow. We're on our way down there at the moment. We'll be with you," he broke off to consult with the driver, *"in about two hours and a bit. Say seven o'clock. Any suggestions as to where we might stay?"*

"Yes. There's a hotel called 'The Grove'. I'm standing outside it right now. It's just by the harbour, actually overlooking Corrigan's boat. It looks rather nice."

"Sounds perfect."

"And there's a sign in the window says they've got vacancies."

"OK. Then that's where we're heading. We'll see you later."

***

Joe was interested in 'Doris', and thought that it would be useful to find out as much as he could about her capabilities. He took careful note of the type of boat. "OK. Let's see if we can find an Internet Café. I want to find as much information as I can about their boat's specs."

"OK."

They located a suitable café down a backstreet nearby, and paid the required fee for internet access. Joe sat down at a terminal, and using the new-fangled 'Google' thing, entered the details of 'Doris': i.e. it was a 'Fairline Squadron 65'. He soon found the information that he wanted:

Length: 65 feet. *"Big!"*

Draft: 4 feet 6 inches.

Cabins: 4.

Hull: Fibreglass. *"That's good,"* he thought, *"That won't stop a bullet!"*.

Twin 1150 horsepower engines, with a bow thruster. *"Hmm. Quite powerful!"*

Maximum speed: 32 knots. *"Holy shit!, That's fast!"*

Cost: £650,000. *"Fucking hell! £650,000! I wonder which pays best: guns, drugs, or prostitutes?"*

He took careful note of all this information. And he sketched a diagram of the boat, in particular, marking the position of the engine and the fuel tanks. He then sat back in his seat, thinking carefully.

Vicki had been looking over his shoulder, and now asked him, "What's a bow thruster?"

He smiled at her. "It's a thing that pushes the front of the boat to one side or the other. It's useful on a big boat like this. It makes it easier to manoeuvre when parking it."

"Oh."

"And that's given me an idea. I need to think about this. But more than anything I need to eat. I'm hungry. In fact, I'm bloody starving.""

"Yeah. So am I."

***

They were sat in a nearby bar, overlooking the harbour,

each with a plate of fish and chips (or 'fish and fries' as Vicki insisted on calling them), and a beer. Joe was anxiously observing the activities outside, on the lookout for Michael Corrigan's bodyguard, Frank Boyle, who he wanted to avoid at all costs. He knew that should Frank see him, then most definitely suspicions would be aroused. While he was watching for Frank, he did notice the same West Indian guy walking along the harbour front, seemingly looking for Joe, but not finding him.

Joe was a little surprised when Vicki suddenly said to him, "That black guy. I think that I've seen him a couple of times before. In London. At one point I thought that he might be following me."

"Hmmm. OK, quickly finish your drink and then let's us follow him, and see if we can find out what he's up to."

"But I have my suspicions," he thought.

Vicki was surprised by Joe's reaction to what she had just said, but decided to go along with his suggestions. They both finished their beers and then left the bar. Immediately outside there was a small shop selling holiday essentials. Joe dipped inside, and quickly came back out with a couple of pairs of sunglasses. He handed one pair to Vicki. "Here's your disguise."

"Oh, wow. What a fantastic disguise. No one will possibly see through that. Why don't we rob a bank while we're at it? We'd be certain to get away with it while we're disguised wearing sunglasses."

"OK, enough of the sarcasm. It's the best I could come up with on the spur of the moment. Anyway that guy's field craft isn't very good."

"How do you know?"

"Because he was tailing me in London, and I easily gave him the slip."

"Oh."

"We need to know what's going on. Who he's working for. I have my suspicions, and I don't think it's Michael Corrigan. I think that he may, somewhat peripherally, be working for MI5. Have you got your gun with you?"

"Yes."

"Good. So have I."

"But do you really think that shooting an MI5 agent would be the best approach? Didn't you say that MI5 are the ones that are paying you to kill Michael Corrigan?"

"Yes. However, it's all starting to look just a little bit complicated. But I don't think that it will be necessary to actually kill the guy. I think that I'll just frighten him a little bit so we can find out who he's working for. I do have my suspicions, but I don't know what's behind it all and I want to find out just what the fuck is going on."

They started down the road, following their target, who was some fifty or more yards in front. He kept looking around, seemingly a bit anxious that he didn't know where Joe and Vicki were. At on point he looked back, and as he did so, Joe grabbed Vicki, pulled her into a shop doorway, and started kissing her passionately. Vicki responded enthusiastically.

After a few minutes they separated and looked at each other.

"Right. Let's get back on his trail," Joe said.

"Wow! Was that for real, or just part of our disguise?"

"Both," admitted Joe. "But for now we need to focus on the job in hand. However, later..." He smiled wickedly at Vicki.

She took hold of Joe's hand. "Maybe he'll turn around again," she added hopefully.

Joe grinned at her. They continued in their pursuit of the West Indian. who stopped, took out his mobile phone and made a call. Joe edged a bit closer, trying to listen in to this end of the conversation. He managed to overhear the odd word here and there.

"...together.....lost....don't know......George..."

Joe stopped dead. His suspicions were finally confirmed. George! Just what the fuck was George up to? He decided that he had to find out just exactly what was going on. He quickly took several steps towards the guy, pulling his gun out as he did so. Joe wasn't actually paying much attention to his surroundings, but thankfully there were no potential onlookers at that moment. He grabbed the guy by the neck, and pushed the barrel of his gun against the side of his head. At the same time he knocked the mobile phone out of the guy's hand, and then stamped on it.

"OK, mother-fucker, what's going on? Why are you following us? And exactly what is George after?"

In the meantime, Vicki was watching this with a slightly shocked expression on her face. Nevertheless, she had the presence of mind to look around and make sure that there was nobody about who was paying attention to what was going on.

"Please don't hurt me, I wasn't doing no harm," the man pleaded.

"That should be: 'I wasn't doing any harm', you fucking illiterate moron. You know, I really think that I ought to put a bullet in your head just to improve the general standards of literacy within the British population."

"No, please don't."

"OK. So. Tell me just what's going on! Exactly why is George having us followed?"

"I don't know why. He just wants to know everything about where you're going, who you're meeting. Everything. I think maybe he doesn't trust you."

"Well, I certainly don't fucking trust him. OK, from now on you don't work for George any more. Open your mouth."

The man did so, looking terrified. Joe pushed the barrel of his gun into his mouth.

"If I see you again, you're fucking dead! Understand?"

The man nodded, looking even more terrified."

"Now disappear. Piss off. Don't ever let me see you again."

The man turned and ran off without even a backward glance.

Joe turned to Vicki who was looking slightly shocked by all that had just taken place. "Well," he said cheerfully, "that's sorted. Though I still don't know why George found it necessary to have me followed."

"Who's George?" asked Vicki faintly.

"Why, he's the chap who's paying me to put a bullet in the head of Michael Corrigan. Well, anyway, let's go have another drink before we retire to bed. In sleeping bags that aren't zipped together," he added hastily.

Vicki was slightly disappointed by Joe's last statement.

***

The next morning, Vicki woke to the delightful smell of frying bacon. She quickly climbed out of her sleeping bag, pulled on jeans and a jumper, then went through to the saloon area where Joe was busily rustling up a full English breakfast – bacon, eggs, sausage, baked beans, and fried bread.

"Wow! That smells fantastic,"

"Sit down and enjoy," Joe said with a broad grin on his face. He put a full plate on the table in front of Vicki, and a second plate opposite her. They both sat and happily tucked in. After they finished, Joe collected the plates and put them in the sink.

"Now. We need to have a pow-wow to decide who we're going to kill first today."

Vicki raised her eyebrows. "Oh?"

"Only kidding," Joe added hastily. "What we actually need to do is meet up with Chaim and his guys. And also keep an eye out for Corrigan and Abd-al-qadir. We need to decide how we're going to play it. Do we, for example, simply wait for them to come back after they liaise with the 'Islamabad' and collected their drugs, and then hit them here on land? Do you see any problems with that approach?"

"Yes. They could easily set off from here, collect their drugs, and then land somewhere else."

"Of course, that's quite possible. So it's going to be better for us to get out there and, hopefully, keep an eye on exactly what they're up to. And then step in at the right time and take appropriate action."

"But will 'Holly Golightly', beautiful as she is, be any match for their boat? Doris is she called?"

"That's a very good point of course. But what's going to happen is that Chaim and his guys will be picking up the motor boat that the Israelis have organised for them, and they'll also be heading out there. Then that won't present a problem. There'll be the two of us. And they'll have a fast boat. We'll be able to simply merge in with all the other sailing boats in the area, And we've got firepower!"

"Why don't we just take care of them on land before they go out there? There'll be enough of us, and we'll be taking them by surprise."

"Yes we could do that. But it would be good to take the heroin out of circulation. Eight million pounds worth. And in any case it will be easier to dispose of their bodies at sea, rather than here in Falmouth."

"Yeah, fair enough."

"Right. I'll contact Chaim, while you do the washing-up."

Vicki gave him an irate expression, and then stuck her tongue out. "Fuck off!"

"No, OK, I'll do the washing-up, then I'll contact Chaim," Joe added hastily.

***

Some time later Joe got on the phone to Chaim. "Shalom, Chaim. How are things going with you guys?"

"*We arrived down here in Falmouth last night. This hotel you*" *recommended is pretty good. They do a great breakfast. It's not that often we get to eat nice bacon back home on the kibbutz. In fact never."* Chaim laughed.

"Well, I'm glad you like it."

"We've got a good view of the harbour. At the moment we're looking down at 'Doris'. And we're watching Abd-al-qadir, and Corrigan and his guys. They're on Doris' deck, talking, and they look like they're about to set off fairly soon. So I think that we'll go down to the boat that we've got, and get going before they do. I think that we know pretty much where they're heading."

"That sounds like a good idea. We'll set sail now so we can get out there as well. By the way, what's your boat called? We'll keep an eye out for you."

"Our boat's called the 'Artige'. I've got absolutely no idea what that name means."

"And have you got an accurate location for the 'Islamabad'?"

"Yes. The Islamabad's most up-to-date location is forty eight degrees forty seven minutes north, six degrees eleven minutes west."

"Hold on." Joe took out the chart that covered the western part of the English channel, and plotted the position of the ship. He thought deeply about possible courses that they might all take. "I'd guess that the Islamabad will be heading pretty much north-east. And that Corrigan and his crew will head pretty much due south from Falmouth to rendezvous with them. For sure it must be today that the meeting is going to take place. So we all need to move out now. I think that you should head out to the approximate location where Corrigan will liaise with the ship. By my reckoning that'll be approximately fifty degrees north, five degrees west. You've got a fast boat, so go now and hang around in that area waiting for them. Pretend to be fishing. We'll be in a slower boat so we'll probably go about half-way to the rendezvous point and keep an eye on things from there. And hopefully our sailing boat will simply blend in and look harmless enough not to attract their attention when they do come back in."

"OK. Sounds good."

"And we need to keep radio silence. But if we have something important to tell each other use channel seventy-two. Let's agree a few code words and phrases. Related to your apparent fishing activities."

"Go on."

"Corrigan and Co. let's refer to as 'Mackerel'. So you could say something like 'the mackerel are biting' to mean they're liaising with the big ship and collecting the drugs. 'The mackerel are running' means they're on their way back. 'There's lots of mackerel' means there's more than one boat rendezvousing with the big ship."

"If that happens I guess that we back off and regroup ashore."

"I guess so. But otherwise you should shadow them back to where we'll be waiting and both of us will take them on together. What weapons have you got?"

"Handguns. Automatic rifles. And a couple of shoulder-fired RPGs."

"Well that should certainly be enough fire-power." Joe was impressed. "And we've got handguns plus a couple of Uzis. And a sniper rifle with a silencer. I think that between the two of us we should be able to take them on."

"Good. Let's do it now. Let's get out there and kill some people. But remember that if possible we need to take both Michael Corrigan and Abd-al-qadir alive. It would be good to be able to locate the guns that the drugs were going to buy. We can 'question' them. One of my men is especially good at extracting information. And I do believe that you have some important questions to ask of Corrigan for your MI5 paymasters. But afterwards we can kill them both. As I promised, you can pull the trigger on Abd-al-qadir. And finally put your demons to rest."

"Thank you. And Vicki wants the privilege of pulling the

trigger on Corrigan."

"Yes, I'm OK with that. Good luck. See you both later."

***

Joe turned to Vicki. "Right. Time to put on your life jacket. And then we'll get going."

"Aye, aye, sir!" Vicki gave a mock salute. Then they both quickly went through the various steps necessary for setting sail. Very soon they had left the marina and were heading south, away from Falmouth harbour. The tide was with them and they were making a good speed. As before, Vicki enjoyed the sun on her face, the wind in her hair. Joe left her in control of the boat as he stood beside her, using a fairly powerful-looking pair of binoculars to examine the activity around them.

"Look!" Vicki pointed excitedly at a small group of dolphins nearby. They both watched, fascinated, as the dolphins playfully swam alongside the 'Holly Golightly'. "Maybe they're Audrey Hepburn fans," she giggled.

Joe laughed with her. "I believe that they are Short-beaked Common Dolphins," he said. "I've seen them before when I've been out sailing. And actually I think that that particular species is far more likely to be fans of Doris Day. I once saw them outside the cinema, queueing up to see 'Calamity Jane'".

Vicki laughed, but grew more serious, and started focussing on the job in hand.

"OK. Back to the job in hand." Joe picked up the binoculars, and continued watching carefully the nearby boats. "There's 'Artige' with Chaim and his friends." he said, pointing, "Just about to pass us on the starboard side." Vicki looked in the direction he was pointing at, and saw Chaim, who gave them a wave. They both waved back.

"I can't as yet see any signs of Corrigan's boat, 'Doris'. Here you take these and keep an eye out for 'Doris', while I pop down below and make us both a cup of tea. Just keep going on this current course. Due south. One hundred and eighty degrees."

Vicki took the binoculars, and using just one hand to hold the wheel, she kept looking around. There was considerable activity, but she was relieved that no other boats were getting particularly close. She kept looking at the compass to make sure that she was sticking to the required course. She happily watched the dolphins, who were still playing around the boat. And then she suddenly realised that 'Doris', with Michael Corrigan and Co. was passing them, some distance off on the starboard side.

"Joe," she hissed, "they're coming past us right now."

Joe quickly came onto the deck and took the binoculars from Vicki, He watched the boat for several minutes as it steadily pulled ahead of their boat.

"Yep. That's them. I could see Michael Corrigan and Frank Boyle, but no signs of Abd-al-qadir. I guess he's down below. Perhaps he suffers from sea-sickness," he added hopefully. "Anyway, keep on this current course. I'll report to Chaim."

He went below and Vicki could hear him on the radio. "Greetings Artige, there's a large shoal of mackerel heading in your direction. And remember. The best bait for catching mackerel is little bits of other mackerel."

"What the fuck are you talking about?"

"Actually I don't know what I'm talking about," Joe admitted. "I think it's highly likely that I'm talking crap, as usual. But anyway, just keep fishing. Hopefully, there's lots of mackerel out there."

"The best bait for catching mackerel is little bits of other mackerel! Hmmm. Actually, I wonder if there's something in that absurd statement."

"Well there you are, see. It came out of nowhere – a total inspiration!"

"Oh, fuck off. Over and Out."

Vicki started giggling.

CHAPTER 25.

In the middle of the English Channel, July 2004.

The 'Islamabad', a medium-sized container ship, was progressing steadily through the western approach to the English Channel. Her hold was filled with containers, mostly twenty-foot units, whilst on the deck a number of forty-foot units were stacked. Each container had a coded label identifying country of origin, owner, serial number, and so on. One specific container contained a very large quantity of heroin. Eight million pounds worth.

There were two men loitering near this container. They were the Hamas terrorists who had earlier been observed by Chaim's Sinai-based spies. Their role was to assist in the transfer of the drugs to Michael Corrigan. The ship would then proceed to Rotterdam, where it would offload the legitimate cargo. It would stay docked in Rotterdam for two weeks, and the crew would be given shore-leave, allowing them ample time to explore the many pleasures of Rotterdam's red-light district.

In the meantime, the drugs would have been sold in England, and the proceeds used to pay for the weaponry required by Hamas. The guns and other weapons were already stacked up in a warehouse on the outskirts of London. Once paid for, they would then be sealed into a forty-foot container, hidden safely behind a load of medical supplies, seemingly destined for Pakistan. This container would be taken to Southampton docks, where, along with a number of other containers, all totally innocent, it would be loaded on to the 'Islamabad', which was scheduled to call at Southampton on it's way back through the Channel from Rotterdam.

That was the plan.

The captain of the 'Islamabad' was privy to this plan. He was himself sympathetic to the Palestinian cause, and, in any case, his cooperation had been guaranteed with the help of a not insignificant sum of money. Which he was looking forward to start spending in the red-light district of Rotterdam.

The two Hamas guys carefully unsealed the container containing the heroin, and soon identified the several packages that they needed. They cautiously lifted the packages out onto the deck, and replaced the seal on the container, taking great care to ensure it looked authentic. They then signalled to the captain on the ship's bridge. He nodded back to them, and turned to the first officer stood next to him, telling him to reduce the engine revs.

The ship started slowing down. Not enough to attract attention from the British Coast Guards or the French Maritime Gendarmerie, but sufficient to facilitate the expected liaison with Doris, and the transfer of the contraband.

*****

Meanwhile Doris and Artige were both speeding towards the anticipated rendezvous point with Islamabad. Artige was considerably ahead of Doris, and as they got near to their destination Chaim decided to heave to, and start fishing. Their was no sign of either Doris or the Islamabad, so Chaim and two of his men got their fishing lines out. A third man was on the bridge.

"So what are we fishing for, Chaim?"

"A fish called mackerel. I believe that it's a local delicacy."

"What do we use for bait?"

"Apparently, the best bait is bits of mackerel."

"So does that mean that we've got to catch some mackerel, before we can start fishing for mackerel? That really doesn't make any sense at all!"

"Oh shut up. Just put your lines over the side. It doesn't matter if we don't fucking catch anything. We're actually after bigger fish. And we need to keep a look out for the big fish. The freighter called Islamabad, and the motor boat called Doris.

After they've rendezvoused, we'll follow Doris back towards Falmouth, discretely of course, and coordinating with Joe and Vicki as we do so. Then we'll take the bastards. Alive, if possible. But if not possible..."

***

On board Doris, Michael Corrigan and Frank Boyle were stood on deck watching carefully the sea traffic around them, whilst another of Corrigan's men was driving the boat. They saw nothing to arouse their suspicions. Down below, they could hear Abd-al-qadir retching into a bucket. They smiled at each other."

"Rather ironic. The most fearsome extremist terrorist known to mankind suffers badly from seasickness," Frank murmured.

Michael Corrigan grinned. "You OK, Abd?" he shouted down through the hatch.

"Fuck off!"

"Well, I don't think that we need him to help us collect the stuff from the boat. Once we get him ashore he should be OK. I guess that maybe we should have brought seasickness tablets with us."

"I guess so. But who would have known that the most fearsome extremist terrorist known to mankind would need seasickness tablets?" They both laughed.

"OK. Back to the job in hand." They each had a pair of binoculars, with which they started scanning their surroundings. There were several small boats about, but they all seemed to be leisure craft, none particularly close. There were no signs of coastguards or other official-looking craft. They did notice Artige, some distance away, but regarded it as harmless, simply out in the middle of the channel to do some serious fishing.

***

On Artige, the man on the bridge in charge of the boat was watching the boats around them, and noticed Doris as she came into view. He called down to Chaim, "There's a boat called Doris bearing five zero off to starboard."

They all looked in the direction that the man had indicated and located Doris. Chaim realised that they were being watched by someone wielding binoculars and hissed at the others, "Keep fishing. We're being watched."

At that very moment, by an extremely fortuitous coincidence, one of Chaim's men caught a fish on his line. He let out a gleeful shout, and reeled in quite a large fish. A mackerel.

"Is that a mackerel?"

"I think so."

"So shall we chop it up and use it for bait to catch other mackerel?"

"No. We'll just keep it and then have it for tea. Just keep fishing."

They went back to their fishing activities with renewed enthusiasm, but at the same time discretely keeping a watchful eye on Doris.

***

On board Doris, Michael Corrigan and Frank Boyle observed the successful fishing activity on board Artige, and were reassured that the crew were just what they appeared to be - harmless fishermen.

"Once we get the drugs on board, what happens then?" enquired Frank.

"Well. We head off to London where we're going to sell half the heroin. I'm buying the other half myself, to feed into my own business, but I haven't got the free cash to buy all of it. We're meeting up with the other guy at a hotel called 'The Strand Palace' in Central London. You heard of it?"

"Yeah. I've been there. It's got rather a nice bar. They do a nice pint of 'London Pride'."

"Then, once we've got all the money together – it's going to be quite a large package, eight million pounds in all – we head off to the warehouse where we're picking up the guns. They'll already be packed in a container for us. We'll check them over and then hand over the money. The guns are actually costing only seven million pounds – there'll be half a million pounds for Abd-al-qadir and half a million for me. Including a nice bonus for you, Frank."

Frank grinned. "Great!"

"Then we, or rather you, will drive the lorry with the container down to Southampton docks, where it will ultimately be loaded onto the Islamabad, on it's way back through the channel from Rotterdam. Simple. What can possibly go wrong?"

"Lots of things, I guess."

"Precisely. I didn't get where I am today without being ultra-careful about the smallest detail. That's why we're keeping a close eye on these boats around us. Including that one over there that's fishing." He nodded towards 'Artige'.

***

Meanwhile, on board 'Holly Golightly', Joe and Vicki were cautiously watching the activities on the few boats around them. Doris and Artige were no longer in sight and Joe was wondering how much further to sail before slowing down and then wait for their return. He worked out their current position and marked it on his chart.

"Fifty degrees, five minutes north and five degrees, one minute west."

Vicki looked at him quizzically.

"That puts us approximately half way to the anticipated rendezvous between 'Doris' and 'Islamabad'. If we hang about here we'll be in a good position to join in with Chaim in taking them out on their return. And if they decide to land elsewhere - quite possibly Helford would be the most likely - then we'll be well positioned to take them there. OK, now let's heave to."

Joe took Vicki through the heave to manoeuvre, then they sat on deck relaxing for the moment, observing their surroundings.

"What happens after this is all over?" Vicki asked.

"You mean after we've killed Michael Corrigan and Abd-al-qadir?"

"Yes."

"Well. We sail this boat back to Fowey, and give it back to Chris."

"And then?"

"We pick up the MX5 and drive it back to London."

"And?"

"I collect the money that I have just earned, from George at MI5."

"Assuming that the bastard doesn't try to double-cross me!" he thought.

"Then?"

"Then you and me disappear out of sight to somewhere really romantic. And then…"

They smiled fondly at each other.

"But we've got a job to do first. People that we need to kill. We have to concentrate on the job in hand."

***

On board the 'Islamabad', the seaman on watch on the bridge had identified 'Doris' through his binoculars. "I can see the boat that we're meeting up with just off the port bow, sir," he called to the Captain.

The captain came and stood beside him. He took hold of the binoculars and looked in the direction that the man was pointing. "Yes, that's her," he said. He looked around and saw nothing to raise his suspicions, just a couple of fishing boats. One was called 'Artige'. "OK. Reduce speed to fifteen knots. Doris will easily be able to match that and then we can transfer the goods across to her as quickly as possible."

The manoeuvre to match the speeds of the two boats was quickly executed. A couple of lines were passed between them and secured, to guaranteed as stable a connexion as possible. Then, with lookouts from both boats watching carefully for Coastguards and other possible threats, the several packages were quickly transferred to 'Doris'. Once the move had been completed successfully, the lines connecting the two ships were released, and they separated. 'Doris' turned away from the 'Islamabad' and quickly set a course back towards Falmouth. Finally, when 'Doris was clear, the Captain of the 'Islamabad' increased the speed and resumed his original course through the Channel towards Rotterdam.

***

All this had been observed furtively, and with great interest, by Chaim and his colleagues on 'Artige'.

"How are we going to handle this?" they asked Chaim.

"Do nothing for the moment. Just let them get ahead. Then we'll start following them, but not too close to start with. In the meantime I'll contact Joe and let him know what's happening."

He switched the radio to channel seventy-two. "Joe. The mackerel are running. The mackerel are running."

There was no reply.

"Joe. The mackerel are running," he repeated anxiously.

Still no reply.

"For fuck's sake, Joe. The fucking mackerel are fucking running!"

"Understood. I'll watch out for them. We'd like some mackerel for our tea."

"OK. I'm going after them now. See you later. Over and out." He turned to his men. "Right, pull in the fishing lines and let's get after them."

"What happens if they see us and decide that they don't like the look of us?"

"It won't matter. We can match them for speed. We've got the RPGs so I think that we most likely outgun them. We're going to go up against them at some point, so it might as well be sooner rather than later. Though I guess that it will be better if we're fairly close to Joe and Vicki and the 'Holly Golightly' when we go up against them. But anyway let's get going now."

***

"*For fuck's sake, Joe. The fucking mackerel are fucking running!*"

"Understood. I'll watch out for them. We'd like some mackerel for our tea."

Joe terminated the radio link to Chaim, and turned to Vicki. "Right, they're on their way. We need to get ready." They dropped the sails, and then started the engine - "*It'll be easy to manoeuvre quickly*" - and turned the boat towards the direction that they expected 'Doris' to come from. Joe pulled out the two Uzis and checked them over once again, making sure that the magazines were full and the guns were ready to go. He did the same for the sniper rifle – he had started to work out in his head what he was going to do, and thought that the sniper rifle was definitely going to play a useful role, to say the least. He loaded the sniper rifle with the explosive-tipped ammunition.

They waited, tense, expecting 'Doris' to materialize at any moment. Vicki kept looking around nervously at the boats around them. "What's going to happen if, or actually when, we open fire on 'Doris'? What are all the people on all these boats around us going to do?"

"Send out an SOS to the Coastguards, I guess. And then we'll have problems. Let's cross that bridge when we come to it." He smiled grimly at Vicki.

They waited, tensely, on the look out for 'Doris'.

***

On board 'Doris', Michael Corrigan and his bodyguard, Frank Boyle, were starting to feel relaxed. They had the heroin in their possession. There had been no hiccups in the transfer between the 'Islamabad' and 'Doris', it had gone according to plan. And they anticipated that everything would go smoothly from now on.

Abd-al-qadir was still down below, retching into a bucket. Corrigan and Frank Boyle grinned at each other."We'll be ashore soon, and then he'll be alright, I guess. Anyway, let's forget about him and celebrate with a drink. Fancy a whisky?"

"Great. I'll go get it." Frank went below, and returned with a bottle of Johnnie Walker, and three glasses. "One for him." He nodded towards the seaman on the bridge. He poured three glasses, handed one to Michael Corrigan, one to the guy in charge of the boat, and one for himself.

"Cheers." The two of them clinked glasses, and then they each took a swig. They saluted the guy on the wheel, who also took a swig and grinned at them.

"How long before we get back to Falmouth?" Michael Corrigan called up to him.

"About an hour or so. No need to hurry. Relax and enjoy yourselves. It should all be straightforward from now on."

Michael Corrigan and Frank Boyle relaxed further, They sipped their whisky and idly watched activities around them. Frank suddenly got excited. "Look over there. A shoal of Short-beaked Common Dolphins."

Michael Corrigan laughed. "I'm glad I've got a wild-life expert on the boat with me. You see anything else?"

Frank suddenly tensed. "Yes. I can see a boat called 'Holly Golightly'. "

"Yeah. So?"

"I think that it's Joe Hurricane's boat."

" Joe Hurricane? That guy from 'The Flying Lobsters'?"

"Yeah."

Michael Corrigan took hold of a pair of binoculars from beside him, and focussed on the 'Holly Golightly'. He looked closely at the boat, and at Joe and Vicki on board, but didn't see anything to alarm him. "After all, it's a sailing yacht, so I don't think it will be a problem. If it comes down to it, we can go an awful lot faster. And he's only the singer from a chicken-shit rock band. It's not as though he's MI5. So. Why are you worried, Frank?" he asked.

"Not sure. It's just a bit of a surprise to see him here"

"But didn't you tell me that he kept this boat – the 'Holly Golightly' – here in Falmouth?"

"Yeah."

"So why do you think that there might be a problem?"

"Because...."

***

Although some distance away, Joe was aware of the interest that the people on board 'Doris' were taking in him. He had the sniper rifle loaded with the explosive-tipped ammunition, and the silencer attached, ready at his feet. He was waiting for just the right moment to use it.

The radio suddenly squawked. *"We're closing in on the mackerel now. I repeat: we're closing in on the mackerel. Get ready!"*

Joe tensed. Waiting.

"Go."

In one swift move, Joe deftly lifted the rifle to his shoulder, lined-up the sight on the side of 'Doris', at the point where he knew that the engine was located, and pulled the trigger. He pulled it twice more in quick succession. 'Doris' immediately slowed, and black smoke started pouring from the exhaust . At that same instant, there was a loud crash as 'Artige' rammed 'Doris' from the other side.

Michael Corrigan and Frank Boyle immediately pulled out their side-arms, but were both knocked off balance and stumbled to the deck. Within seconds they were overpowered by Chaim and two of his men who had jumped aboard 'Doris'.

Joe steered 'Holly Golightly' towards 'Doris'. As he got close he saw that Chaim was holding four men at gunpoint, their wrists fastened with zip ties. Michael Corrigan, Frank Boyle, Abd-al-qadir, and a fourth man who was probably simply nothing more than a hired crew member. He tied up his boat alongside and climbed aboard. Frank Boyle glared angrily at him, but Joe ignored him. He addressed Chaim.

"OK, Chaim. This is good. We've got the ones we wanted." He looked coldly at Michael Corrigan and Abd-al-Qadir. "But what shall we do with these two?" He gestured at Frank Boyle and the scared looking seaman with him.

Chaim briefly studied the two men. "Can you swim?" he asked them. The crew member nodded nervously. Frank Boyle shook his head.

"No, I fucking can't. What are you going to do about it?"

"Well, I think that it's time to give you a swimming lesson." He nodded at his Mossad colleagues who pulled the two men to their feet, cut the zip ties on their wrists, then pushed them off the boat and into the sea.

"That way!" one of them shouted, pointing at the land, some three miles away. "Good luck!"

"Right, now which of these two do you want?" Chaim smiled grimly at Joe, nodding towards Corrigan and Abd-al-qadir.

"I'll take him. He's the one that I'm getting paid for." He nodded towards Michael Corrigan. "But remember. I want to be the one that puts the bullet into that one's head." He looked at Abd-al-Qadir. "But you do whatever you need to do first."

"So where shall we meet up?"

"I've looked at the charts, and I think that we can go ashore at a place called Towan Beach. It's the other side of the headland from Falmouth. But it's very quiet. So we'll be able to question them without any witnesses."

"We'll sink this boat. Drugs and all. Eight million pounds."

He grinned at Michael Corrigan, who looked back at him with loathing, "Right, come along now!" He dragged Abd-al-qadir onto 'Artige'. At the same time Joe dragged Michael Corrigan onto 'Holly Golightly'.

Chaim then picked up one of his RPGs and pointed it at 'Doris'.

"Whoa." said Joe, looking around nervously. Luckily, there were no other boats around.

"I'll count to ten, and then - BANG!", said Chaim, with a broad grin on his face.

Joe hastily cast off from Doris, and motored away as quickly as he could. He looked back to see 'Doris' blow up, and quickly disappear beneath the sea. He looked at Michael Corrigan, who looked back at him with hatred.

"You bastard! That boat cost me six hundred and fifty thousand pounds. I guess that's more than you earned in your entire career with the so-called 'Flying Lobsters'."

Joe laughed. "And lets add to it eight million pounds of heroin. Whew! That's an awful lot of money."

"Go fuck yourself!"

CHAPTER 26.

Towan Beach, Cornwall, July 2004.

'Holly Golightly' and 'Artige' were both anchored about a hundred yards from the beach. Joe considered it an ideal location; there were no other boats to be seen and the beach was totally deserted. Joe was absent-mindedly watching the glint of the sun on the sea, enjoying the warmth on his face. The final endgame was about to be played. He waved at Chaim on board 'Artige', which was only about twenty yards away from 'Holly Golightly'. Then he took a deep breath and turned towards Michael Corrigan with a grim expression on his face.

"Right. Let's get started."

Michael Corrigan looked back at him with loathing. "You're going to fucking regret this. I've got friends in high places. They're going to come down on you like a ton of bricks. And you as well, bitch," he said to Vicki.

Joe shrugged. "I don't think so. Your 'friends in high places' won't ever know what's happened to you. It might even be that one of your 'friends in high places' is actually the person who's paying me to kill you. Paying me an awful lot of money, by the way. Enough for the two of us," he smiled at Vicki, "to retire and disappear. But first I need to ask you a few questions. How well you answer them will be the difference between a quick, painless, death and a slow, extremely painful, death. Do you understand what I'm getting at?"

"Do your worst. You're getting nothing from me, you bastard."

"Oh, I can guarantee that I will. We're going to start off the old-fashioned, traditional way." Joe grinned, waving a large, evil-looking knife. "But that's just for a bit of fun. When we're all nicely warmed up, I'll switch to a more modern approach." He then waved a hypodermic syringe in his other hand. "Sodium thiopental. The original truth drug."

Vicki looked a bit pale at all this. And Michael Corrigan started to look a little bit worried.

"But first. It's Gin and Tonic time." He explained to Michael Corrigan. "We always finish off a day's sailing with a Gin and Tonic." He turned to Vicki, "Be a dear and pop down below and make us all a Gin and Tonic."

"Should I make two or three?"

"Let's make it three. One last drink for the condemned man." He winked at Michael Corrigan who glared back at him.

While Vicki was down below, Joe leant back against the yacht's gunwale. "OK. The first question I'm going to ask you is: where did the heroin come from?"

"Fuck off."

Joe picked up the knife. "You sure about that's the right answer?"

"Yes. Fuck off."

Joe leaned forward with the knife. "Last chance. Where did the heroin come from?"

"Fuck off."

Joe leaned forward and carefully inserted the tip of the knife into Michael Corrigan's left nostril. And then he gave a small sideways flick of the wrist and cut through the side of his nose. It started bleeding heavily.

"You bastard!" Corrigan shouted. "You're getting nothing from me!"

Joe repeated the action with the right nostril.

Corrigan screamed loudly. "You fucking bastard! You're dead, you understand? I've got friends who will be coming for you!"

"Oh, do shut up." With a sudden downward lunge, Joe

brought his arm down, slicing off Michael Corrigan's right ear. Corrigan let out an even louder scream. Joe laughed, then picked up the ear, and started singing the Stealers Wheel song, 'Stuck in the Middle with You'. He laughed again and waved the ear at Chaim, who was sitting on the 'Artige', watching the goings-on onboard Joe's boat with a somewhat sombre expression on his face.

Chaim looked across at him. "So what are you going to do with that?"

"I think that we'll feed the fishes." Joe tossed the ear overboard.

Just then Vicki came back onto the deck, holding three glasses of Gin and Tonic. She gave a slightly shocked look towards Michael Corrigan. She handed one Gin and Tonic to Joe, and sat down next to him with her own drink. "OK, so now it's Mr Blonde is it? What shall I do with his?" she asked, nodding towards Corrigan.

"He'll have to earn it by telling us what we want to know." They both sat back, sipping their drinks, looking at Michael Corrigan. Blood was streaming down his face onto the deck. He seemed suddenly deflated and just about to open up and start talking. Joe was, however, slightly suspicious, wondering if Corrigan was somehow trying to pull a fast one, and that he was about to get fed a load of crap. Nevertheless, he leaned forwards towards Corrigan, and smiled.

"So, Michael, shall we start over? Now are you going to tell us where the heroin came from?"

"From Afghanistan. Through Karachi. On a ship called 'Islamabad'. On it's way to Rotterdam."

Joe knew this to be true, and started thinking that maybe Corrigan's capitulation was genuine. He decided to quickly push on quickly with his questions, while he had him under his thumb.

***

Meanwhile, on 'Artige', Chaim and his men had started questioning Abd-al-Qadir, but were initially meeting with considerably more resistance than Joe. Chaim's first question, "What is your name?" was answered by Abd-al-Qadir spitting into Chaim's face. Chaim backhanded him across the face and was spat at again. This time Chaim used his clenched fist to hit him full force in the middle of his face, breaking his nose, Chaim observed with a degree of satisfaction, the blood streaming down Abd-al-Qadir's face, and dripping off his chin.

"Right. That's it. No more mister nice guy." He nodded towards his Mossad colleagues. "Take his shoes off and pass the hammer to me." They did as Chaim had asked and passed him the hammer. They sat Abd-al-Qadir down on the side of the cockpit and held him in place. He struggled but was outnumbered. One of Chaim's men was firmly holding his right foot flat on the deck.

"Let's start again. What is your name?"

"Fuck off!"

Chaim smiled. "There's an old English nursery rhyme. Let's see if I can remember it correctly. It goes something like this:"

"This little piggy went to market." He playfully tweaked Add-al-Qadir's big toe, and gave him a mischievous grin..

"This little piggy stayed at home." He tweaked the next toe.

"This little piggy had roast beef. This little piggy had none." He gently worked his way along the toes.

"And this little piggy went … wee, wee, wee, all the way home!" Each time he said the word 'wee', Chaim brought the hammer down on Abd-al-Qadir's little toe, totally destroying it.

Abd-al-Qadir let out a loud scream.

"What is your name?" Chaim shouted. "What is your fucking name?" He brought the hammer down on the next toe, destroying that one as well.

"Abd-al-Qadir. My name is Abd-al-Qadir. Abd-al-Qadir."

"Good. Now we're getting somewhere," Chaim said, patting him on the cheek. "Next question. Who are your contacts in Hamas? And who were you shipping the guns to? And where were they collecting them? Just keep talking! While you've still got some toes left."

"If I tell you, do I get to live?"

"No, sorry. I'm afraid that that's not an option. You've got two choices. They are: dying quickly, with a bullet in your head. Or dying slowly. Painfully. And I can guarantee that you will eventually give me the information that I'm asking for. After all you've got eight more toes for me to work on. And ten fingers. And last but not least, two balls and a dick. Or maybe we'll do them first. So what's it to be?"

"Yes. OK, OK."

"Do you want a drink?" Chaim gestured towards one of his men, who passed him a bottle of water. Chaim unscrewed the top, then held it to Abd-al-Qadir's lips, who drank deeply. He looked at Chaim, then started speaking hurriedly, almost gabbling.

"The 'Islamabad', the boat which brought the drugs in, will be calling at Southampton on the way back from Rotterdam. It will be picking up several containers; I don't know how many, but one of them will contain guns. There are two Hamas men on that boat: Abdullah Badawi and Kadeem Hussein. Once the boat leaves the port, those guys will check the container with the weapons. Then the boat will carry on, past Gibraltar and into the Mediterranean. It's ultimate destination is through the Suez canal to Karachi. But it will be met near Cyprus by another boat – I don't know the name of the boat – and the weapons will then be transferred to it. The two Hamas guys on the 'Islamabad' will also join that boat, and the guns will then be taken and landed somewhere near Shifa in Gaza. And used to kill you fucking Jewish bastards," he added, bitterly.

"Now that was rather uncalled for," Chaim said, and brought the hammer down again and again. Totally destroying the rest of the toes on Abd-al-Qadir's foot. He then sat back, thinking over what he had just learnt, and how he could take advantage of it.

***

On 'Holly Golightly', Joe was busily questioning Michael Corrigan.

"What were you going to do with the drugs?"

"We were taking them down to London. Then I was buying half. Someone else was buying the other half."

"What is the name of this other person? And where are you meeting him?"

"Dan Plummer. We're meeting in the bar of a hotel called the 'Strand Palace'. It's on the Strand in London."

Joe pondered over this, and wondered if sinking the heroin to the bottom of the English Channel early on had been the right approach. Well, too late to worry about that now. "So. Between the two of you, you're putting together eight million pounds? That'll be rather a large package of cash. When, exactly, are you meeting him?"

"Wednesday evening, Six o'clock'"

"And then what?"

"We take the money to a warehouse. Hand it over. Then pick up a container filled with weapons."

"Where is this warehouse?"

"It's in East London. Chequers Lane. Just off the A13. Signed as 'Dawson Products'."

Joe carefully wrote this down. "And after?"

"Then we drive it to Southampton docks. The 'Islamabad' will stop off at Southampton on its return journey, collect this container, along with several others, and then continue on its way. At some point it will rendezvous with another boat and the guns will be transferred. I don't know the details of that."

"OK. Fair enough. I believe you. Now. Give me some names. People on your payroll, people who you are paying off. Police, MPs, and so on."

Michael Corrigan suddenly clammed up. "There's no way that you're getting that information from me. No fucking way. You can cut off my other ear, you can cut off whatever you fucking want, but there's no fucking way that I'm grassing on those people."

"I could cut off your dick."

"You're going to kill me anyway. Just do what you fucking want."

Joe grinned at him, then waved the hypodermic containing Sodium thiopental. "OK. We'll switch to plan B. And then you will tell me what I want to know."

Vicki interrupted, "Before you do that, I want to ask him a question."

"Go ahead."

"Janet Delaney. Did you kill her?"

"The FBI girl?"

"Yes."

"Actually, no, I personally didn't. But she was sticking her nose in where it wasn't wanted. So she had to go."

Vicki looked at him coldly for several seconds, then turned to Joe. "Remember, I want to pull the trigger."

"OK. You've got it. But first..." He brandished the hypodermic syringe. Michael Corrigan looked rather apprehensive. "Don't worry, Michael, this isn't going to hurt." He grinned and patted him on the knee. Corrigan tried to resist, but Joe and Vicki together subdued him, and Joe stuck the hypodermic needle into his upper arm, and emptied the contents into his blood stream. They sat back and waited. Gradually, Michael Corrigan's eyes glazed over.

While they waited, Vicki was reading the label on the bottle of Sodium Thiopental. She read out loud, "It says here that 'Sodium Thiopental should only be administered by, or under the direct supervision of, personnel experienced in its use, with adequate training in anaesthesia and airway management, and when resuscitation equipment is available.'" She looked at Joe and smiled. "I didn't realize that you were experienced in all that sort of stuff."

Joe laughed. "Well, actually I aren't. But I don't think it matters, he's going to die anyway. So let's get started with the questions." He leaned forward and gently patted Michael Corrigan's knee. "So, Michael, tell me. Who's on your payroll? Police, MPs, and so on. You said earlier that you really wanted to tell me," He winked at Vicki.

"Yes, that's right. I really want to tell you."

"So. Any policemen in that list?"

"Detective chief inspector Roger Kenworthy. Superintendent Dan Spiers. Chief inspector Dave Boorman." He rattled off a couple more. Joe carefully noted them all down.

"What about MPs?"

"Joe Osborn. Tom Radcliffe. And the shadow home secretary, Donald Thomas."

"Wow! Shit! The shadow home secretary!" thought Joe.

"Anyone else that I need to know about?"

Corrigan named the editor of a national newspaper, together with a well-known high court judge.

"And Frank Moxon in MI5."

Suddenly, time stood still for Joe. He went pale. *"Frank Moxon! Shit! That's an alias that George occasionally uses. What's George up to? Why is he paying me to take out this guy?"*

And then it suddenly hit him."*George is doing some sort of cover-up to get rid of all traces of all his past misdeeds. And once I've done what he wants, then I'm going to be surplus to requirements. I think that from now on I"m going to have to be very careful about how I handle this. And I really do want my money!"*

Vicki recognized Joe's shocked reaction. "Joe. You OK? What's happening?"

Joe turned to Vicki. "I...I'm not sure. I need to think. Let's take him down below."

They dragged Michael Corrigan down below, and hand-cuffed him to the toilet. "If you need to take a piss..." He turned to Vicki. "Let's go back up on deck. I need to think. And I need another Gin and Tonic. A large Gin and Tonic. A very, very large one."

"OK. I'll make it," said Vicki, slightly alarmed by Joe's re-action to what Michael Corrigan had said. But she thought it best not to question Joe just yet. She thought that he would eventually tell her what was going on. In his own time.

They sat on deck drinking their Gin and Tonics. Joe was thinking furiously. He certainly had information that he could usefully pass on to George, in exchange for the second instal-ment of his four hundred thousand pounds. The names of police and MPs. Possibly George would then blackmail them. The location of the arms warehouse. George could use that to win a feather in his cap with MI5. Dan Plummer with his four million pounds. Although, Joe thought, maybe he'd hang on to that bit of information, and see if he could get his hands on the four million pounds for himself. And in any case he'd definitely need to be very wary of George. But as he turned things over in his mind, he realized that it was highly unlikely that George would know Joe was aware of the Frank Moxon alias. And therefore he wouldn't suspect that his involvement with Michael Corrigan had been uncovered. Joe started to feel a bit more relaxed.

"Right," he said, with a more cheerful expression on his face. "Let's get together with Chaim, and work out what we're going to do next. Like, who we're going to kill first. But for now let's just enjoy our Gin and Tonic."

***

Some time later, they were all sitting on the deck of 'Artige', watching the sun set.

"So. Have we got the information that we wanted? asked Chaim.

"Well. I don't know about you but I've got rather more than I wanted," Joe said with a grim smile.

Chaim raised his eyebrow. "Oh?"

"Let's just kill the two of them and move on. After we do that, what will be your next step?"

"Well, I've got the names of the two Hamas guys on the 'Islamabad'. We'll take them out. But, most importantly, we've screwed up the whole conspiracy. The eight million pounds-worth of guns aren't going to be used against us. What about you?"

"It's gotten a bit complicated." Joe was thoughtful. "Me and Vicki will be heading for London. We've got rather a lot to take care of."

Vicki looked a bit surprised at hearing this.

"Could you help me by taking out the warehouse containing the guns? You can get to keep them if you want."

Chaim examined Joe's face. "I thought that would be MI5 doing that."

"Change of plan. I'm keeping my MI5 contact out of the loop for now. I'm going to be handling things myself. So, can you help?"

"I guess we can. Where is this warehouse?"

Joe gave him the details.

"OK. We're onto it. What now?"

"Now we kill some people."

Chaim looked steadily at Joe, then nodded towards one of his men. He went below deck and came back dragging Abd-al-Qadir. Who had his wrists zip-tied together in front of him. Joe looked at the bloody mess of Abd-al-Qadir's right foot and smiled at Chaim.

"I guess he needed a bit of help to jog his memory."

Chaim laughed.

Joe pushed Abd-al-Qadir to the side of the boat. He stood in front of him, examining him closely. "Do you remember me?" he demanded. Abd-al-Qadir looked back at him impassively, saying nothing. "You killed the woman that I loved. You fucking murderous bastard." Joe shouted. He spat at him, then quickly pulled out his gun, held it against Abd-al-Qadir's forehead.

"Now, am I going to kill you with this gun. Or would you prefer it that I use a knife." He pulled out a large, evil-looking, knife. He stared impassively into Abd-al-Qadir's eyes. Then in one swift movement, he stuck his knife into his lower abdomen, and pulled it up, spilling out his intestines. For a few moments he savoured the look of horror in Abd-al-Qadir's eyes, then he quickly brought the knife up and very deftly slit his throat. In a final movement Joe pushed him off the side of the boat into the sea.

Chaim, Vicki, and the other guys all went quiet at what had just happened. Then one of the Mossad guys, watching the body, suddenly said, "You know, it rather looks like bits of human are just as good a bait for catching mackerel, as are bits of mackerel." He turned to Chaim. "And are we still having mackerel for our tea?" The tension was broken, and everyone started laughing.

Joe looked at the body floating in the sea for several seconds, then turned towards the others and smiled grimly. "They say that revenge is a dish best served cold." He looked again at the body floating in the sea, then turned towards Vicki. "One down, one to go. And then we're heading back to London." He looked at Chaim. "We've got a few things to take care of there. What about you?"

"We're also heading to London. To sort out the warehouse

full of guns. And then we'll take out the Hamas guys on the Is-lamabad. But don't hesitate to get in touch if you need any help."

"Likewise." They shook hands, then embraced.

"And after all this is over," he looked at Vicki, "we'll both come and visit you at Ashdot Yaakov Meuhad. Sometime soon."

"I'll look forward to it. And I know Malka will."

"Malka! Don't tell me that she's still still around?"

"She sure is. In her nineties now. And as cranky as ever."

***

Back on 'Holly Golightly' Joe and Vicki embraced. "So. Do you want to do this, or shall I?" said Joe.

Vicki looked serious. "I've never killed anyone before," she admitted. "But I really want to see him dead. I want to pull the trigger."

"OK. I think that you've earned that privilege." He placed a gun in her hand. He gave her a reassuring smile. Then he went below to where Michael Corrigan was handcuffed to the toilet. He released him and dragged him upright. "Do you want a last piss?"

Corrigan shook his head. With a resigned expression he said to Joe, "No. Just do your fucking worst."

Joe smiled grimly, then dragged him onto the deck. He pulled him upright, looked into his eyes, and smiled at Vicki. She stepped forward, quickly lifted her handgun, pushed the barrel against Corrigan's forehead, and without hesitating, pulled the trigger. The body dropped to the deck.

Joe looked at Vicki. He smiled at her. She smiled back.

"Good. There's actually one more thing I need to do," said Joe. "And I think that maybe you should look away."

"You and me are on the same page now. So, do what you have to do."

Joe shrugged, smiled apologetically, and pulled out his knife. "Last chance to look away." Vicki shook her head. Wearing a grim expression, Joe used the knife to saw through Michael Corrigan's right wrist, and cut his hand off.

Vicki gasped. "Why are you doing that?"

"I'm sorry, but I think that its very likely that I'm going to have to provide evidence he's dead before I can collect my money. And this is the evidence that I need."

"Oh."

He then pushed Michael Corrigan's corpse into the sea. "More mackerel food! Right, let's go..."

CHAPTER 27.

London, July 2004.

The next day, Joe and Vicki were sat in the MX5, driving along the M4 near Heathrow airport, and as usual the motorway was congested with slow-moving traffic. When she saw the sign to Heathrow, Vicki gave a start as she realised that it was scarcely more than a week since she had landed there, having flown in from America. She started turning over in her mind all the events of the past week. Flying to Amsterdam. Michael Corrigan's bodyguard. Meeting with Joe. The train back to London. The 'Tarantula'. The 'Flying Lobsters'. (*"The Flying Lobsters! Was there ever such a group?"*) Sailing from Fowey to Falmouth. Ambushing the Artige and seeing Corrigan suffer. Watching Joe kill Abd-al-Qadir. Herself killing Michael Corrigan. And realising that she was falling in love with Joe. She smiled at Joe, reached across and took hold of his hand. Joe smiled back at her.

They were both feeling rather tired, having spent some eight hours sailing the 'Holly Golightly' back to Fowey, plus another five hours in the car.

In Fowey Chris had been thankful that the 'Holly Golightly' had been returned in one piece. Without any bullet holes. And admitted that he had really had a lot of fun driving the MX5 around the roads of Cornwall.

"I hope that you didn't get caught on any speed cameras."

Chris laughed. "Sorry, mate!"

"Oh well, never mind. Fairly insignificant compared to the other stuff we've been up to. Anyway, we're left your weapons on the boat. We didn't actually use the Uzis, but the sniper rifle proved to be very useful."

"Right. Off you go and carry on making the world a better place!"

"We'll do our best."

***

They were now approaching central London, heading along Brompton Road. "I think that I'll get another room in the Dorchester," said Joe. "A double room." He winked at Vicki. "It's just that I don't trust George, the MI5 guy. I need to do things on my terms."

Vicki nodded agreement. "I totally trust you to do what's best. And I... I think I love you."

Joe smile fondly at her. "And I think I love you too. In fact, I know that I love you. But first we've got some things to sort out before we go down that road. Like get the money that I'm owed."

"Get the money! Get the money! Oh you're always so fucking romantic!" They both laughed, but then got more serious about what was ahead of them."

"So. What do we do first?" asked Vicki.

"Number one: set up a meeting with George." He suddenly swerved onto the motorway's hard shoulder and stopped the car. "OK, here goes." He pulled out his phone, and punched in George's contact number. The phone rang and was quickly answered.

"Joe. So you're finally reporting back to me?"

Sounded a bit irritable, Joe thought. Possibly the West Indian guy who had been tailing him, had reported back to George what had happened in Falmouth. He smiled.

"Well, George, I've completed the mission you gave me. Michael Corrigan is well and truly dead, and I've got a list of names for you."

"But how do I know that he's really dead?"

"I guessed that you were probably going to say that, you suspicious bugger," Joe answered cheerfully. "Do you, by any chance, have Michael Corrigan's fingerprints on file?"

"Yes. Why?"

"I thought that you might have. In that case, I'm going to drop a package off for you at reception in Thames House. And then I'll phone you again tomorrow morning." He terminated the call, and laughed.

He turned to Vicki, and smiled. "Right. Next stop, MI5 headquarters at Millbank in the centre of London. Thames House, it's called." He picked up the plastic bag containing Michael Corrigan's severed hand. "And this is the proof that he's well and truly dead. This bit of meat is worth four hundred thousand pounds!"

Vicki smiled back at him.

"And then. Step number two: head off to the 'Strand Palace' hotel and see if we can get the money off this guy, Dan Plummer. If we can get our hands on that, then I think that our futures will be well and truly taken care of. However, at the moment I'm still trying to work out exactly how to do that. But I've got an idea."

"Whether or not we get Dan Plummer's money, step number three will be to meet up with George and collect the second half of the four hundred thousand that he owes me for killing Michael Corrigan. There's going to be a bit of a problem that I haven't told you about. Yet. I'm still trying to work out how to address it."

Vicki was a little concerned by what Joe was saying. "What problem?"

Joe turned and looked at her. "It seems that George was corrupt, on Michael Corrigan's payroll. I think that is going to complicate things quite a bit."

Vicki looked back at Joe with her eyebrows raised, "Well yes, I suppose it will. But I'm sure that you'll be able to handle it."

"Of course I will. And, in the end, we're going to have a shitload of money." He gleefully rubbed his hands together. "And then we'll head off into the sunset. Together." They smiled, then leaned towards each other and tenderly kissed. "Right." He stared the car, and rejoined the motorway. "First stop, Thames House."

***

A little while later, they were driving along Millbank. "That's the Tate Gallery of British art. Very famous." he pointed out to Vicki as they passed. "I think it used to be a prison. Millbank prison or some such," he added vaguely.

"Yes, it looks like a prison."

Joe pulled the car into the side of the road, and put it into neutral, leaving the engine running, "And that's Thames house. MI5 headquarters." He nodded towards the building they had stopped near.

"That's an even grimmer looking building, for sure."

"OK. We can't hang about. Any cars stopping around here will instantly raise suspicions and bring people out to investigate. You stay in the car whilst I drop this off." He brandished the plastic bag containing Michael Corrigan's hand. "Anyone comes near the car, you have my permission to shoot them." The expression on Vicki's face prompted him to hastily add, "Sorry, only kidding." He then got out of the car and hurried into the building. Less than a minute later he ran out, and got into the car. He put it into gear and they quickly rejoined the traffic.

As they were driving along, he pulled out his mobile phone, and hit the redial button.

"Yes, Joe?"

"There's a package waiting for you in the reception at Thames house. I'll call you again tomorrow morning when you've had a good look at it." He terminated the call.

"Right! Next stop, Park Lane, 'The Dorchester'."

***

They had checked into the hotel under false names: John and Margaret Sharpe. Posing as a married couple.

"Wow, this fantastic." Vicki excitedly explored the room, admiring the furnishings, the pictures on the wall, the freebie shampoo and soap, the contents of the mini bar, the view across Hyde Park.

"Nicer than your hotel, is it?" asked Joe.

"No. Actually mine is just as nice," said Vicki, defensively.

After checking in, they slowly made their way to the Strand, grabbing a sandwich, and admiring the sights on the way: Buckingham Palace, Admiralty Arch, Trafalgar Square. Joe was now sat in the bar of the 'Strand Palace' hotel, with a newspaper and a beer, surreptitiously watching the other customers. He identified a possible match for Dan Plummer. He was sat with another couple of guys, probably bodyguards, and had a briefcase with him.

"*Surely there can't be four million pounds in that,*" he thought. "*Well, first I need Vicki to do her stuff so I can get a positive ID on him.*"

Meanwhile, as prearranged, Vicki approached the hotel reception. She was wearing dark sunglasses, partially hiding her face. "Please could you arrange to deliver this to a Mister Dan Plummer. It's quite urgent. I think that he might be in the bar. But I don't want him to see me. It's a surprise," She smiled at the man, and handed him an envelope and a ten pound note.

"Certainly, Miss. Leave it with me."

Vicki quickly left the hotel, as the receptionist walked through into the bar." Message for Mister Dan Plummer," he announced loudly.

The man whom Joe had provisionally identified as Dan Plummer raised his hand. "Over here," he answered to the receptionist, who handed him the note that Vicki had left. Dan Plummer opened and read the note, and the said something to his companions wearing an irritated expression. Joe knew that the note was supposedly from Michael Corrigan (*"From beyond the grave"*) delaying the arranged meeting by an hour.

Looking around, Joe was pleased to see that the bar was getting quite full, presumably the after-work crowd. He could also see that there were quite a number of people milling around in the reception area, busy checking in. *"Maybe this might work,"* he thought. He waited for about fifteen minutes, giving Vicki chance to sneak back into the hotel through the side entrance, and get in position. The bar was getting busier all the time. Eventually he pulled his phone out of his pocket and phoned Vicki. "Time to activate phase two," he murmured.

He stood up and started moving through the crowd, positioning himself closer to Dan Plummer. Suddenly the fire alarm went off; a loud ringing noise, accompanied by an automated voice repeating "Evacuate... Evacuate... Evacuate..." Everyone in the bar got to their feet and started moving towards the exit, mingling with the people in reception, and also the residents of the hotel who were streaming down the stairs.

Within this crowd, Joe moved very close to Dan Plummer, taking note of the nearest exit, such features as the pillars in the reception area, and most importantly, the proximity of the bodyguards. Suddenly, as the chance presented itself; he moved alongside Plummer, and in one swift move, took out his silenced handgun, thrust it into his side, and pulled the trigger. He grabbed the briefcase and ducked behind the nearest pillar in the reception area.

The bodyguards reacted immediately, realising that their boss had just been shot, but unaware of where the shot had come from, or who was responsible. They both pulled out their own handguns and brandished them, looking about wildly. Everyone around started screaming, and pandemonium ensued.

Taking advantage of the chaos, Joe managed to make his way out of the hotel's side door. He quickly starting walking up the Strand towards Trafalgar Square. A couple of police cars raced past, sirens blaring, but he didn't react and just carried on walking. He soon reached Trafalgar Square, and saw Vicki already there, leaning on one of the lions. He smiled at her, and took hold of her hand. "I think that it worked," he murmured, "so far. Let's get to the hotel and see what we've got here."

They walked along The Mall, hand in hand, mingling with the tourists. They cut through Green Park, and very quickly reached the 'Dorchester' hotel. Once in their room, they eagerly examined the briefcase that Joe had taken from Dan Plummer. It was locked, but Joe's lock-picking skills soon sorted that. They opened the briefcase and stared, mesmerised at bundles of five hundred euro notes, hundred dollar bills, fifty pound and twenty pound notes, a couple of bars of gold, and what looked like a little bag of diamonds.

"Wow!" said Joe. "I wasn't sure that there could possibly be four million pounds in a briefcase this size. But I think that maybe I was wrong."

"Wow, indeed!"

"And now, Mrs. Sharpe, I think that it's time to celebrate our new-found wealth!" They turned to each other, smiling happily, and slowly drew together. They tenderly looked in each others eyes, smiled, and then exchanged a long and tender kiss, which very quickly turned into a fierce, passionate kiss. And then they frenziedly started pulling each others clothes off, and they made love there and then on the bedroom floor. They both climaxed within minutes.

"Wow!"

"Wow!"

They climbed into the bed and started exploring each others bodies more leisurely and sensitively. They quickly became aroused and made love again, this time slowly and gently, taking their time, until eventually they both climaxed again. They lay next to each other, looking into each others eyes, smiling happily.

"So, Mister Sharpe, what next?"

Joe smiled. "Give me time to catch my breath, and I'll show you what's next."

Vicki giggled. "I don't think I can wait that long." She squirmed under the bed sheet and started tenderly kissing Joe's penis. She took it into her mouth, and Joe quickly became hard once more. This time Vicki climbed on top of Joe and inserted him into her. They gently made love again, slowly, and finally they both climaxed for the third time. Vicki climbed off Joe, and they lay side by side, this time starting to feel just a little bit worn out.

"You know, for a fifty something year old, you're not too bad."

"Cheeky cow." They both laughed, then grew a bit more serious.

"So what now?" Vicki asked.

"Now we raid the mini bar." Joe climbed out of bed and crossed the room. He opened the mini bar, and looked inquisitively at Vicki. "Gin and Tonic?"

She nodded happily. "Yes, please."

Joe mixed two Gin and Tonics and brought them back to the bed. He switched on the television and they started watching the news. The headlines were about a notorious London criminal, who had been murdered in a hotel called the 'Strand Palace' near Trafalgar Square. Apparently, police were looking for two men who had been seen brandishing guns in the foyer of the hotel. Joe smiled.

"Well, I think that worked out better than I expected it would. OK. Next stop: George."

CHAPTER 28.

The Dorchester Hotel, July 2004.

The next morning, Joe and Vicki ordered a room service breakfast, which they quickly, and hungrily, ate. Then they sat and finalised the details of Joe's meeting with George.

"Since, for obvious reasons, I don't trust George a fucking inch, I'd like you to hide in the bathroom when he comes here. With your gun. If my plan goes pear-shaped..."

"Pear-shaped?"

"Sorry. It's an expression us Brits use. It means horribly wrong. Anyway, if my plan goes pear-shaped, then I'd like you to be in a position to step in. Take him out if necessary."

Vicki looked alarmed. "Take him out?"

"Take him out means..."

"Yes I know what it means. It's just that, then it will be two in two days. Starting to be a bit of a habit. Normally the only thing that I take out is the trash."

"Well, that's exactly what you'll be doing here," Joe said. "Sorry," he added hastily, seeing the annoyed expression on Vicki's face. "That was a bad joke. Anyway, I don't believe it will come to that. It would be an absolute last resort. But, just in case..."

When they were both satisfied with the finer details of the plan, Joe rang George.

"Good morning George. Did you receive the package that I left for you?"

"Good morning Joe. Yes I received the package, thank you. And the fingerprints do match up, so it does seem that Michael Corrigan is no more."

"OK, so we need to meet. I want my money, and I'm going to give you a list of names."

"So. When and where?"

"Noon. The Dorchester. Room six sixteen."

"Room six sixteen? That's not the room that I set you up in."

"No. There was a problem with the original room. I drank the mini-bar dry," Joe added, cheerfully.

"Hmmm.... OK, room six sixteen. Noon." George rang off.

***

As noon approached, Joe and Vicki psyched themselves up for George's arrival. Eventually the hotel's phone rang.

"There's a gentleman in reception for you, sir."

"Yes. I'm expecting him. Send him up, please."

Vicki took her gun into the bathroom. She almost closed the door, leaving it slightly ajar. Joe sat on one of the chairs in the room, with the coffee table in front of him. He placed his silenced handgun on the coffee table and covered it with a newspaper. A couple of minutes later, there was a knock on the door. Joe stood up and crossed the room. He opened the door and ushered George in, directing him to the chair that faced his own. George sat on the chair, with his back towards the bathroom door.

He had brought a briefcase with him, which Joe eyed with interest. "Can I get you a drink, George?"

"No, thank you. Let's just get our business over and done with." He placed the briefcase on the table, turned it towards Joe, and opened it. It was filled with bundles of ten and twenty pound notes. "Would you like to count it?"

"I trust you, George." He inwardly smiled to himself. "I have a list of people who are, sorry were, being paid off by Michael Corrigan." He handed George a folded sheet of paper.

George unfolded it and started reading down the list of name. Suddenly, when he reached the bottom of the page, he froze and looked up at Joe. With a cold smile, Joe swiftly lifted his handgun from the table and shot George in the centre of his forehead.

***

Joe and Vicki both looked down at George's body. He was laid flat on his back, his lifeless eyes staring at the ceiling. With a bullet hole in the centre of his forehead. "So now what?" asked Vicki.

"First I need to go through his pockets. Then we'll need to bring in an 'clean-up specialist'. I know just the person. But I don't want to leave any ID on the body." He quickly searched George, and found his wallet. From it he took his MI5 ID, and a couple of bank cards. He left money and one of the newfangled Oyster cards and then replaced the wallet. The cards he had removed, he cut into small pieces and flushed down the toilet. There was also a gun. He debated removing that, but in the end decided to leave it. "*Maybe Debbie would like it,*" he mused.

"Now we'll have to contact the 'clean-up specialist'." He smiled grimly, pulled out his phone, and from memory punched in a number. It was quickly answered.

"Hi, Debbie, it's Joe."

"*Joe? Don't tell me that you've got yet another clean-up job for me?*"

"Yes, sorry Debbie," he replied apologetically. "But it's not going to present too much of a problem," he added, looking down at George's fairly trim body. "Hopefully, you can take care of it today?"

"*Certainly, Joe. Whereabouts is the item that needs clearing?*"

"It's in room six sixteen at the Dorchester Hotel. I'll leave the usual ten grand plus a small bonus. And there's a handgun in one of the pockets. You want me to leave it there?"

"*Like a souvenir, you mean?*"

He laughed. "Yes. Like a souvenir."

"OK. I'll be on to it straight-away." Debbie said, and broke the connection,

Joe turned to Vicki. "Right. Time to go." They quickly collected all their possessions, including the two cases of money. And as before, Joe made sure that he packed all the little bottles of free shampoo, bath gel, and the little bars of soap from the bathroom. And the hotel pen, of course.

Vicki smiled, and shook her head despairingly. *"Four million pounds and he still rips off the toiletries..."*

"OK. That's everything. We're leaving no traces behind..."

"Well, apart from a bit of DNA on the bed sheets."

Joe laughed. "Yes, apart from a bit of DNA on the bed sheets."

One final scan around the room, and they left, hanging the 'Do Not Disturb' sign on the door handle. On the way out, they detoured via Joe's original room, and he emptied the room safe which contained George's original two hundred thousand pound down-payment.

"So. Where to now?" asked Vicki.

"As far away as possible."

***

On the way to the airport, Joe posted four letters. To 'The Guardian', 'The Times', 'The Daily Telegraph', and 'The Independent'. Each letter contained a copy of the list of names that Michael Corrigan had given him. The editor of one of those papers was actually on Corrigan's list, and Joe felt a mischievous sense of glee at the furore that would be following very soon.

EPILOGUE.

Australia. Some eight days later.

Joe and Vicki had flown from London to Sydney the previous week. First class. Vicki had never flown first class before, and she found the whole experience breath-takingly wonderful. The champagne, the 'a la carte' menu, the luxuriously comfortable seating.

"Can we fly first class again sometime? Please! Pretty please!"

"Of course. With the money we've got now, we'll always be travelling first class. So let's give a big thanks to George and to Dan Plummer!"

Once they arrived in Australia, they kept a close eye on the news coming out of Britain. A major scandal was developing that involved several politicians, including the shadow home secretary. Plus, several senior policemen, a high court judge, and the editor of a well-known national newspaper, were also implicated.

The other news items that interested them were firstly: the discovery of two corpses that had been washed ashore in Cornwall. Both badly decomposed, they had been partially eaten by the mackerel that were very abundant in that area. One of the corpses was missing its right hand and had died as a result of a gunshot wound to the head. It had been identified as Michael Corrigan, a notorious underworld figure. The police believed that his death was the result of an inter-gang feud. The second corpse was an unidentified Arab male.

And the second news item: a suitcase had been discovered in the Thames containing a human body part. It was not specified which actual body part was in the suitcase, though it was reported that it had definitely come from a male! Police divers had subsequently found two more suitcases containing further body parts. It had been confirmed by DNA comparison that they all belonged to the same person. The search was continuing....

***

Joe and Vicki were walking hand in hand along Bondi Beach. "So what's the plan for the future?" asked Vicki, smiling lovingly at him.

"Well, my Australian friends are in a very good position to pull a few strings, and they are going to organize a pair of Australian passports for us. 'Genuine' Australian passports. And from now on, we will be known as Mr. and Mrs. Jeff and Lindsay Palmer. Then I want to take you on a trip to Israel, now my demons have finally been laid to rest. You'll love it there. We can visit the historic sites in Jerusalem, go walking in the Golan heights, go swimming in the Dead sea, and... pick olives!"

Just then there was a loud and piercing whistle from higher up the beach. They looked up to see Scott waving at them. "Hey, you pommy bastard, come up here and bring your sheila with you. The tucker's ready on the barbie, and the stubbies are nice and cold. Get your arses in gear before Matina drinks all the beer..."

ABOUT THE AUTHOR

Pete Burnell

In describing many of the locations in this book, Pete is drawing on his own personal experiences. For example, in his younger days, Pete worked as a volunteer on Kibbutz Ashdot Yaakov Meuhad picking olives. Following that spell of his youth, and a period spent teaching, he worked in the IT industry in many different places, including Beirut and Kuwait.

But it should be pointed out, that he has never worked as a freelance agent in any of the security organisations mentioned in the book, and he has never pointed a gun at anyone!

This is his first novel. More will follow.

Printed in Great Britain
by Amazon

79403292R00132